POKER FACE

Jess Sturman-Coombs is a debut writer of fiction to include, but not limited to, sci-fi, romance and thrillers. Poker Face is the first in a series of crossover fiction so, if you like what you find in the following pages, please keep a look out for the next instalment of gritty storytelling.

Jess graduated from The University of Northampton with a degree in law and lives in Northamptonshire with her son, daughter and husband - and a big black fluffy dog called Alfie. More details can be found about the author of this book on her official website, **www.wix.com/jesssturman/jess-sturman-coombs**, where you can also connect to her blog **'Lock, stock and barrel'**.

POKER FACE

Jess Sturman-Coombs

www.wix.com/jesssturman/jess-sturman-coombs

Poker Face. Copyright © 2011 Jess Sturman-Coombs.

The moral right of the author has been asserted.

All rights reserved.

Printed and bound in the UK. Second edition February 2012

Published by Jess Sturman-Coombs

ISBN 978-0-9571012-1-0

This is a work of fiction. Names, characters, places, incidents and dialogues are products of the author's imagination or are used fictitiously. Any resemblance to actual people, living or dead, events or locales is entirely coincidental.

A CIP record for this book is available from the British Library

Cover design: Ivan Waldock

Dedications

Writing books can be a long and difficult journey and I'm not just talking about the 88,000 word count, the plot, or even the grammatical minefield. When you write a book you give birth to places, characters and circumstances, and as you write they grow like children. They soon become as much a part of your life as they do a part of fiction.

When someone offers to read your work, someone who shows the same level of enthusiasm and love for it that you worried only you would ever feel, someone who offers constructive feedback and advice and is excited about what the future might hold, I believe it is only fitting to dedicate your proud and finished work to them. So, here it is, as promised, a list of all those who have helped me to springboard my 'literary children' into the big wide paperback and e-world. Thank you for reading and a big thank you to the following very important people:

Ben, Dave, Heather, Ivan, Jen, Olivia, Paul, Robin, Sally, Sam, Sandra, Tamara and last, but only because someone has to go last (it is in alphabetical order) and definitely not because she's least, Tracy!

I would also particularly like to thank my two children Ollie and Madeline and my fabarooney husband, Robin, for always believing, whether in Star Wars, fairies or my ability to produce a book that other people will enjoy. The world would be a lonely and less creative place without believers.

CONTENTS

1. End of school	7
2. Have you GOT an appointment?	16
3. The interview	21
4. First day nerves	29
5. Mr Alessi's criminal tower	36
6. An eye for an eye	42
7. I just don't think you should be here	46
8. The price you pay for being a woman	54
9. Verbal warning	59
10. A romantic gesture	67
11. Pablo's little secret	72
12. Special delivery	77
13. A birthday not to remember	81
14. The hangover from hell	89
15. Life is full of lessons	95
16. Next stop	101
17. Almond Blossoms	108
18. Danny slips	116
19. Running away	124
20. New shoes well worn	128
21. The demand	133
22. Who can you trust?	140
23. The set up	145
24. A little inside knowledge	154
25. A secret shared is a problem halved	159
26. With family like this, who needs enemies?	166
27. A step too far	172

28. Brother or informer?	178
29. Family values	185
30. Bang, bang, you're dead	190
31. Counting the losses	198
32. Home sweet...mansion!	205
33. The truth hurts	214
34. The siege	221
35. Don't forget to look under the bed	229
36. The Ruby prize	238
37. Candy from a baby	244

1
End of school

He pushed down on the handle of the back door, it was locked. He immediately became agitated, that would make things harder, but not impossible. Through the glass he could see the key in the door and the shadows of a house in darkness. A light blinked on the cooker illuminating a digital clock, 12am. He didn't care much for the unsociable hour. He was determined to get inside one way or another.

The neighbouring houses were silent, everything peaceful. No cars could be heard on the main road running through the estate and no footsteps on the surrounding network of footpaths. The darkly dressed figure stood alone in the moonlight as he put his elbow to the window and slammed hard. The glass gave way easily and he put his hand through, turning the key in the lock. He smiled and took a step forward, he was in. He moved through the kitchen and into the hallway, then, quietly, he climbed the stairs.

Pushing open the first bedroom door he stopped to admire the teenage girl sleeping there. She was curled up, innocent and blissfully unaware of his presence as her eyelids flickered over a dream. Her dark hair covered the pillow and reached right down to her waist as it fanned across her back and fell over her pale face. She was petite, beautiful and about to suffer horribly. He walked across the room and crouched down beside her bed. She looked just like his wife and for a moment he enjoyed having her there with him, close and warm, her breath on his face, but then he felt fury boil up inside. She was going to pay for looking like *her*, in tears.

Suddenly and cruelly the covers were ripped away and she woke feeling confused and disorientated. *He* labelled it 'ignorant'. He couldn't care less when she started to cry as he grabbed her by the back of the neck and dragged her down the stairs. She begged him to leave her alone but he mocked and laughed at her. He pushed and shoved, yanked her hair, brought his hands down on her head and slapped her hard. Gripping her arms so tightly they felt as though they might break he pushed her down to the floor, and there he kicked her ruthlessly. She scrambled as fast as she could over to the waste paper bin where she was violently and painfully sick. The muscles in her abdomen protested against the impact of his size eleven boot in a wave of tight nauseating cramps. She covered the area with her hands protectively as she shivered and sobbed on the carpet.

It was while removing his belt to beat her more savagely that he spotted an empty bottle of alcohol on the mantelpiece and that was him distracted - it was *that* easy.

"I'll be back for you, Ruby Palmer, you mark my words," he threatened. "I haven't nearly finished with you. Disobedient animals get beaten until they obey do you understand me?" he slurred at her drunkenly and she shook her head as the tears rolled down her face.

"No, I don't understand and I'm *not* an animal!" she pleaded bitterly but he turned his nose up at her like she was dirty.

"You locked me out you stupid little cow!" he yelled at her furiously, spit flying from his hard whitened lips.

"No you were out and it was late. I have school tomorrow. I wanted to go to bed. I was tired. I was scared somebody might come in so I locked the door, that's all I did. You have a key, dad!" He threw his head back and laughed before crouching and gripping her chin as he snarled.

"Nice try, Ruby. You left the key in the door so mine wouldn't work, would it?"

"By accident!" she argued pulling back his fingers and forcing his hand away. "I never locked you out on purpose, I swear." He stood and pushed her with his foot before leaving the room to search for a fresh bottle of gin in the kitchen.

She took her chance and, still holding her stomach, she headed for the sofa. He was busy slamming cupboard doors as she climbed over the back and hid. The gap was small but then so was she, which made it perfect. She shook and sobbed silently as she listened to him return, trying to recall what he'd been doing before he went to get more drink. He mumbled angrily and paced the room feeling disorientated. She heard the swish of his belt as he pulled it free from the loops on his trousers, quickly. It made her shudder. He threw it down onto the table, the metal buckle clattering loudly. Would that buckle be enough to remind him of what he'd started? She hid her face in her pulled up knees and waited to see.

Silence followed and then the sound of relief as her attacker drained half a bottle in one effortless swig. The sofa creaked and she clenched herself tightly into a ball, praying that he wouldn't look over at her. He would smile like he was pleased with his find and then grab her hair and yank her out to finish her off.

Before long he had emptied the bottle and he slung it carelessly at the fireplace, laughing when it smashed into tiny shards. Within the hour she could hear him snoring but she never went back to her bed. At least now he didn't know where she was. If he woke and went looking for her again she'd be safe. She stayed awake all night too frightened to let her guard down. If he went upstairs shouting her name she would run away...and *never* come back.

"Hey, Ruby," a low shameful voice called her as she stopped in at the living room to grab her school bag from the floor. She took a deep breath and turned to face him, her mouth defiant her jaw rigid. He dropped his head and sighed guiltily before looking back up at her. "You off to school?" he asked and she nodded, but said nothing. She hated him and he could see it in her pretty blue eyes. "Look...I'm sorry..."

"You hurt me," she interrupted him. He nodded in acceptance looking away again. "You're always hurting me," she went on.

"Ruby, I..."

"You treat me like an animal. *No*, second thoughts, you treat me worse than that. I'm hurting, dad, and now I have to go to school and pretend everything's OK when it's not. It's not OK, dad! It's my last day today and I'm covered in bruises thanks to you. Even on my last day I have to find excuses and lies to explain how *this* happened," she told him bitterly pulling down her collar to show him the green and brown marks on her neck and collar bone. It looked terrible. "And you're lucky I don't have PE else someone would definitely spot *this!*" she seethed pulling up her shirt and showing him the bruising to her side and stomach. He could hardly bear to look. "All I want is for you to stop drinking," she whined in despair.

"And I will," he protested sadly. "I promise I will. I'll stop...today."

"That's what you always say...the morning after!" she reminded him. "What's the point in wasting my breath, I'm going to school." She wearily hooked her bag strap over her shoulder and then paused to press the balls of her hands into her eyes. "The last thing I need is to be yelled at by Mr Manning for being late. I have a headache," she grumbled. "*And* I'm tired but don't worry I'll get the blame for that too when I can't concentrate. I'll be told I'm rude for not listening and argumentative when I refuse to take the rollicking dished out when I finally snap. It's not fair, dad, I've had enough!"

"Ruby, wait!" he cried after her but she slammed the back door with its broken window and wrestled with the crappy gate, wishing she could pull it right off its rusty and seized up hinges.

It was hard to stay focused at school and not just because of the pounding head and stomach ache from the night before. It was also her last day...*ever*. They had survived school life and made it to the final bell and now Sasha was finishing off her *'Happy life I'll miss you!'* message across the front of Ruby's school shirt in permanent red marker.

"That better not go right through and stain my skin, Sasha, or I'll be wearing jumpers for the next three months!" she warned. Sasha giggled, thinking it would be hilariously funny to draw a rude picture while she was at it.

"Don't worry, Ruby, and hold still or you'll smudge my work and you know how I'm aiming for an 'A' in art."

"Art?" Ruby repeated looking down to see what Sasha had just finished putting the final touches to. She screeched out: "Sasha, no! I have to get the bus looking like this! Ugh that's disgusting! Mr Carter was right, you *always* lower the tone!"

Sasha had trouble standing she was laughing so hard. "When he said *'lower the tone'*, Ruby, he meant add more shading that's all!" she declared innocently knowing perfectly well he meant stop drawing filthy pictures else you'll end up in Mr Manning's office. Ruby belted Sasha with her bag but then stopped as she spotted Matthew Dean and three of his friends approaching.

"Ugh what does he want *now?*" she complained suddenly feeling exhausted. "Can't he just leave me alone?" Sasha looked over her shoulder in the boys' direction as Ruby cringed and rubbed at the picture on her shirt, desperately wishing it would go away and take Matthew with it. "He hardly needs encouraging, Sasha!"

"Look forget him, Ruby, you've made your feelings clear. You've made your decision and you don't want to be just another name on his list. He might be fit but he's disgusting! I mean who makes a list of girls and then sets about trying to conquer *all* of them? He's called it his 'Hit List' you know?" Sasha filled her in and Ruby nodded slowly.

"Yeah I know but I'll tell you what I don't know. I don't know why *I'm* on it. He must have been getting desperate for names!"

"Don't say that, Ruby," Sasha argued shoving her friend slightly. "I hate it when you say bad stuff about yourself. It's not fair, it's not true *and* it's mean. You're gorgeous and *that's* why you're on his list. It's that idiot dad of yours that makes you feel so low about yourself." She hated Ruby's dad for the way he treated her. "You tell yourself, Ruby, *I'm beautiful, I'm clever, I deserve a life and I'm damn well going to get one!"*

Ruby smiled and hugged her friend, a strong meaningful cuddle she wished would never end. But this *was* the end. It was the end of school and things were going to change, for everyone. What they had known and done for the last five years was over. The people they saw every day of the week, sat with, chatted with, got into trouble with, would be doing *other* things. They would be taking different paths and Ruby felt overwhelmingly sad. She wasn't usually one to dwell or get down. Ruby was bouncy, electric, a real live wire, but she was going to miss her friends and, in a strange way, she was going to miss school too. She wouldn't miss it for the work and the angry teachers but for the escape it provided from home and the social support it was going to be a huge hole in her life.

"Hey girls," Matthew greeted smoothly as he reached them. They let each other go, the final goodbye interrupted by the school's resident player. "Are you going to kiss now?" he asked raising his eyebrows hopefully. Sasha giggled and pouted sexily, as if to tease, but Ruby glared at him suspiciously. He made her feel under pressure, chased and, when he was with his friends, he also made her feel stupid. "So, Ruby, what's the plan for the summer, lots of topless sunbathing?" he sniggered and she shook her head at him trying desperately not to blush, they would *love* that!

Sasha was safe from Matthew. He was best friends with one of her brothers and that meant she was *officially* off- limits. No lists, rating or two timing for her. Matthew sidled up more closely now. "I'm good with suntan lotion, Ruby," he confessed, checking her out in the most blatant and toe curling way. She sighed and straightened herself trying to appear confident, though feeling anything but.

"To be honest, Matthew, I'm going to be *really* busy over the summer, too busy to be your toy. If you want something to play with...get yourself a Barbie," she suggested collecting up her bag and blazer from the floor to a chorus of laughter and jeering. "I'll see you soon, Sasha...I hope. I'm really going to miss you. Oh god this is so crap!" She wanted to cry and wished that Matthew and his silly crew weren't all staring at her. He'd gate crashed her goodbye and as much as she wanted to storm off she also wanted to let Sasha know how much she meant to her *before* she moved on and forgot Ruby ever existed. "We will *definitely* have to go clubbing," she suggested feeling insecure. "I mean it's my birthday in four months. You'll come won't you...for that?"

"Of course I'll come! Listen I wouldn't miss your seventeenth for the world, Ruby Palmer," Sasha pointed at her sternly. "We are going to party hard and you are going to be *so* hot we won't need to pay for a thing. We might even find you a bloke," she told her looking at Matthew as she said it. "One who *doesn't* make lists!" He laughed it off and Ruby glanced at him cautiously, like he might pounce if she didn't keep an eye on him.

"OK, I'll see you around then," she just about managed with a smile but her big blue eyes looked sad and lost. "I Love you, Sasha," she whispered shyly, not liking that her feelings were so exposed.

"Love ya too, babe," Sasha sang out more confidently. "I'll call you...later...OK? I promise!"

Ruby nodded, fighting the tears, and moved to walk away but Matthew stepped in front of her before she could leave. "How about me, do you love me?" he asked eagerly but she shook her head and tried to sidestep him. He sidestepped too, blocking her. "Come on, Ruby, that's not very friendly. What's got into you?"

"Nothing!" she flayed her arms helplessly at him. "I just get tired of you hitting on me all the time. It's like you think I'm not capable of anything else. "I'm not here for your enjoyment, Matthew, so give up!" she finally snapped at him. She'd had enough. His friends let out a wave of painful groans and she rolled her eyes at them. There was no such thing as a private conversation. Matthew narrowed his eyes looking every bit the menace that he was.

"So what *are* you here for then?" he teased spitefully. "You got better plans?" he asked, daring to smirk as he said it. His little gang laughed and clicked their fingers, enjoying the entertainment, while Sasha slapped her brother round the shoulder and told him to shut up. It was one all now but Ruby was competitive. She *never* gave up without a fight. Living alone with her drunk and abusive dad had made her hard, not confident necessarily, but determined and feisty.

"A better plan wouldn't be hard to think of, Matthew," she told him boldly and Sasha clicked her fingers in her brother's face loving the fact that Ruby was now giving as good as she got. She loved that about Ruby, never afraid to tell someone, no matter how much bigger they were, to go jump. Matthew's face had taken on a challenging look. She could see him calculating his next move as he ran his tongue along his teeth. She could feel the adrenalin starting to pump but she wasn't about to show it or back down. Backing down just wasn't in her.

"I give you two weeks," he nodded like he was capping some big *special offer*. "Before you're bored out of your little mind and begging me to come round and help you bronze up...or...*whatever*," he sniggered managing to make *'whatever'* sound dirty. She clenched her jaw and hoisted her long dark hair around and over her right shoulder out of the way of her bag strap. It was getting hot!

"Yeah...well...don't put your life on hold, Matthew, because it's *not* happening. I wouldn't want you to miss out on anything life changing while you're sitting in with your mum waiting for *me* to ring." Another burst of laughter erupted and he looked her up and down slowly.

"So, why are *you* going to be so busy?" he snorted at her. "Got some high flying job lined up? Have you lied to them about how well your exams went?" he tormented, reaching forward to touch her face with the back of his fingers. She tilted her head out of the way frostily and folded her arms across her chest.

"Why are you always such an idiot?" she asked looking indignant.

"Chill, Ruby, you said you'd be busy. I'm just asking *that's all*," he defended poorly. He was trying to make a fool of her and she knew it. Her eyes fixed him with a burning fiery glare.

"You're *saying* that I'm thick, so thick I can't get a job, so thick I'd be content with letting you get all over me for the whole summer. Well *newsflash*, Matthew, the thick girl doesn't want you and she *has* got a job...actually..."

"Where?" he interrupted quickly, testing her.

"A law firm in town," she responded just as quickly, not knowing where that had come from but glad of the timing. It *definitely* sounded true. "So...so...you can just take your suntan lotion and find some other *thick girl* to rub it into because you're not coming anywhere near *me!*"

She turned and stormed off, feeling defiant for all of the five minutes it took her to get round the corner and out of his sight. Oh god why had she told him she had a job? Why? Why? Why? *Nobody* was going to give her a job. Matthew was right she had no qualifications. She was nearly seventeen and going nowhere...*fast!* She was destined to end up like her old man, unemployed, depressed and *heavily* dependent on alcohol.

She watched as the bus approached and wearily pushed her body away from the wall that she'd flattened herself against. After joining the queue and jumping on she sank against the window wishing she didn't have to go home. A whole summer cooped up with her dad and his incoherent ramblings and aggressive outbursts *ughh* she was destined for misery. Maybe Matthew was right, but would two weeks be all it took for her to go running to *him*?

Matthew wasn't such a bad excuse to be out of the house, and it certainly wouldn't be the first time she'd tipped up on his doorstep when her dad had lost it, but now she was on his list. From now on turning up at his house would mean much more than mucking about and watching films. It would mean getting signed off officially on his *'Hit List'*. She tried to reason it through in her head, it didn't take long. He certainly wasn't bad looking, just a using, disrespectful two timing idiot...with idiot friends.

2
Have you GOT an appointment?

She sighed and watched the town go by outside her window as the bus crawled through the slow moving traffic. Everywhere was busy, thanks to the *'regeneration work'* going on in the town centre. Roads were being dug up, crossings put in, cycle paths and bus lanes appearing all over the place. The whole thing was a nightmare but rather than tackle the town centre in stages the workmen, planning officers and monster sized equipment had descended on it like a tornado, ripping *everything* up.

Ruby's bus continued to make slow progress up the hill and was now sitting at temporary traffic lights. It rumbled, squeaked and hissed as it waited and edged, waited and edged, while the driver huffed and mumbled something about the colour green. They were stuck on the High Street and they could have walked to the bus stop quicker, it was only round the corner! It was getting hot, the sun beaming through the rows of windows and the engine temperature, a bit like Ruby's impatience, was rising steadily. The thick air had started to smell of warm bodies and combined with diesel it made Ruby shift uncomfortably in her seat.

She looked out of the window, desperately trying to focus on something else, and right in front of her was a tall grand looking building that she'd never noticed before. She'd lived in the same place all her life but was looking at a building that had been there longer than she had. It had taken being stuck in traffic to appreciate the beautifully crafted facade, a facade that she wouldn't have second glanced otherwise. So much detail had gone into the stonework, the ornate window design, the red brick, the concrete pillars, and *that's* when she noticed the sign above the door; **Tangle and Alessi Solicitors.** Her heart skipped a beat and without thinking it through she stood and made her way to the front of the bus.

"Can I get off please?" she asked politely but the driver glanced back and grunted at her.

"*This* isn't a bus stop. I'm waiting for the lights to turn green."

"Yeah I know but..."

"Health and safety says we can only drop off at designated..."

"Does health and safety say anything about passengers suffering from heat stroke who are about to throw up all over the floor of your bus?" she asked and in answer got the hiss of hydraulics as the doors swung open. "Thanks for that!" she called over her shoulder, jumping off and looking nothing like a sick person as she made her way to the kerb.

She paused at the official looking black door before pushing it open and stepping inside. The hallway floor was tiled in red with frosted glass doors leading to separate rooms. A grand looking staircase covered in green carpet curved gently up to the first floor. It was cool and airy, especially after the build up of fumes on the High Street. One of the doors had a gold metal plate fixed to it telling her *that's* where she'd find reception, so she quickly tucked her shirt into her skirt and shrugged her arms into her blazer. Taking her tie from her top pocket she passed it behind her neck, effortlessly making herself look smart and tidy. It was second nature now having worn a tie every day for the last five years but, as of Monday, no more tie. That should have made her feel ecstatic but, again, it only reminded her of all that she was losing.

She took a deep breath, allowing a flash memory of Matthew's mockery and a reminder of her father's drunken leery face to spur her on. With Sasha's worldly wise words repeated on her lips one last time, *'I'm beautiful, I'm clever, I deserve a life and I'm damn well going to get one!'* she pushed down on the handle and let herself in.

Chairs sat against one wall and a long curved reception desk sat further back under the windows. There were bookshelves, floor to ceiling, with impressive mammoth legal texts on them and a grand fire place sat exactly central against the back wall. The wooden shutters were pulled back from the huge windows and she could just see the back end of her bus, the No.47, making its way slowly around the corner. A man sat to the right of the doorway clearly in the middle of something important and quite complex looking. She guessed he was a client waiting to be seen. He was so engrossed he didn't bother to look up as she walked over the dark green rug to the desk and waited patiently for the receptionist to finish her telephone conversation.

Ruby played with the hem of her blazer and looked about feeling awkward. Her fingers moved to fiddle with her collar, trying to keep the marks on her neck hidden. Her attention was drawn to the seated man. He was wearing black shiny shoes and black socks. He had on a smart dark suit with the jacket open to expose a professional looking tie, not a comical or musical one like her science teacher wore. He had dark hair, a slight covering of stubble on the lower half of his good looking face and when she looked to his eyes she noticed they were looking right back at her. She was startled. She hadn't been expecting that!

The man narrowed his green eyes on her looking ever so slightly interested and then lowered them back to the papers balanced on his knees. She bit down on her lip nervously and turned back to the receptionist to catch her completing a full head to toe analysis of Ruby in her uniform. Finally done assessing her for worthiness, and no doubt she didn't pass, she looked up to her face, no smile, no customer service, just a snappy,

"Have you *got* an appointment?" Ruby shook her head feeling hopeless.

"No...I just wondered..." she looked back over her shoulder and the man was watching her again, still the same intense gaze as he waited to see what she would say. She took a deep breath and turned back. Now lying she was good at. She had needed to do it from a very young age. She'd lied that the bruises were caused by accident. She'd pretended to school that her father gave a toss and pretended to her father that school was going great. She had made it work for her at school and at home and now she would make it work for her again. She wanted this, she *needed* this.

"An appointment?" she repeated casually. "Yeah of course, the careers office told me to pop in. I was just having a chat with them about my skills...and...and...talents." *That sounded weird coming from her.* "And they said that I would be well suited to office type work. Mrs...Mrs..." She half laughed suddenly realising she had no idea who her careers teacher was and whether they even had one at St Marys. "Malloney," she plumped for, and basically because it sounded like baloney which was what she was talking a lot of, "Well, she said that she would call ahead and arrange the meeting. She told me to make my way straight here from school. You know, *no time like the present!*" she tacked on sounding all positive and eager. She heard the seated man to the right of her and she wasn't sure whether he had coughed or covered up a laugh. She at him but he still appeared to be sorting through paperwork.

"What like for a...*job?*" the receptionist asked with contempt, making no attempt to hide her disapproval.

"Not *like* a job. A job!" Ruby corrected and the receptionist glared at her while the man clearly laughed that time.

"Well who are you supposed to be seeing?" she questioned like it was all such a huge inconvenience.

"The person responsible for offering jobs?" she hazard a guess then, pushing the cocky card further, she pretended she'd forgotten her name. "Erm I think it's a Mrs...Oh I forget now...Mrs..." she raised her eyes to the ceiling thoughtfully and bit down on her lip. Her acting was in full swing and going well.

"Hughes?" the receptionist offered, more helpfully than she realised or meant to be. Ruby grinned, *how easy had that been?* She nodded.

"Yeah that's right, thanks, Mrs Hughes. *That's* who I need to see."

"Right, well, if you want to take a seat I will speak to her but I doubt she'll see you without an appointment. There's nothing on my list and you can't just come in when you want and expect to see someone. You *need* to make an appointment."

Ruby went and sat down choosing to ignore the moaning. The stroppy cow was at least going to ask for her to be seen. The seated man collected up his papers, shoved them into his briefcase, and then stood and approached the reception desk in a couple of smooth strides.

"I'll talk to Mrs Hughes, Amanda," he told her rapping his knuckles once on the desk. "I'll inform her of our young visitor and she'll ring down for her in a minute...I'm sure," he nodded sounding confident as he turned and looked over Ruby with a totally unreadable expression.

"Very well, Mr Alessi," the receptionist acknowledged before grabbing the ringing phone and glaring one more time at Ruby.

Ruby dropped her head and cringed at the floor. She had blagged it and right in front of one of the senior partners too! Mr Alessi, the man whose name was above the door, snorted in amusement as he left the room.

3
The interview

Five minutes later the telephone rang and Amanda sent Ruby up to Mrs Hughes' office. She climbed the gently curving staircase with its immaculately clean green carpet and polished dark wood banister. The office was on the first floor towards the front of the building and she paused at the door, taking another in a long line of deep breaths before knocking.

"*Come in,*" chirped the voice from inside and this time Ruby was relieved to find her next interrogator much nicer than her last. Mrs Hughes stood and smiled warmly, inviting her to sit down.

"Would you like to remove your jacket my dear you must be stifling. I'm so sorry this office is like a furnace today and it won't get much better now we're at the start of summer. It's these old buildings you see, single pane glass and ill fitting windows mean it's freezing in the winter. Some bright spark has actually painted them shut so in the summer it's completely the opposite!" Ruby was melting under the pressure as she removed her blazer. Placing it over her lap she crushed the material between her hands nervously and mumbled.

"Thank you."

"Not a problem my dear," Mrs Hughes smiled kindly. "So, I hear you've come straight from school?" she asked sounding impressed and Ruby nodded. "Your careers teacher sent you, is that right?" Ruby nodded again but this time the squint in her eyes made it look like the nod hurt. Mrs Hughes gave her a searching look "Hmmm, a..." she looked down at some jottings she'd made on a piece of paper as she spoke "Mrs...Mrs..." she looked back up at Ruby's mortified expression, "Mrs...*Maloney* so Mr Alessi informs me." Ruby stayed deadly still. There was no point nodding she had been well and truly busted. Mrs Hughes continued, tapping her pen against the notes in front of her, "Now that's *interesting* because Mr Alessi and I know your careers teacher quite well." Ruby's eyes widened and she stiffened in her seat. "Ruby, for future reference *his* name is Mr Dunlop, like the tyres," she clarified. Her firm expression quickly turned to amusement as she smiled widely. "Don't worry my dear I haven't brought you up here to give you a grilling."

Ruby began to breathe again and her shoulders lowered slightly. She was like a coiled spring and so on edge that a knock at the door made her jump. "You're OK, relax," Mrs Hughes whispered just as the door opened and a young man leaned in.

"I'm really sorry, Lottie, I know you're busy..." He turned and looked over Ruby, his deep brown eyes taking her all in quickly before turning back. "Have they made some alterations to the uniform at St Marys?" he asked with a frown and Mrs Hughes shook her head disapprovingly at him. "I have to say I think it's an improvement...don't you?" he smirked.

"Mr Glover do you mind I'm in the middle of a meeting?" she informed him sternly, caving into a smile. He grinned back, *very* sexy!

"It's not a meeting though is it because *apparently* she never made an appointment," he reminded, thumbing over his shoulder towards Ruby. "In Amanda's book that's tantamount to reception abuse. I'm surprised she's not being detained in the strong room awaiting trial." Mrs Hughes gave a chuckle and Ruby cringed wondering if there was anybody in the building who didn't know what she'd done. "Anyway, sorry for interrupting your *'drop-in'* session but I'm off to court and I really need that document, Lottie, the one Mr Alessi gave you? It's District Judge Whalton and if you don't give it to me then *I'm* brown bread! You may as well toast me now," he submitted with a shudder. Ruby smirked. He was very cute, very funny and obviously way too intelligent to ever feel the same way about her.

"For interrupting like you have, commandeering my office doorway *yet again* and referring to me using my first name during a meeting, whether it was scheduled or not, I should withhold what you need and let you take the flack," Mrs Hughes threatened and he cringed, the kind of cringe that was hard to resist. "*But* I'm feeling generous today *so*..." she scooped a document out of a red tray and the young man slipped into the room to keep her from having to get up. At least that's what Ruby *thought* he was doing. He grabbed the document with one hand and stole two sweets from her open bag of jelly babies with the other. "Danny!" she objected but he just bit one in half and looked at her innocently.

"What, a man's got to eat hasn't he?" he spoke with his mouth full. "I am a student you know and, just for the record, my name is Mr Glover. This *is* a meeting!" he chuckled naughtily, glancing again at Ruby before slipping back out of the room as if he'd never been there.

Mrs Hughes moved her cup onto a pile of loose papers and placed a heavy file on some others. She then turned the desk fan on with a deep sigh. "Do you know that boy is like a whirlwind? He comes in here, leans all over the place with his cheeky grin, steals my sweets, nicks my grapes and then he's gone again and I can't remember what I was doing." She looked about her and retrieved her hand written note which she'd accidently placed with the papers under her cup. "Ahhh yes so, Ruby, why are you here? Why drop in just like that and make up some story to get through reception?" She leaned back in her chair preparing to listen and it creaked under the strain. Ruby stammered nervously.

"I...I'm desperate for a job. I'm really sorry because I never meant to lie. I was going to come in and ask...outright. But the receptionist was so stuck up that I knew I wouldn't get anywhere and so I kind of...panicked. I'm sorry." She sounded and looked very regretful and Mrs Hughes smiled.

"*Why* are you so desperate? Is it the money? Are you in trouble? I'm asking because most young people are dragged here kicking and screaming for summer jobs by their parents and just because they want them to have a reference for their CV. It's clear they would much rather be sunbathing and hanging out with friends over the summer so why don't you?"

Ruby steadied herself, twisting her blazer in her hands as she looked helplessly into Mrs Hughes' pale blue eyes. She was sincere and she made Ruby feel at ease. "How about the truth this time, Ruby?" she urged.

Ruby played with her hands in her lap, twisting her fingers and wondering what to do while Mrs Hughes waited patiently.

"My exam results are going to be awful," she confessed. "I've had more important things to worry about..."

"More important than exams?" Mrs Hughes asked sounding unconvinced.

"Yes," Ruby nodded. "But now all of a sudden the exams are done and I have nothing to look forward to. My future stopped today as soon as I walked out of the school gates. I have nothing planned after the last bell and it's *really* scary. My friends have *everything* sorted. They are going to college and then on to university. They are getting jobs with the family business or going travelling..."

"And you?" she asked gently, seeming genuinely interested.

"I...well I...Oh god this is so embarrassing!"

"Go on," Mrs Hughes encouraged and Ruby took a deep breath preparing to do something she had never done before, confide in someone.

"My dad's an alcoholic and I can't bear the thought of spending the whole summer with him," she reeled off quickly as if ashamed. Mrs Hughes nodded as if she understood. She didn't look shocked or repulsed and so Ruby went on more slowly, feeling a little more confident. "Everyone at school thinks I'm thick but I'm not! I can do so much better I know I can. I just need the chance to show it. I will work *really* hard. I will turn up every day and do *whatever* you want."

"So why did you choose here of all places?" Mrs Hughes wanted to know and Ruby knew she was supposed to say. *Well I researched the most respectable firms and out of all of them this was the one I would give my right arm to work for,* but Mrs Hughes had asked for the truth and so Ruby was going to give it to her, straight.

"Because the bus stopped outside...and...because I told a boy at school today that I had a job...in a law firm. He was being mean to me."

"Like how?" Mrs Hughes demanded forcefully like she might just go and sort him out. It made Ruby smile sweetly.

"He suggested that all I was good for was sunbathing and keeping *him* happy over the summer so I told him I wouldn't be around. I told him I would be too busy," she whispered and lowered her eyes now like she was ashamed. "I told him I had a job." Her eyes turned pleading again and she leaned forward in her seat. "I desperately want to show everyone I can do it...please?" she begged and Mrs Hughes frowned sympathetically.

"Well it's unusual I have to say...but I like you. You have come in here off your own back, stood your ground and stated your case. You have the makings of a solicitor in you my girl," she told her smiling proudly. "It's not the end of your life if your grades aren't up to much. It's easier, yes, but with the right kind of determination you have years to achieve the qualifications you want. I'd say *you're* pretty determined, Ruby! I graduated as a mature student when I was thirty-seven you know. So, how about you come back here on Monday at 9.00am and we will set you up with some tasks, see how you get on? I will probably give you to Sarah to do some matrimonial work, that's family to you and me, or maybe Tom Marshall could do with a hand in civil litigation. I'm sure once everyone knows we have a helper on board they will *all* be trying to steal you for themselves," she laughed. "I think I know who will win *that* battle."

"Who?" Ruby asked praying it would be the young man who'd commandeered Mrs Hughes' doorway and stole her wine gums.

"Ahhh I'm not telling," she answered tapping her nose like it was a big secret. "Let's just see shall we?"

Ruby was baffled but nodded, almost in tears. She'd done it! She didn't care who got her as long as they kept her. She wanted to scream and jump up and down but Mrs Hughes smiled and moved across the room to place a steadying hand on her shoulder, "Ruby, dear, do you think you could be a little bit smarter on Monday?" she asked and Ruby looked down. She gasped out suddenly, having completely forgotten about the abusive messages and childish pictures permanently marking her school shirt. *Now* the sexy, sweet stealer's comment made sense! She cringed painfully.

"Oh that's so embarrassing. I'm so sorry. It's the last day...I could kill Sasha, my friend, *she* did it. It really wasn't my idea!" she tried to explain, desperately fearing everything might be ruined, but Mrs Hughes laughed.

"I understand, Ruby. I've had teenagers of my own and I remember the last day ritual trashing of the uniform *very* well. I'll see you on Monday and well done on getting your first job," she praised. *That* was something Ruby had never experienced before. Mrs Hughes reached out to shake and Ruby let her take her right hand. It was the first time she'd ever shook hands and she hoped she'd done it right!

Nothing was going to dampen her happiness she vowed, not even her dad. It was official she now had a job! The first thing she noticed as she walked down the path to her backdoor was that the smashed hole in the window had been covered up with a thin board, a poor effort but an effort nonetheless. She was confused now and gingerly pushed the door open feeling apprehensive.

"Hey, Rubes," her dad greeted from the kitchen table. He smiled and then quickly looked away, spotting the bruises now spreading out from under her collar up towards her ear and jaw. There was no way she'd have managed to cover those all day, someone must have noticed this time.

"Hey," she replied, lingering in the doorway like she'd just walked into the wrong house. She wasn't quite sure if she would be staying.

"Baby, take a seat, come chat to your old dad," he encouraged kindly and she frowned.

"Why?" she demanded cautiously, keeping the backdoor close just in case he suddenly lunged for her. He stayed quiet as she looked about the kitchen and then, after giving him a brief glance, she edged towards the living room to take a look in there. "What's going on?" she asked accusingly and he laughed and patted the surface of the table.

"Sit, Ruby, please. Look I feel awful for what I did to you last night. This morning I cried, Ruby, after you left for school. I cried like a baby."

"Oh," she seemed shocked and a flicker of guilt crossed her pretty and tired little face.

"No, don't feel bad, sweetheart, it's my fault not yours. I'm a changed man," he declared softly and she nodded and gave him a strained smile. He could see that she didn't believe him.

"I haven't had a drink all day and I fixed the door."

"Yeah I noticed...thanks," she stammered and he smiled and pushed out the chair opposite with his foot. She eyed it like it might bite her and then bravely moved forward and slipped into the gap to take a seat.

"I tidied up too and I cleared up the broken glass in the living room. I made myself lunch, I even had a cup of tea instead of my usual tipple," he laughed and she smiled more hopefully now, even her eyes lit up slightly. "I've changed, Ruby, please believe me. I hate myself for what I did to you, what I've constantly done to you. You must hate me so much...and I don't blame you..."

"No...I don't hate you, dad," she told him awkwardly and he reached forward and placed his large strong hand over hers.

"I wouldn't blame you if you did but I want to make up for it now. I thought we could watch TV tonight, just you and me eh...what do you say?" She smiled and relaxed into her seat. "We could have pizza?" he suggested and she nodded and struggled to contain how excited she was. Everything was working out. She had a job, he was going to stop drinking and they could fix the house up and make it a home again. The end of school wasn't the end of her life like she'd thought, it was just the beginning.

"I'll go check the magazine and see what's on," she declared jumping up and making her way towards the living room."

"Yeah you do that...and I'll go get the pizza," he offered. Ruby stopped suddenly and spun round holding her hands up in front of her to object.

"No please, dad, stay here. We can ring for a pizza...or I can go. Please I don't even want pizza. I'll *make* dinner...I'll make...beans on toast...or...if we don't have beans...toast. It will still be nice. We can both stay here all night, in the living room and then tomorrow you can go to the doctors and tell them you've quit drinking and you might need some help."

"I don't need any help, Ruby," he smiled and she shook her head.

"Oh...I know that but what I mean is...like perhaps they could make it easier...you know...the cravings and that. Don't go, dad, please!" she begged as he stood and made his way to the door. He kissed her on the head and smiled.

"Stop worrying, Ruby, I'm just going to grab a pizza...and stop off to see a man about a dog," which was his way of saying some dodgy geezer on a dark corner of the estate. Tears welled up in her eyes and he cupped her chin in his hand. "Ruby, you have my word. I've stopped drinking, I'm a changed man. I'll not be more than half hour. You stick the TV on, get cosy and wait for your old dad to come back," he told her before turning and leaving through the backdoor.

Ruby sighed deeply and turned off the living room light. She didn't bother to lock the back door, not after last night, and then she made her way straight up to bed. Tears pooled in her eyes as she stared helplessly at the ceiling and when they were full they tipped over the edge and rolled silently towards her ears. She closed her eyes trying to keep from screaming at the injustice of it all but she was so exhausted she soon fell asleep, on top of her quilt, still in her uniform.

In her dream she was walking along the ledge of Tangle and Alessi Solicitors. It was high and she could feel a warm breeze on her face, the breeze carried the distinct smell of alcohol. Below she could see her bus, the number 47, waiting at the temporary traffic lights and suddenly a strong pair of hands pushed her from behind. She fell, fast. She braced herself for pain. As her body hit the floor she jolted in shock, her eyes opening wide. She was on her bed. Her father was right over her, his hands either side of her head as he breathed the smell of alcohol all over her.

"Hello, Ruby," he greeted. "You left the backdoor unlocked, anybody could have come in. You need to be more careful or you're going to get hurt," he grinned and she clenched her eyes tightly shut, waiting for the pain to begin...again.

4
First day nerves

When she arrived on Monday she wandered into reception wishing she'd found out *exactly* where she was meant to go on Friday. Amanda was playing with the answer machine and she glanced up briefly. Ruby smiled but immediately wished she hadn't when Amanda's face didn't crack in the slightest. It was still hard and stony. She hadn't been forgiven for getting past her without an appointment and Ruby doubted she ever would be. She lingered uncomfortably but Amanda clearly wasn't going to make the first move so she did.

"I was asked to come in...by Mrs Hughes...Monday morning...first thing," she stammered out nervously but there was nothing in response. Amanda didn't even bother to look up as she fussed about behind her desk. "Do you know what she wants me to do?" she tried again.

"No!"

"Well is she about then?" Ruby persisted and Amanda sighed and looked her over. Even without the defaced uniform it seemed Ruby was still just as offensive.

"No, she's not here and I don't know what people expect *me* to do about it. They tell people to turn up and then expect *me* to deal with them. Well it's not my job, I'm busy. The answer machine is playing up, I've still got to get the DX and date stamp the post and then they'll be expecting tea..."

"DX?" Ruby asked, confused.

"Yes, documents that come over night, like a secure post. It's the safest and quickest way to send important things. Oh why am I even telling *you?*" she waved Ruby off like she was incapable of understanding.

"Well can *I* help...if you're busy? I could get the DX or make the tea or stamp the post?" She was trying to be helpful but it seemed Amanda liked to moan. She liked her million and one jobs as much as she liked to moan about them and she was actually very protective of them. In her eyes nobody could collect the post quite like she could or be trusted to date stamp correctly and in exactly the right place and nobody would *ever* get the tea and coffee orders right. Ruby was just an annoying schoolgirl no doubt after *her* job.

"No dear I don't think you can. It's not that simple you see." She left it at that letting Ruby read between the lines. She was simple! She was now also furious and ready to put Amanda in her place, right before storming out.

"For your information, *Amanda,* I'm not as stupid as *you* seem to think. If anyone's stupid it's the woman who couldn't keep a sixteen year old girl from landing a meeting that she'd never even arranged! So, as far as your date stamping is concerned, let me clarify just to make sure *you* get it right. It's very simple really, a bit like *you*. The year is two thousand and eleven, the month is May, *that's the fifth month if you're numbering*, and the day is...,"

"Twenty-fifth," Mr Alessi confirmed stepping out from the strong room with a dusty packet of deeds and documents. He looked at Ruby with those same eyes, full of intrigue and amusement. "Shall we find you something to keep you out of trouble, Ruby?" he asked her, not waiting for a reply but expecting her to follow him out of reception and up the stairs. She did. "Right, why don't you start off with Sarah in matrimonial?" he suggested, like she had an option. "Her office is here. Pop your head round and see if she needs you. I'm sure she will." He continued up the stairs without a backward glance or goodbye and Ruby was left standing outside the office door, her tummy twisting in knots. She knocked and Sarah called her in.

Sarah Matrimonial, which Ruby had renamed for ease of reference, was lovely. Her secretary had called in sick so she was also incredibly stressed and flustered. It was a warm sunny day and plenty of hints were banded around about how nice weather seemed to bring on bouts of illness. The other secretaries were all placing bets on whether she would arrive back with a suntan. Ruby was placed in front of a computer, her ears were plugged into a machine, her foot was forced to hover over a pedal and she was asked to see if she could type. She was awful at it and when she accidently hit erase instead of rewind on four hours worth of dictation she was quickly assigned to something *less* stressful; photocopying. That wouldn't have been quite so bad had the copier not been in reception and she not been told to ask Amanda how it worked. That went down like a lead balloon.

"It's so easy a brainless idiot could do it," Amanda told her, demonstrating again how even someone like Ruby could manage it. "This here is the A4 paper tray. This here is the A3 paper tray. You lift this, put the document this way up, tap the screen for what size you want, then what quantity you want, then how dark you want it and *then* you hit the green button...*gently!* Don't slam the lid, don't press the buttons too hard, don't pull the paper out if it jams and never *ever* photocopy with the lid open." Ugh Ruby was getting seriously sick and tired of Amanda.

"Why not?" she demanded to know, crossing her arms.

"I beg your pardon?"

"Why not photocopy with the lid open? Is it shy?" she tormented sarcastically. "Would it like me to turn the lights off? Will I be blinded permanently? Maybe it might take a picture of my face by accident. Perhaps it *might* like to take a picture of my..."

"Thank you, Ruby! *Perhaps* we should see if Tom Marshall has anything for you to do?" Mr Alessi suggested as he stepped from the strong room *again*. This time he had a small white review card in his hand and he was flapping it in front of his face thoughtfully. Ruby rolled her eyes. *How was that possible, did he live in the strong room?* "Amanda," he called out. "All the deeds seem to be mixed up and I'm looking for these ones can you find them for me? I've spent just about as long as I can take in that damn room so perhaps you could just...*sort it?*" he requested placing the small white card on her desk and attracting a huff and an eye roll. He frowned like he didn't like Amanda much and then turned and squinted at Ruby. "You come with me," he ordered.

Tom Marshall was also lovely and this time Mr Alessi took her into the office. There was no uncomfortable having to knock and offer her services to a complete stranger. "Mr Marshall I have a young lady here, Ruby Palmer," he introduced. "Perhaps you could use her for something? I don't know what, maybe some filing? Not photocopying or typing, unless you're feeling brave or masochistic, but if she's no good at filing just...I don't know...get her to make tea or something," he suggested making Ruby feel like an unskilled spare part.

They both looked at her and Ruby looked at her feet, her face fed up. Mr Alessi raised his eyebrows before turning back to Tom. "You heard about the increase in tuition fees then? Bet you're glad you missed all of that, qualifying when you did? Danny's still got another year left." Tom smiled at Ruby standing like a lemon with her hand on her hip, trying unsuccessfully to blend into the corner of the room. He looked back to Mr Alessi.

"Yeah, I heard that Danny's uni just increased their tuition fees to £9,000 per year!" he declared sounding appalled "Apparently it only applies to new students though so hopefully Danny should be OK," he added glancing at Ruby again. She was checking out the room. He continued, "Not cheap eh and all because of government cuts in teaching grants." This time Ruby accidently made eye contact with him *big* mistake. "What do you think, Ruby, will it put *you* off going to uni?" he asked.

"What?" she asked flatly looking from Mr Alessi to Tom. Tom laughed kindly.

"Tuition fees, the cost of studying, will it put you off going to university?" he repeated and she frowned at him and shook her head.

"No but the whole lot of 'U's I'm expected to get in my GCSE's will," she told him widening her eyes and daring him to try and push the subject. She'd had enough. She was stupid, she didn't fit in, she wasn't any good at anything and she couldn't be sure whether Mr Marshall's attempt to join her in the conversation was out of politeness or cruelty. He cringed like he'd done something wrong and Mr Alessi smirked.

"Good luck," he warned and turned to leave the room. Tom lowered himself back into his chair cautiously.

"So, Ruby, why don't you take a seat?"

"Why?" she demanded fiercely and he couldn't help but smile.

"Well maybe then I can tell you what I do. I can tell you what I need to help me do those things and you can tell me if you think there's anything you can do to help me. How about that?" he asked softly and she looked up and smiled at him. Tom Marshall was nice.

Three days later Ruby was still sat in the middle of Tom's floor. She was surrounded by grey files, tidying them, putting things in order, making sure they had account numbers and then making sure they had suspension files in the cabinet for them to go into. He needed them out of the way. They were starting to take over and his room had become a tripping hazard. He only had a narrow pathway through from the door to his desk and he was constantly falling over toppled piles. It was lunchtime and Ruby didn't feel much like going out so Tom offered to grab her a roll from the bakers. He'd been gone half an hour and now she could hear him coming back up the stairs talking.

"I know £9,000! I was speaking to Mr Alessi about it only a few days ago." Then she heard the voice she'd been so eager for. The one she hadn't heard in days and was beginning to worry she would never hear again. She hadn't seen him since Friday, when he rudely and cutely interrupted her non booked meeting. It was Danny, the sweet stealing, doorway lounging, insanely gorgeous reason for her still being there. She had wanted to walk out *so* many times.

"Yeah well Mr Alessi keeps going on about it but then I suppose in his day it was all grants and quills!" he laughed. "Today you kind of come to expect it don't you?"

"Hmmmm, yeah, I suppose," Tom answered regretfully.

"I don't agree with it, Tom, but I'm not so extreme that I would shelf my degree for it. So it's more money. I might just have to ask Mr Alessi for a pay rise. That's what he's *really* worried about, Tom, graduates and trainees looking to recover their costs through *him!* It's not about the poor young students who are starving to death because they only have enough money for ten pints of lager and a kebab. Don't let him fool you, Marshall!" he warned with a laugh and Tom laughed too.

"Well he can't be too hard up he's just taken on another body, quite good she is too. I like her."

"Oh yeah I heard he placed her with you. She's certainly doing the rounds isn't she? First Sarah and then you and all in one day, that's not bad!" he chuckled cheekily. "Or is it? Depends on how you look at it I suppose. He's trying to keep her out of reception did you know?" he went on sounding all gossipy.

"Is he really? He did say something about not getting her to photocopy, is that why?" Tom wondered sounding intrigued.

"Yeah she and Amanda haven't exactly hit it off and you know how volatile Amanda can be. It looks like she's finally met her match. The last thing Mr Alessi wants is Amanda walking. He'd have to put Ruby on reception while he waited for an agency to provide someone else. The clients would *love* that!" he teased and Ruby cringed. *What a git!*

"Ahhh come on, Danny, she's lovely," Tom defended. "She's in there right now as it happens sorting my files out. A very good job she's doing of it too. I'm more than happy to keep her."

"Oh...is she in *there? Now?*" Ruby heard him whisper. "Ooops!" He spoke a little louder than before and she knew it was for her benefit. "Yeah well...you know...if you're getting on great guns with her and she's really helpful...and professional...and...*great*...then as much as I'd like to pinch her and take advantage of her skills I think *you* should keep her. No really, Tom, I insist!" Tom chuckled and then she heard whispering but try as she might she couldn't make out what they were saying. She wanted to slap Danny, hard!

At 4pm that day Mr Alessi strode into Tom's office after just one forceful knock, which made them both jump.

"Ah, Mr Marshall, I'm glad you're here! I need to steal Ruby. I have a big appeal coming up and a backlog."

He didn't wait around to find out whether it was OK or whether she was in the middle of something, which she was. He didn't even ask *her* he just spun round and ordered over his shoulder. "Send her up in ten please." Ruby dropped the file she was halfway through and clenched her hands into fists. Tom looked down at her sympathetically.

"Tick tock," he smirked. "Was nice working with you, Miss Palmer, and thanks for all your help. You've now *officially* been placed. I very much doubt you'll be back now."

5
Mr Alessi's criminal tower

Ruby hated having to leave Tom in the lurch. He'd been so nice to her that she made sure his files were back in the cabinet before making her way up the stairs to Mr Alessi's criminal department. She wandered onto the landing cautiously and felt flustered when she stepped into the office adjoining Mr Alessi's. It was Danny's office and he was sat at his desk. His head was bowed as he sifted through a pile of papers, pen poised. Hearing her arrive he raised his deep brown eyes.

"Hello," he greeted with a smile sounding a little surprised. "Are you lost?"

"No, she's not lost but she *is* late!" a voice boomed out of nowhere. "I told you ten minutes, Ruby, and it's now 4.45. You're thirty-five minutes late!" She glanced at Danny feeling her face flush and he gritted his teeth and scrunched his nose at her.

"Do we need her then?" he asked turning to Mr Alessi who had just stepped into the doorway of his own office. She scowled at Danny for being so rude right in front of her. She would happily go back to Tom Marshall's office.

"Let's find out shall we?" he responded. "Anything you want her to do?"

"Copying," Danny answered distantly like he couldn't care less as he circled something and made a note next to it. "And lots of it," he added on with a laugh. She rolled her eyes and sighed. "Don't worry," he reassured, still making notes, "We have a copier up here so you don't even need to upset anyone." She bit her tongue and kept from responding. He looked up at her waiting to see if she would and then stood, pushing his leather chair out, and left the office. He banged about in the room across the hall for a few minutes and then leaned back through the doorway into her view. "Are you coming?" he asked.

"Why don't you just click your fingers, pat your knees and say *'here girl'?*" she grumbled feeling like a pet. Mr Alessi gave her a blank look and then went back to his own room, leaving her to drag her feet to join a grinning Danny.

The room was small, windowless and white. It contained only boxes of copier paper, a copier, a chair, a desk and a shredder. It screamed minimal and stark.

"Right, these documents here need to be copied three times, please," he requested. She stared at the pile of loose papers resting on top of a bunch of fat lever arch files and took a deep breath. She picked up a sheet, placed it on the glass screen, lowered the lid, increased the quantity to three and then pushed the green button. "Ahhh you're a natural," he grinned patting the lid of the copier and leaving her to it.

At 6pm she made her way back into Danny's office and hung about nervously in the doorway.

"I haven't finished," she told him and his mouth turned up slightly as if amused.

"*And?*"

"And it's 6pm, everyone else has gone home but I still haven't finished. What do you want me to do?"

"Oh yeah of course it is," he confirmed glancing at his watch. "I always stay late but you don't have to. It's easy to forget up here what time it is. You go, Ruby, that's fine," he sounded understanding, nice even, until he added with a grin "You can finish it all in the morning!" She shook her head at him and grabbed her coat wearily from the chair opposite his desk. He watched her leave and then went back to checking, circling and making notes.

The following day she was determined to be more positive. She got in early and tackled the copying immediately. At 10am Danny arrived and put his head round the door.

"Morning. *Very good.* I need that done by 12 lunch time please," he told her before disappearing again. She cracked on and at 11.45 she had it completed. She hadn't stopped for a break, not even for a cup of tea, and she was *very* pleased with herself. She had it all done, three neat stacks of papers and fifteen minutes early too. She could handle this. She went through to see Danny feeling confident.

"Finished," she declared, trying to sound casual. He scribbled something out and jotted something else before looking up at her. He could do casual so much better than she could.

"Have you?" he asked and she nodded feeling competent.

"Well done." He looked at his watch, "And fifteen minutes early too." He'd noticed! "You know what that means?" She narrowed her eyes at him and shook her head carefully.

"No. What?"

"You can go and get Mr Alessi's lunch!" he told her like it was exciting though he knew full well it wasn't. "There's a twenty in my blazer hanging up on the stand. Just check the pockets I've got nothing to hide. He wants a prawn mayo on brown, a juice and a piece of fruit. Thanks, Ruby, and well done again." She wanted to cry but obediently walked over to the stand and rifled through his pockets for the money. It felt a bit strange going though his things and playing with the fabric of his jacket, it felt nice. She could smell the aftershave that clung to it. It smelt *great*. She turned and looked at him, forcing the words out just to be polite.

"Did *you* want anything?" she asked and he smirked.

"Was that painful? It *looked* painful," he observed seeming highly amused before shaking his head. "No I'm fine. I'm being taken out to lunch...*by a lady*."

"That's nice," Ruby managed feeling insanely jealous but not quite sure why. It wasn't like he was in any way hers. She imagined Danny's girlfriend to be beautiful, clever, tall, *blonde,* and probably studying to be a lawyer too.

"Ah that will be her now," he declared hearing footsteps on the stairs and giving her a wink. Ruby turned to leave and nearly walked right into Mrs Hughes.

"Ah, Ruby, I was hoping to bump into you. I was right wasn't I? Mr Alessi got his way in the end. I knew you would end up here. So, *how are you getting on?*" she sung out eagerly and Ruby forced a smile.

"Yeah great thanks. *Just* copying," she emphasised then looked down at the note in her hand. "Oh and getting lunch."

"Ahhh that's really helpful. Isn't that helpful, Danny? I hope you're making her feel welcome *and* valued?"

"Of course, welcome and valued, that's Ruby," he teased. "Now come on where are you taking me for lunch Mrs Hughes, or is it Lottie, are we business or pleasure here?" Mrs Hughes laughed and shook her head at him.

"Behave, Danny, please," she tried to be serious but found it impossible. "How about that nice little coffee shop on the corner?" she proposed. "Oh, and why doesn't Ruby come along too that would be nice wouldn't it?" He frowned like that wouldn't be nice at all.

"She can't she's getting Mr Alessi's lunch," he uninvited quickly. "Come on before the phone rings." He linked her arm and pulled her towards the stairs. "If it does ring, Ruby, just take a message yeah?" he ordered over his shoulder.

Ruby arrived back with Mr Alessi's lunch and placed it on his desk with the change. He was in the middle of a telephone conversation so she didn't even get a thank you. She went back out again and wandered the streets aimlessly for an hour. When she returned her mood felt a little lighter. An hour in the sunshine had helped her recover her morning in a white box with nothing but white paper and a white copier. She was nearly snow blind! She dumped her jacket and bag on the chair opposite Danny's desk, took a deep breath, and forced a smile for him.

"What now?" she asked as helpfully as she could and he folded his arms and leaned forward to look her over. It wasn't a *checking her out* once over it was more like he was intrigued by her, *all* of her. He shook his head like she'd just said something unbelievable and then slammed his hands down on the desk making her jump.

"I have a *really* important job for you, follow me," he told her walking to the far side of the room and opening the filing cabinet drawers. What he wanted wasn't in there and he slammed them shut again. He moved into Mr Alessi's office and she followed. He opened the filing cabinet drawers in there and slammed them shut again. He then opened a cupboard built into an alcove. "Ah ha, here we are. Take these," he told her handing her a bunch of huge lever arch files and letting her struggle with them as they slipped and slid in her arms. He then walked out of the room and she followed, awkwardly.

He led her straight back to the copier room where he pointed at the fat lever arch files on the floor. "Right, we have a very important appeal coming up and those lever arch files contain some of the evidence and supporting documents we need to take with us. It's a *big* appeal. Now that lot there is our copy, but we need a copy for the judge, a copy for the other side and a copy for the barrister," he informed her, ticking all interested parties off on his fingers and then holding them up to make his point. "Three, see! *So,* can you copy that little lot, three times, keeping it all in order? You need to hole punch it and place it, *in order*, in those lever arch files you're holding right there." He tapped them with his pen and her face dropped. The enormity of it all was just too much.

"Are you joking?" she asked desperately.

"Is it funny?" he asked and she shook her head.

"No not really."

"Well then I'm not joking am I?"

He left her feeling like nothing more than a tool. She was expected to dress smartly so they could shut her in a white box for the *whole* day. They wanted her to be polite as she ferried tea and coffee at their every demand and then wait quietly like a good little girl while they talked about things she didn't understand - before she could ask if there was *anything else* they wanted her to do. She hated him, she hated Mr Alessi and she hated the bloody firm too. She went home at 6.30pm, forgetting the time because she was at the top of the building where everybody was left to fend for themselves. It was a whole different world up there, separate from the rest of the firm. It was Mr Alessi's criminal tower.

Danny was too engrossed in his work to even say goodbye or thank you as she scooped her belongings from the chair opposite his desk and left to go home.

6
An eye for an eye

The following morning Mr Alessi and Danny stayed shut in Mr Alessi's room while they had their weekly meeting. Mr Alessi telephoned through to ask Ruby to bring in two coffees as soon as she arrived and she immediately set to it. She managed to open the door while juggling both cups, without any help from them, and they only stopped talking to watch her struggle to find space to put them down.

Danny asked if she was enjoying the copying. She scowled at him, it *wasn't* funny. He then told her if she didn't like it perhaps she could do it more quickly and get it over and done with. She could always ask someone in the building who knew what they were doing for some advice on how to speed things up a bit. The appeal was in four months but they were kind of hoping it wouldn't *take* four months to get the files duplicated.

She could have hit him but instead she stayed quiet choosing not to inform him that she had other important jobs to do aside from the photocopying, like mundane file opening. Mr Alessi watched in silence while Danny wound her up. He didn't join in but neither did he stick up for her and tell Danny to shut his face. She hated both of them but took the moral high ground. She ignored all of Danny's comments and left the room. She heard him chuckle as she closed the door.

She sat at her desk, opposite Danny's, and went back to filling in forms and opening new files. Twenty minutes later he emerged, leaving his empty cup on *her* desk.

"Right I'm off to the police station," he declared and Ruby smiled to herself as she put her head down and continued to pen client details into blank boxes.

He grabbed at the handle of his top drawer but it wouldn't open. He then tried the two below but they wouldn't open either. "My drawers are locked?" he exclaimed, baffled. When Ruby looked up he was frowning and trying to work out how that had happened. He *never* locked his drawers. The key was always in the top lock but he had never even turned it, he hadn't needed to. Now the key wasn't there. He was leaning on his elbow deep in thought his thumb nail turning in his mouth.

"Do you need to take you drawer to the police station then?" Ruby asked innocently and he pinned her with his dark eyes and scowled.

"No, I need my *keys* from the top drawer so I can *drive* to the police station," he responded dropping his arm to the desk and concentrating solely on her now.

"Ahhh I see. Then I wonder where it could be," she mused with a very thoughtful expression. She stood and made her way to his desk, perching on the edge confidently. "Hmmm it's such a small key isn't it? It could be *anywhere!*" she teased, leaning her head back and moving it gracefully so that the curls in the end of her long dark hair swayed and brushed across his paperwork. The paperwork he had spent days working on and which she was now *sitting* on! He looked over her suspiciously.

"Ruby, if you're hitting on me I really don't have the time and anyway...you're *too* young," he told her firmly.

"Get over yourself, Danny. Do you really think I'd *be* interested in someone your age? You're old enough to be my dad and that's pervy!" she scrunched her nose at him in disgust and he frowned back like he was offended.

"I'm three years older than you, Ruby, and I'm *not* old enough to be your dad. Nor am I pervy *thank you!*" he argued. "If you're not hitting on me then what are you doing lounging all over my desk like you might have something I want?" He clenched his jaw, she saw it flex. He'd finally worked it out. "Have you got the key?" he demanded.

"Do you know if I were in a police station I'd be gutted if they sent me you because *you're* crap!" she declared spitefully. He leaned back in his chair and huffed.

"And you're rude so what's your point?"

"*I'm* rude?" she laughed like he'd said something ironic.

"Look if you've got the key..."

"Yes, Danny, I have got the key and *you're* just going to have to find a way of getting it back aren't you? Maybe if you think hard enough you can work it out. Why don't you try...*for me?*" she pleaded mockingly. He narrowed his eyes on her in frustration.

"I'll search you if you don't give it to me *now*," he threatened. "I'm *going* to be late and I don't have time for your childish games!"

"Would you really...*search me?*" she asked seeming both amused and surprised. "I don't think you'd get away with that, Danny!"

"Then I'll just have to tell Alessi you've got it and..."

"*And what?*" she goaded fearlessly. "I'll tell him exactly the same thing as I told you. If *you* want it then *you* find it. To be honest he owes me an apology too. I could kill two very annoying birds with one big fat stone!" she told him angrily.

"Right, so this is about an apology then is it?"

"Well done, Danny, though technically you cheated. Why don't you see if you can manage to work out what the apology is for *without* my help? Be quick it's nearly 10.30am and *you* have to be at the police station," she reminded glancing at her watch and swinging her crossed legs slightly to distract him. It did and he sighed trying to remain focused.

"Erm...because I've been an idiot?" he asked and she smiled and raised her eyebrows like he'd done well but she wanted more. "Because I've been rude to you, mean to you, given you the most horrible jobs I could think of, made you look incompetent in front of Mr Alessi at every opportunity and begged Tom Marshall to have the balls to come up here and demand to take you back?" She glowered at him. The list had been longer than she'd thought. He checked his watch and then looked back at her. He could tell she was hurt now and he melted slightly. Taking the file and blazer from under his arm he placed them in front of him giving her his full attention. "Look I'm sorry, Ruby, OK...I..."

She slipped off his desk immediately, that was all she wanted to hear. She crossed the room, slid open her top drawer and removed the key. Swinging it around her finger she brought it back and placed it down on the surface of his desk. She pushed it towards him keeping her finger on top and he hovered, waiting for permission to take it. She lowered herself in front of him, her eyes burning so wildly he could almost feel her energy. She was like a whirlwind ready to cause devastation faster than he could click his fingers. She spoke low, everything about her determined and undeniably clear.

"Word of warning, Danny, if you bully me expect to get bullied right back. I won't take it, not without a fight. Don't make an enemy out of me if you don't have to," she cautioned before lifting her finger and walking away.

Sliding into her chair she picked up her pen and began filling out boxes as if she'd never stopped. He took the key, opened his drawer, and grabbed his car keys out. He then placed the small key in his inside pocket so she couldn't do it again. He spied his bottle of water sitting on the desk, looked at her and then opened the drawer and locked it inside. She was dangerous and he was bound to upset her again, he didn't want poisoning.

He leaned back in his chair and watched her. She refused to allow herself to be flustered as she hummed and continued to flick through her paperwork like he wasn't even there. He grinned, she was brilliant. He shook his head and collected up his things before walking out and leaving her to it.

7
I just don't think you should be here

That night after work was a long one for Ruby with lots of arguing and torment. Her dad was insanely drunk, again. He had slept the whole day so his body clock was *all* wrong. While she just wanted to sleep he wanted to rant. He stormed into her bedroom while she was dreaming and pulled off her covers just to tell her that she wasn't good enough. He followed the usual routine, dragging her down the stairs in tears and punishing her until he grew bored. Then he collapsed on the sofa and fell into a deep sleep. She crept over him and snuck into the gap behind the settee where she spent the rest of the night praying he wouldn't go looking for her. It was too late to run away, to hide it out at Matthew's house, and she was only wearing shorts and a vest top anyway. She wasn't dressed for roaming the estate in the middle of the night.

By morning Ruby was exhausted and when Matthew stopped to give her a lift into town she gladly accepted. He walked her to the office and she knew he was testing to see if she really *did* work in a law firm. She stopped outside with no intention of inviting him in and folded her arms across her chest.

"OK thanks, Matthew," she told him hoping he would get the message and go away.

"So, what's it like...in there?" he asked trying to peer through a window.

"It's like...*a job,* Matthew. What do you think it's like?"

"Still got the hump then I see?" he smirked at her and she huffed.

"I haven't got the hump and I never did have the hump either. I'm tired, Matthew, and the reason I snapped at you on the last day of school was because I was tired of your stupid games. I know what you're up to and I've heard all about your little *'Hit List'*. You seem to forget that your best mate is my best mate's brother and she tells me *everything*. I'm on the list aren't I?" she demanded to know and he grinned at her.

"I don't know what you're talking about, sorry," he played.

"Right," she went to leave but he grabbed her sore arm making her wince. He pulled her back, stepping forward and pushing her hair behind her ear like he always did. He leaned in but she titled her face away so he couldn't kiss her and as she did so she saw Danny approaching. He smiled smugly and raised his eyebrows at her.

"Morning, Ruby," he greeted pushing open the door and entering the building. She sighed and wriggled away from Matthew. Now she would look like she was making out on the High Street right in front of the firm! She was seriously fed up.

"Leave me alone, Matthew!" she ordered and pushed the door open to go inside.

Heading straight for the coffee room she began to make herself a drink in the hopes that it would keep her awake. Flicking on the kettle she placed some granules in a cup with some milk, a spoon and some sugar. She bent over and rested her arms on the sink and her head on her arms, groaning in frustration. Her head was aching and she felt a bit sick, but after last night that was no surprise.

"That your boyfriend then?" Danny asked her and she sighed. Why couldn't he just wait to make his coffee? Why did he have to do it *right now?* She didn't answer him. "He seems nice. Maybe a little bit pushy but...*nice*," he teased and she turned and glared at him.

"Does he?" she asked angrily and he smirked taking her cup and grabbing another one to put a tea bag in. He then proceeded to pour in hot water and she guessed he was making a drink for himself and his best mate, Mr Alessi. Solicitors and trainees didn't make drinks for the secretaries, they were far too important for that. It was always the other way round, the refreshment pecking order. "Why don't you just stop messing with me, Danny? I know you don't like me. I heard you pretty much say I was rubbish outside Tom Marshall's office. I know you don't want me up here but I'm afraid that's where I've been put. If I'm perfectly honest I don't *want* to be up here but *I* don't have a choice do I? I was quite happy with Tom..."

"Were you?" he asked sounding astonished.

"Yes! He was nice to me. He at least asked me if I was OK..."

"And are you?"

"What?"

"OK?"

"Yes!" She felt confused why was he so smooth and *soooo* cute? He had managed to take the wind out of her sails and she tried to recover herself. She was *meant* to be angry with him. "But that's not the point is it? I felt like *he* appreciated me. I'm tired and I've had a horrible night. I've still got all that copying to do and the room is like a coffin!"

"It's white and airy," he pointed out.

"So it's like a white and airy coffin...and I hate it! There's no view, no windows, no air. It's hot and it stinks of photocopier!"

"It stinks of photocopier?" he clarified with a grin and she gritted her teeth. He stirred the coffee and tapped the spoon annoyingly on the side of the cup. "So what do you want *me* to do about it?" he asked her like she was being slightly unreasonable.

"Can't you just move it in here where there's a window and a view...and air?" she exclaimed.

"I can't just go moving things around, Ruby, stuff like that needs to be given the OK. It's not *my* firm. Mr Alessi asked for it to be put in that small box room and so that's where it was put. He's the boss do you want to take it up with him?" he asked her doubtfully and she shook her head just as tears began to stream down her face. He frowned uncomfortably, the last thing he'd been expecting from her were tears. "Here...this is yours," he handed her the coffee. "You want to talk?" he asked softly but she shook her head. "Is there anybody here you want to talk to, Mrs Hughes is nice...*apparently so is Marshall?*" he joked and she smiled wiping the tears with her hand and snuffling. "OK...well...take a few minutes, yeah?" he encouraged as he grabbed his tea and walked to the door.

He stopped and turned back to look at her. "Oh and by the way Mr Alessi isn't in till later so just in case you thought I'd stolen your coffee, I hadn't. Don't go getting me back or anything." He smiled mischievously and then left the room. She cried a little bit more and then grabbed her coffee and a glass of water to take back to the photocopier room.

Danny was meeting a barrister in court at 9.45am and he returned at 12pm in a foul mood. It clearly hadn't gone well. He banged about and argued with clients over the telephone. Mr Alessi came in and their voices dropped to a whisper. Ruby stayed in the copier room and even closed the door to keep from being dragged into anything, but intrigue eventually got the better of her. Spotting her glass of water on the shelf she downed it and put it to the wall to listen. She knew what she was doing was wrong and her heart raced so loudly she was almost unable to hear as Mr Alessi snapped quietly at Danny.

"Well where the bloody hell did they get it from? This is bad, Danny, *very* bad!"

"Well obviously someone's spoken with the police. We may as well hand over a signed piece of paper saying *'Yeah actually our man did do it. Sorry about the appeal and for wasting everyone's time!'*" Danny fumed.

"So that will be why I've just had a message telling me they're coming in this afternoon," Mr Alessi informed him. "I take it you've been keeping the file safe because what goes on in our meetings, Danny, it is highly confidential. You of all people should know that! It all goes on that file so how the hell has someone got hold of it?"

"Oh come off it are you really trying to pin the blame on *me?*"

"That's not what I'm doing. I'm asking whether the file has been kept secure. That's different!"

"*No* it's the same, Alessi!" he ranted and Ruby noticed that he'd dropped the 'Mr'. She'd also picked up on the fact that the perfection seeking Mr Alessi hadn't challenged it. Now the argument seemed more personal and she was riveted. "What about your new little recruit in there?" Danny went on making her eyes grow wide. *Why was he bringing her into it?* "Has *she* had access to the file? What about the people who were actually *in* the meeting, have you considered them?"

"I'm pretty sure me and Johnny aren't saying anything, Danny," Mr Alessi responded sarcastically.

"Yeah but that still leaves Carlito, right?"

"I don't think Johnny is going to buy that do you? That's his main man. They go back a long way and he's proved his loyalty time and again. No I'm sorry, Danny, but it must have come from that file and this firm." Danny laughed though he clearly wasn't amused.

"I'm sick of all this, busting a gut to keep you and them happy then being asked to come up with a reason for being made to look like an idiot in court!" Something was slammed down on the desk and it made Ruby jump. She almost dropped the glass. "Does she have any idea, Alessi? Does she have a clue because I really don't think you're being fair here? She's just a girl, she can't handle this and she's a liability too. Information on Johnny Giavani's file gets leaked and you've just taken on someone new. Have you worked out what that means yet?" Ruby couldn't believe how cruel he was being about her and she frowned, feeling hurt. Why couldn't he just be more like Tom Marshall and appreciate her for once?

"She *can* handle it and she's fine," Mr Alessi told him firmly refusing to budge on the matter.

"If fingers get pointed that includes her too. Send her back to Tom Marshall she was happy there, she said so herself this morning! Do everyone a favour, Alessi!" Ruby was gobsmacked not only was he ordering Mr Alessi around, his boss and senior partner, he was trying to get rid of her too! He'd been on the verge of nice earlier and now he just wanted shot of her.

"If fingers get pointed, Danny, she will tell them what she knows, which is nothing," Mr Alessi clarified coolly. "She will be fine. She's tough and I've never seen anything like it. She's a one off and I like her. She stays, Danny!"

"You like her and she can handle it," he clarified with a hint of sarcasm. "OK let's see shall we?" She heard footsteps approaching and quickly returned the glass to the shelf in a panic. She felt sure they would know what she'd been up to. She grabbed a pile of papers and held them against her chest, *as if that would protect her!* She then backed quickly up to the copier as Danny shoved the door open causing it to slam hard against the wall. He glared at her, his hair ruffled, his tie undone, his shirt out under his blazer and his hands balled into fists at his sides. She looked frightened and when Mr Alessi joined him in the doorway, *completely* blocking her exit, her big blue eyes grew even wider. There was no escape.

"What?" she whispered looking from one to the other.

"Why are you here?" Danny demanded but she didn't answer. "Do you even know?" Still no answer, she was stunned. "Have you been sent or are you blissfully ignorant, Ruby?" She looked to Mr Alessi for help, her mouth slightly open.

"Get some air, Danny, you're being an idiot," Mr Alessi told him, sticking up for her *at last*.

"Right, so it's OK to point the finger at me but not at her? Are you going to tell *them* that? I thought you said she could handle it. Is that what she's going to do, stand there catching flies, refusing to talk, or are you going to tell them to stop being idiots and settle for fresh air over answers? Do you think they're going to let her off that lightly, Alessi, just because she's attractive, just because she's female? I'm telling you now that they won't and, if anything, *that* will make it worse...for her."

"What have I done?" Ruby found her voice at last. "I've been in here copying the whole time and I'm not ignorant either. I know I'm not as clever as you with your eighteen year practice certificate," she pointed at Mr Alessi. "Or *you* with your degree," she jabbed her finger more forcefully at Danny. "But I'm *not* ignorant! It's been hard that's all. I've had other things to deal with. Nobody told me to come. I wasn't...*sent*. I wanted to prove that I could get a job, hold it down and be good for more than just pleasing that creep who you saw me with this morning, Danny. I don't understand what's going on here. I think you're right I haven't got a clue." She flayed her arms helplessly. "I think I should go. I don't think this is working." She put her hands on top of her head and took a deep breath trying not to cry. They stared at her, putting her under more pressure. She just wanted to be left alone but they hadn't budged. "I just keep getting it wrong and I'm trying, I *really* am. I can't seem to get *anything* right!"

Danny took a long deep steadying breath and rubbed his forehead and eyes with the tips of his fingers like he had a headache.

"Ruby...I'm sorry. I never meant that you were thick. I really don't think that. Please...look...don't go, you're doing great. I just lost it that's all, bad day I guess." He turned to lean against the frame and face Mr Alessi. "She will have to be somewhere else when your clients come in, Alessi," he informed him.

"Yes I know that," he nodded.

"No, I know you *'know that'* but I mean you *really* have to make sure she's somewhere else because it's doing my head in having her here. I'm not comfortable with it at all."

"Relax she *won't* be here. I will make it absolutely clear when the time comes that she has to be out."

"Why don't you want me here, Danny? Why do you hate me *so* much? What have I done to you?" Ruby demanded softly and he looked at her for a long minute, searching her face all pale and upset.

"I don't hate you," he told her simply before turning and walking back to his office.

She stared at the gap left beside Mr Alessi and when she looked up into his green eyes hoping for an explanation he stepped into the room and approached her. Reaching out he pushed her hair gently away from her face to expose the marks that covered her neck. She quickly moved his hand away and he spotted the bruises on her wrist too. She couldn't look him in the eye as she slung the paper she was holding onto the floor in frustration. She crossed her arms over her chest feeling defiant. *Why did he have to go and interfere?*

"Who did it?" he asked her in a whisper and she shook her head still looking at the floor.

"Accident," she told him flatly.

"Hmmm." He didn't sound convinced. "Is there a problem, Ruby?" he asked her softly and she looked up into his eyes, her face hard and determined.

"I never came here for counselling, Mr Alessi, I came here for a job so just let me get on with it," she told him. His eyes seemed to sparkle with surprise at just how resilient such a small girl could be.

"Very well, Ruby, but remember I am a lawyer by profession and sorting problems is my job. I'm very good at my job and to employees like you I offer my services for free."

"Thanks," she acknowledged just wanting to leave the awkward conversation behind. He smiled warmly for a second and then reverted back to Mr Alessi mode as if someone had flicked a switch.

"Ruby, I need a file retrieved from storage. Go down and get it for me," he ordered handing her a white review card. This time she didn't bother to huff about it. She reached out and took the card from his left hand and the keys for the basement from his right. She immediately went to search for it, glad to be away from the both of them.

8
The price you pay for being a woman

It took over an hour and it was lunch time before she eventually found the file she was looking for. She felt icky and dizzy and her head was *really* hurting now. She tried to work out when she'd last had her period but since starting work and with her usual timetable being all different it was impossible. Was she half way through her cycle or was she actually due for a week of hell, she just couldn't be sure. Then, as she was climbing the stairs back to the office the cramps suddenly hit and she gripped the banister fighting the wave of nausea that came with it. The firm appeared to be deserted and she was glad of it. The last thing she wanted was for someone to come and make a fuss of her.

She sat on the stairs doubled over for a little while longer. When the cramp passed she stopped in at the ladies to splash water on her face. The night of no sleep wasn't helping. It was impossible to catch up after losing a whole night like that and being tired just made her already bad periods so much worse. It meant she couldn't eat and that meant she had no energy. Being tired made her feel cold and emotional and now all she wanted to do was curl up and sleep.

She slowly and wearily made her way to the top of the building with the file but as she passed the box room she gasped out in shock.

"The photocopier, it's gone!" she declared loudly and Danny popped his head round the office door. His forehead creased and his eyes looking delighted at how funny she was.

"Are you serious? You're not worried that the copier's been stolen are you?" he asked, poorly trying to hide his amusement.

"Yes, *look* it's not here. It was here when I went down to get this file and now it's...it's gone! I'm not lying, Danny, come and look! It definitely wasn't my fault this time. I've been gone for over an hour so don't blame me!" she exclaimed defensively and he threw his pen behind him onto the desk and hooked her elbow with his hand to lead her into the coffee room.

"Copier!" he announced and her mouth dropped open. She recovered it with a grin and a giggle. It was so good to hear her laugh and he realised it was the first time he'd ever heard it. It was a really sweet infectious laugh and it made him want to say something else funny. He nudged her with his elbow, "Window, air and view," he reminded her of her wish list.

"But how?" she asked feeling stunned.

"Permission was requested as soon as you went down to storage and *unusually* granted just like that. So here it all is just as the lady ordered," he told her. "I'm sorry for going off at you, Ruby. I don't hate you," he confirmed looking deep into her eyes for a *very* long moment. God she wanted to kiss him so bad he was so incredibly gorgeous. "I just would rather you wasn't here that's all. Try not to take it personally," he smiled sympathetically and then turned to walk back to his desk. She was mortified. It wasn't personal he just didn't want her around! How personal could it get?

The joy of finding the copier relocated had been swallowed up whole by Danny's open and honest admission. Ruby, feeling unwanted and sad, went back to the box room to continue sorting paperwork into the three evidence files.

"Right I'm off to court if anyone calls," he suddenly interrupted her looking round the doorway and sounding much happier now he'd made her life a misery. "I probably won't see you till tomorrow because I'll be back late but have a good afternoon...it's nice outside," he told her and she nodded, hole punching a wad of papers, splitting them into three piles and then placing them into each of the lever arch files in order.

"Got it," she told him feeling unwell and fed up. The pains were strong and regular but she was battling them admirably. Mr Alessi was next to put his head round the door.

"Ruby, you look very pale I suggest you go out and enjoy the sunshine over lunch." She nodded just to get rid of him but she had no intention of trying to top up her tan. "Right I'm popping out for ten minutes then I need to be back. I've got clients," he told her while she continued to punch holes. "Ruby!" he called her sternly and she looked up, trying to remember whether she'd put the last document in all three piles or just the one pile, that would put *everything* out of order. "I have clients," he repeated and she frowned at him. *So what? He always had clients why was he telling her now?* He was still looking at her and she was frowning back at him like she didn't understand. "I have clients in ten minutes and you're going out, *yes?*" he confirmed more slowly.

"Yeah cool, clients, ten minutes, I'm going out, got it," she mumbled trying to concentrate but feeling weak enough to faint.

"So...I'll see you after lunch then shall I?" he asked her and she nodded, again paying no attention. If she messed up the lever arch files she would no doubt be cornered and shouted at again so she was paying close attention. If that meant ignoring Mr Alessi then so be it."

"OK see you later then," she confirmed trying to sound interested and he nodded feeling satisfied .

"Very good."

As soon as Mr Alessi was gone and she knew she was finally alone she took herself into Danny's office to pop some pain killers. She curled into a ball in his deep comfy chair and pushed her hands into her abdomen, her head on the armrest. She tried not to think about the thumping headache or the urge to be sick that flowed over her in waves every time her stomach cramped. Every now and then she'd get a big one and the agony made her knees pull in more tightly.

Tiredness got the better of her and as the tablets began to take the edge off she managed to doze. The sound of Mr Alessi's voice slowly brought her back again. He was climbing the stairs and chatting and as she tried to get her body to respond and wake up he reached the office and spotted a sleepy Ruby in the chair. He stopped dead and his face looked different, he looked concerned. He was unsure whether to continue, frowning at her like he was furious, like she'd done something terribly wrong. She uncurled herself from the seat, feeling tight and stiff.

"Is there a problem?" she heard a voice from behind him and she suddenly remembered he said he had clients. Had they arrived already she wondered feeling dazed and disorientated. He paused a little longer staring right into her eyes like he hoped they might contain the answer to his dilemma, but nothing came.

"No, there's no problem, please come right through," he invited breaking eye contact with Ruby as he walked passed her to make the journey to his room. The first man stepped through the doorway and stopped. He was a large older looking man, handsome, distinguished and everything about him hair raising. Ruby was petrified and her heart began to race.

He started to move again but his eyes didn't leave Ruby's until he was standing in the doorway with Mr Alessi. "Please go through, take a seat," he encouraged but his client paused as his eyes moved to settle on Mr Alessi's. They appeared to be able to send messages without words and Ruby was picking up on the vibe, he wasn't happy! As soon as the first man was out of view, claiming one of Mr Alessi's client chairs, a second man stepped into the room filling the doorway with his broad, towering frame. He immediately smiled upon seeing Ruby and stepped right up to the desk to shake her hand.

"Please forgive my companion, Johnny Giavani, he's not in the best of moods right now," he told her, stating the obvious. "You're a new face," he continued. "That's not *always* a bad thing, especially when it's as pretty as yours," he grinned and winked. "I'm Carlito. Pleased to meet you Miss...?" he waited for her to fill in the gap but Ruby was rigid in her seat, her small hand in his warm clutches. She looked to Mr Alessi unsure what to do and he cut in for her.

"Just an office junior that's all, Carlito, you're unlikely to see her again. She doesn't get involved in cases."

"She looks quite cosy in Danny's chair, she looks like she's been here for years," he observed sceptically looking back over his large shoulder.

"Well she *was* asleep and sleeping on the job is always a *very* bad sign," he responded staring at Ruby now and sounding more than a little hacked off at her.

"Hmmm, if you say so," Carlito mumbled. "Well it was nice to meet you anyway Miss...*office junior*," he smiled, letting her hand slip from his. She immediately placed it under her thigh and sat on it so he couldn't try and shake it again. He stared at her a little longer as if waiting for her to break and confess something and then finally turned away. He chuckled before making his way into Mr Alessi's office to join his colleague.

Ruby worried for the rest of the afternoon. Heading straight for the door she roamed the streets of the town centre until at least 1.30pm. She knew she would be returning late from lunch but she'd rather that than meet Mr Alessi's clients again. They had properly freaked her out. The first guy was scary in a, *I don't talk* kind of way but the second guy was creepy and friendly in a, *I would smile whilst breaking every one of your fingers* kind of way. She wasn't keen on either of them.

Eventually she went back to the office but Mr Alessi wasn't there and he didn't come back. Danny didn't come back either so she locked the door at the top of the stairs feeling scared. She was worried their clients might return and find her alone. She continued to pick her way through the stacks of papers that needed copying and for the first time she was glad when it was time to go home.

She made sure she left at 5.30pm with everyone else, there was no way she was staying another minute longer than she had to. She definitely didn't want to face Mr Alessi who might come back and rant at her, she didn't want to see Danny who had made it quite clear that he didn't want to see her and nor did she want to be in the building on her own.

9
Verbal warning

The following day Ruby arrived to find Mr Alessi's door closed and though it looked like Danny had been there, having left behind his blazer and coffee cup, he wasn't in the box room or the coffee room. She went back to her copying but was disturbed half an hour later when the phone rang. She followed the ring all the way to Danny's phone and begrudgingly picked it up.

"Hello," she answered cautiously. Technically the phone was Danny's, it was on his desk, but she was always worried someone might try and put an angry client through to *her*. In fairness the firm had enough of them!

"Ruby, can you come in here please?" It was Mr Alessi and she panicked. Before she could say anything he hung up on her with a slam. Her legs felt like jelly as she stood at the door to his office and tapped lightly. "Come in," he ordered and she stepped inside to see him sat at his desk with Danny stood just to the side of him. Danny smiled slightly in acknowledgement but Mr Alessi didn't, he just sighed cupping his hands together and placing them in front of him.

"You wanted me?" she asked meekly.

"Ruby, do you have a problem with instructions?" he asked her sternly and she shook her head.

"No," she whispered.

"I told you yesterday to go out at lunch time and get some fresh air. I told you it was sunny..."

"What? You can't tell me what to do on my lunch break! Look I felt ill OK..." she argued but he cut in.

"Ill! All of a sudden you were ill?"

"I had stomach cramps. I felt sick..."

"A bout of appendicitis was it? Sounds like a convenient excuse for not doing as you're told to me." he accused. She frowned at him, refusing to respond as she pressed her mouth into an obstinate line. He raised his clasped hands and brought them down onto the table, hard. "Ruby!" he prompted angrily and she clenched her jaw.

"OK! It was my period, Mr Alessi, if you must know! I felt rough and, *yes,* it came on suddenly and, *no,* it wasn't a convenient excuse at all. In fact, after the way you two treated me yesterday, him attacking me and you doing nothing to stand up for me, it was very *in*convenient actually. I didn't *want* to go out and if I'm honest all I really wanted to do was go home to bed!"

"Well you should have," he told her.

"Is that a sackable offence then, not going out at lunch time?" she asked sarcastically.

"No but it might well be a new one young lady if you don't lose the attitude!" he barked at her fiercely. She frowned and sobered up slightly.

"Mr Alessi, you're not really going to sack me are you just because I stayed in? I can't get sacked I have to be out of the house for the whole summer...*at least*. Please, Mr Alessi, you're being completely unreasonable. I can't help that I was ill. I can't help that I was suffering. I get really bad sometimes, especially if I'm stressed and tired. I can't help it. Ugh this is *so* unfair!" she grumbled and he frowned and held up his hand to stop her.

"Ruby, can you please just shut up for a minute? I do know about periods, I'm not stupid. I also appreciate that you didn't want to tell me that's what was wrong with you but if you get that bad again then I'd rather you told me you were sick and went home, particularly if I've asked you to do or not to do something. Do you understand me?"

"I thought you'd think I was shirking and to be honest there's no point going home anyway, I wouldn't get a break. I was trying to be responsible, Mr Alessi," she tried to defend herself and he nodded formally.

"And I am grateful for that but when I make a request there is usually a good reason. I wouldn't suggest you go out for lunch unless I *thought* it was necessary."

She sighed feeling ganged up on and she couldn't believe that she'd just declared to both of them that she had periods! "Ruby, please sit down." Mr Alessi gestured to the leather chairs in front of his desk and she frowned. *What now,* she was screaming in her head. She moved to take one and he watched as she glanced about the room with unease. "Did you read my client's file yesterday by any chance?" he asked her and her mouth opened slightly but no words came. She glanced up towards Danny and saw the slightest of head movements. Was it a nod, she couldn't be sure? She looked back at Mr Alessi.

"Yes," she lowered her gaze knowing she'd definitely done it now. "You left it out and I wanted to know why he was a client. He gave me the creeps yesterday, they both did, and then you went out and never came back. You were both out and I was alone. It was on your desk. I didn't go looking for it, I swear. I was dropping something off, a letter that had been hand delivered..."

"Yes I got that thank you," he confirmed.

"I know it doesn't make it right but I only read the first page and it didn't tell me much. I was curious but then I chickened out. I kind of wanted to know why I felt the way I did about them but then I wasn't so sure I really wanted to know. I'm thinking it's not good. My intuition was telling me to run, jump, whatever it took to get out of here when they turned up yesterday. I trust my feelings, Mr Alessi, they've got me out of a lot of situations in the past. I'm really sorry," she told him sincerely and he nodded and smiled.

"Very good, truthful, I like that. I demand complete honesty from my team. You can lie as much as you like to everyone else, Ruby, hell most of the time you'll have to, but not to me. I expect the truth the whole truth and nothing but the truth. Do you understand me?"

"I understand, but aren't you going to bawl me out for it? Aren't you going to sack me for..."

"Right this sacking issue seems to be a real problem for you," he interrupted. "So, let me make myself clear right now and before we go any further. I am *not* sacking you. I have no intention of sacking you and while we're on the subject of honesty I can't really sack you, not now, you know too much."

"Too much?" she echoed and he nodded, "What does that mean?"

"Do you really need me to explain what 'too much' means, Ruby? I know you're set to get an 'F' in your GCSE English but I at least expected you to understand that."

"How do you know about my exam results?" she protested, looking horrified, and he laughed.

"Ruby, since you ignored my instructions and stuck around over lunch to see the faces of my *very* private clients, and then had the cheek to read one of their files, I made it my business to know *everything* about you. I've looked into your predicted exam results, your shocking behaviour at school, your social life, your home life, even your *love* life." Danny dropped his head and concentrated on his shoes awkwardly.

"What the...but how...why? I don't understand!" she exclaimed looking from Mr Alessi to Danny, who was still wishing he wasn't there. Mr Alessi glanced at him too and shook his head in despair.

"Stand please, Ruby," he instructed as he pushed his chair back and made his way across the room. He stopped right in front of her, invading her personal space, and she felt flustered as he reached out towards her. He ran his fingers inside the collar of her shirt and she tried to step backwards thinking he was making a pass at her.

"Whoa, Mr Alessi! I don't know what you think the deal is here but I'm really not that kind of..."

"Shhhh," he reassured, his mouth creasing into a grin as he brushed the back of her neck. He then removed his hand bringing it back for her to see. Perched on his index finger was a clear round plaster, almost invisible to the eye. When it was flat against his skin it was impossible to see it but when he peeled it off and let her see sideways on she could tell there was definitely something there. He then took hold of her hand and turned it palm up so he could lay the floppy silicone disk on it for her to examine.

She prodded it with her finger and then looked up into his eyes, searching for answers. "It's a bug, Ruby," he explained. "I had to be sure you weren't spying for someone else. It would be a good cover, young pretty schoolgirl walks in for a summer job and lands one just like that, ignores requests, sees my clients and reads their files. The file you found on my desk was a set up, an old file from storage put in a fresh cardboard folder. I checked for your fingerprints and they only appeared on the first page so you were telling the truth. You eventually did as you were told yesterday and went out until 1.30pm."

"How do you know that, you were out when I came back?"

"As soon as my clients were comfortable in my office I had you followed. Do you remember the gentleman who kindly informed you that the label in the collar of your shirt was showing?"

"He tucked it back in for me while I was chatting to a trader on the market," she recalled not liking how much he knew. Someone had been watching her and they had even come close enough to touch her. It made her shudder at the thought.

"He wasn't tucking your label in, Ruby, he was planting this...for me." He removed the *thing* from her hand. "It tracks too," he informed her, seeming pleased with its multitude of uses.

"Great," she responded dryly her mind feeling completely blown.

"I know where you went last night, who you talked to and what you said. I also know what you did...or *didn't* do," he informed her and she suddenly collapsed back into her chair in disbelief. She placed her hands over her face to try and hide from the humiliation.

"My god, you were...*spying*...on me! There has to be laws against that. I'm here to file, fax and photocopy. That's a serious breach of my human rights, Mr Alessi!"

"Spoken like a true lawyer," he laughed. "What do your teachers know, Ruby Palmer?"

"But you listened in...to...*everything?*" she clarified uncomfortably and he nodded.

"I'm sorry, Ruby, but I had to. It's my neck on the line and I really mean my neck. If you happened to go straight to the police and tell them what you'd seen in that file, if you gave names of the corrupt officers we hold information on, we would be looking at a serious problem. Problems need dealing with, Ruby, and my clients are dangerous. I don't just handle petty theft and drunken street brawls. I deal with arson, armed robbery, murder, torture, drugs, trafficking and corruption. I'm talking gangland stuff, Ruby. The question is can you handle it? If you can then you might be looking at more than just a summer job here." Danny had stayed quiet for the whole of the meeting but now he stepped in.

"Mr Alessi, look, I really think you should just pay her and offer her a reference for another firm. She's young, she's...she's a liability," he protested and Ruby glared at him. He could be such an idiot sometimes.

"She is young but she also has the perfect background. No pushy overbearing parents to worry about. She has the looks, the talk, the determination and the drive. I think she's perfect. They've already seen her, Danny. I tried to make out she was just a junior but they didn't buy it. They humoured me but they think she's part of the team and they are fully expecting to see her again. She's seen their faces and Carlito told her their names..."

"He did what?" Danny sounded mortified. "Why would he do something as stupid as that? Their names are none of her god damn business!" he half shouted and Ruby frowned at him, her mouth open once again. What *was* his problem? He half laughed looking defeated. "So basically because of Carlito she *has* to stay now. *He's* just made her permanent! Why, Alessi?" he demanded to know and Mr Alessi shook his head at him.

"Maybe it was an accident but either way they won't want their visits jeopardised by our allowing an office junior access to clients and information like that..."

"We didn't!"

"Look we can't go back on what's happened. She knows. Whether you want to blame Carlito, me, or her for not obeying orders, the result is still the same and they will now want to grill her themselves..."

"What?" Ruby sat forward in her chair preparing to walk.

"We are talking about the Cosa Nostra, Ruby, the Mafia," he smiled. "That's who *you* shook hands with yesterday. Your instincts, gut feeling, intuition, whatever you want to call it, it's very acute."

"But they will want to grill me? Just for being here at lunchtime? Grill? Me? What like broken fingers?" She was almost in tears and Danny, who was holding his body weight against the table, dropped his head and shook it from side to side slowly.

"See she can't take it," he spoke firmly. "It's not fair. Just let them monitor her. If she consents to being bugged they will soon see she has nothing to do with anything and eventually leave her alone." For once Ruby was starting to like the sound of Danny's advice. She would be bugged for the rest of her life if they would just keep from torturing her.

"Red hot pokers, electricity, my pet dog's head?" she fretted and Mr Alessi looked amused.

"That was the Godfather, it was a horse's head and anyway you don't have a pet dog...I checked," he told her.

"Ugh, is there anything you don't know about me?" she demanded feeling completely exposed, but not as exposed as she was about to be.

"Nothing, Ruby, I know *everything* and, by the way, if Matthew tries to tell you again that you should be having sex with him he's wrong." Danny groaned and Ruby tried to turn her chair so he couldn't see her face. "He's only after one thing you know..."

"Oh I know thanks very much," Ruby cut him off raising the palm of her hand for him to look at. "I've worked that out *all by myself* and I didn't need to breach *anybody's* privacy to do it!"

"I can see that he gets a little talking to if you feel pressured. I'm sure Danny here would be more than happy to speak with him...wouldn't you, Danny?" he asked raising his eyebrows and grinning.

"I'm sure she can handle some school boy, let's face it you're offering her a job with the mafia," he reminded him and Mr Alessi laughed.

"Very true," he agreed. "Well, anyway, if you need your boyfriend sorting I can arrange it," he confirmed helpfully and she slammed her hands down on the armrests.

"He's *not* my boyfriend!" she objected but then stopped fuming for a second and frowned. "What do you mean by sorting?"

"Gentle talking to, nasty trap, poison, a hole in the head? There are many ways to deal with vermin, Ruby."

"He's *not* vermin! He's a pain in the arse, yes, but he's *not* vermin. I've known him for years and I can't *believe* you were even listening to our conversation..."

"Argument, Ruby, say it how it is," Mr Alessi had the nerve to correct. "It wasn't a conversation. He was piling on the pressure and you were arguing."

"IT WAS PRIVATE!" she shouted back at him her face so flushed it felt ready to explode.

"Ruby, from now on *nothing's* private. If I think you need bugging, following or grilling, I will sanction it and with regard to Matthew, trust me, I was a teenage boy once and the lines and moves he's pulling *all* lead to the same thing."

"Great, a sex talk from my boss!" Ruby stropped raising her knees and hiding her face behind them.

"Just you remember to follow the rules, young lady, starting with this one," he told her slapping her leg, "Feet off the chair!"

10
A romantic gesture

Ruby couldn't wait to get the day over and done with. She spent the rest of it avoiding both Mr Alessi and Danny at all costs. She closed the door of the box room while she hid and got on with hole punching and pouring through paperwork. She didn't even come out for lunch and she worked through *all* of her breaks too. Mr Alessi pointed out to Danny that the firm had never seemed so quiet but Danny felt sorry for Ruby. It was clear she never wanted to have another conversation like that again, especially with Mr Alessi! She was glad when it was eventually time to go home and for the second day in a row she made sure she left on time.

"I'm off!" she declared forcing herself to enter Danny's office and acknowledge him, but just so she could grab her things from the chair and get out again.

"Ruby," he called softly and she stopped in the doorway but didn't turn. "Are you OK?" he asked her and she nodded vigorously as her face flushed. She was so glad he could only see the back of her head.

"Yep fine," she told him quickly and untruthfully. He smiled. He could tell that she was eager to leave but she didn't want to seem rude as she hung on to see if he was all done.

"Have you decided what you want to do about the Johnny Giavani thing? It's your call you know. Alessi might insist on you staying but you still have a chance to get out. All you have to do is hand your notice in and agree to being tracked for a while. I'm assuming you have nothing to hide?" he queried kindly and she shook her head and turned to look at him.

"You'd like that wouldn't you, Danny? Would it really make you happy if I handed in my notice?" He bit on his thumb nail and gave a long sigh.

"Yes. It's complicated, Ruby. It's not as simple as you think. I'm trying to help you here. By your own admission Carlito and Johnny frightened the life out of you. Do you really want a job that involves rubbing shoulders with people who make you feel like that?"

"Danny, I've rubbed shoulders with people who make me feel like that every day of my life. I can handle it and you can't get rid of me that easily. My exam results are going to be crap, my teachers will vouch for the fact that I was nothing but a pain in the arse and a trouble maker and jobs are hard to come by. I need this job because it's this or nothing and there's no way I'm going to sit at home with my dad for the rest of my life, unemployed. Give me Mr Giavani and Carlito any day over *him*," she joked sadly.

"What if I lined up another job for you, the same kind of thing...but different clients? I know a lot of people, a lot of firms. I could easily get you placed somewhere else. I would give you a glowing reference. You *are* a very good worker, Ruby," he confessed and she narrowed her eyes on him.

"I do believe you just gave me a compliment, Mr Glover," she smirked and he smirked back, it was *very* cute. "Thanks for the offer, Danny, but I'm not that stupid. If you get me a job elsewhere and I mess up they will kick me out just like that. Then I'm back to square one again. For some reason, and I don't quite know why, Mr Alessi seems to like me and he's made it clear that he can't just get rid of me. I know too much, remember?" she told him cheekily and he dropped his head to the desk as if exasperated. She was very clever and also spot on. "I'm kind of guaranteed my job here so why would I take a risk by going elsewhere? Until Mr Alessi kicks me out I'm here to stay so you'd better just get used to it."

She turned and left the room descending the stairs quickly and silently, only the slam of the front door gave any indication that she'd left the building. Danny leaned back in his chair, either she had no idea what she was letting herself in for or she was much tougher than he thought.

She started her walk up the High Street and a voice called out to her from behind.

"Hey, Rubes!"

She huffed, not needing to look round to know who it was. She didn't stop but she did let him run to catch her up. "You are *so* rude, Ruby

Palmer, do you know that?" Matthew complained falling in with her pace and nudging her with his elbow. She looked him up and down.

"New trainers, Matthew? How'd you afford those, your mum get a pay rise?" she goaded and he sucked his teeth at her.

"Shut up, Ruby, you're not the only one with a job you know."

"Huh what *you've* got a job, and you expect me to believe that?" she giggled, highly amused. It annoyed him but there was something about Ruby that had him hooked, he always had been. There had been plenty of other girls for Matthew but Ruby was difficult, hard work *and* a challenge. He was determined to have her one day, to win her over, to get her to give in to him. She needed him and she went to him for safety, he was half way there already. It was only a matter of time before he would have her worn down and ticked off his Hit List. But he wouldn't be letting her go again. He knew he wouldn't stay faithful to her, he wasn't the faithful type, but she was *definitely* a keeper and he had no intention of sharing her with anyone.

"OK so I don't have a job...yet," he admitted, "but that's just because I'm concentrating on my school work. Some of us *are* going on to do A' Levels, Rubes, remember?"

"Are you saying I'm too stupid to do A' Levels?" she stopped and glared at him, her face so defiant he couldn't help but smile. He loved their fall outs and fights. Ruby was physical and he had the scars to show for it. He shook his head because right now he *didn't* want to fall out.

"No, babe, I'm definitely not saying that," he told her as sincerely as he could manage while trying not to laugh.

"Listen I'll have you know that I'm doing my exams again, my boss is paying for it and *he* says I *will* go on to university. So if you're taking the piss, Matthew, you'd better just shut your face else..."

"*Ruby!* I'm not taking the piss come on listen to me." He took her hand and she stepped backwards. He pulled her forwards. "Hit defrost for a second will you, Ruby. I mean come on it's not like I'm some stranger is it? Can you not just be friendly for once? Are you like permanently due on or something?" She pulled her hand away from his and carried on walking but he caught her up and slipped in front making walking difficult. When he tripped and fell backwards she finally stopped and broke into laughter.

He held his hand out and she offered hers to pull him back up. "Thank you! I'm surprised you didn't let someone trample me. Listen I came into some money the other day and I'd really like to take you for dinner, Pablo's, what do you say?" She frowned, that was unexpected. It wasn't like Matthew to be romantic.

"How did you get the money?" she asked suspiciously.

"Does it matter?"

"Well, yes, because if it's dirty money I don't want to know, Matthew. If someone's been hurt or mugged..."

"No, nobody was hurt. It was just a bit of gambling, nothing heavy," he explained sounding hopeful. "Come on what do you say?"

"You and me?" she confirmed and he nodded keenly.

"Yes, Ruby, you and me...and my new trainers," he reminded and she giggled before sobering up again.

"Why, Matthew? What do you want?"

"Dinner with you," he rolled his eyes. "Come on there's no ulterior motive here I just want to spend time without the rest of the crew and not in my bedroom either. What do you say?" She was seriously confused now. They never spent time alone unless she was hiding out at his house and then, guaranteed, he was trying it on. She *was* hungry though, she'd worked through all of her breaks and lunch and they definitely wouldn't have any food at home, other than a couple of stale pieces of bread. She agreed hesitantly.

"OK, but then I'm going straight home. This isn't leading to anything, Matthew," she informed him firmly and he grinned.

"Ohhhh I do believe someone just hit refreeze. You do know you should never refreeze once defrosted, Ruby?" he chuckled and she shook her head at him as if he were wrong.

"Nobody defrosted, Matthew, I'm still good."

"Yes you are," he confessed, wishing she wasn't.

11
Pablo's little secret

Pablo's was a nice restaurant not too posh and *always* popular. On the first floor it had function rooms for Christmas dinners and wedding receptions and on the ground floor it was split into a dining area, take out area and a colourful ice cream parlour where young people, who knew better than to hang about on dangerous estates, hung out. It was rumoured that in the basement Pablo ran illegal betting rooms where people played cards for money. This area could be accessed from the back by a metal staircase which came up from the basement into an alley. Pablo maintained that the back access to his building was for *'deliveries only'* and that's what all the signs read. Ruby preferred the more sinister story, it was exciting and dark and it sent chills up her spine.

A waitress seated them quickly and Ruby ordered spaghetti while Matthew asked for pizza.

"So come on tell me all about work," he pried.

"Oh you know it's just copying and stuff really. I like it and it pays quite well but really it means less time at home with my dad. My boss can be really nice when he wants to be. Like I say he's determined to make sure I get my exam results and do well."

"And what about that guy I saw going in there yesterday? He's pretty good looking...you know from a girl's point of view, right?"

"Who, Danny?" she squirmed. "Yeah I suppose he is but...well...we just work together...that's all," she explained wondering why she felt so nervous talking about Danny to Matthew, she wasn't *with* either of them.

"Right," he nodded like he didn't quite believe her. "So what's he like this Danny?"

"He's OK. He's getting better. He was hard work to start with but he's getting a little bit easier to work with."

"What is he then?"

"A trainee lawyer, Matthew! What's the sudden interest in Danny?" she felt harassed and she didn't like it.

"I'm just being friendly, Ruby, chill. You sound guilty that's all. Are you seeing him?"

"What?" Ruby coughed on her first mouthful of food and put her fork down to drink some water. "No, Matthew, I'm not seeing him, not that it's any of *your* business!"

"I'm just looking out for you that's all," he defended.

"No you're not! Why would *you* care?"

"Because I like you...and I happen to know that he's not *really* your type..."

"Why isn't he?" She was on the defensive now and he shrugged like it was obvious.

"Because, Ruby, you come from our estate and that's where you belong, always have, always will. People live in separate worlds, they move and stay in their own circles. Danny has his world with his suits, nice car, money, uni mates and qualifications and you live in ours with our crew and your good friends that look out for you. Don't turn your back on the people you need, Ruby," he warned her and it sounded ever so slightly like a threat. He'd reached forward and she now noticed that his hand was pressing down on hers firmly to keep her from moving away. She looked up into his eyes.

"Matthew," she breathed softly, "Please don't cause a scene. I'm not turning my back on anyone. I'm not with Danny...or anybody else for that matter. I think I want to go home."

"I've looked out for you, I've given you a place to stay and you treat me like crap do you know that?" he snarled and she shook her head looking like she might cry. "I could so easily shut the door on you and then you'd be alone. Do you want to be alone, Ruby?" She shook again biting down on her lip, the conversation had turned nasty and she hated it when he was like this. "You have nobody else just you remember that. We are your family, me and the crew. People who grass or desert get excluded and punished. *You* need to decide if you want to be in or out, Ruby."

"In," she whispered. "I don't want to be on my own."

"Well then stop mucking about and playing at being a grown up with a proper job and snobby friends and prove where your loyalties lie. I bet they only employed you for a laugh. I bet they all look down their noses at you. You should hand your notice in so they can't take the piss out of you anymore. You should rinse them for all they've got before you leave too. Do they have a safe, Ruby?"

"I...I don't know," she looked frightened now. "Matthew, please, they've been really good to me," she begged.

"And I haven't? Have they given you a place to stay when your dad beats the crap out of you? They've got equipment, expensive stuff too, it would sell for a fortune on the estate. Do you have a key, Ruby?"

"No, Matthew, I don't have a key! I want to go home," she told him eagerly. He lifted his hand from hers and smiled. The dark cloud that had come over him lifted and he shook his head at her as if she were unbelievable.

"I'm messing with you, Ruby, can't you take it? You can keep your stupid little job if you want it. If you're happy to let people treat you like you're a joke then that's your problem. You never did seem to notice stuff like that but then I suppose that's why some of us stayed on at school and some of us didn't." She wanted to slap him so hard but she didn't like it when people stared and she didn't want to cause a scene in Pablo's. "I'll take you home in a minute," he told her. "I haven't finished yet and I want to see the dessert menu. Anyway, after dessert I thought we could go back to mine. My mum's out all night so we've got the place to ourselves...we could watch a film?" He stopped chewing to watch her and she nodded with the slightest of movements and then pushed her chair out.

"I need the toilet," she declared. "I'll be back in a minute."

She made her way to the ladies, weaving through the maze of tables and chairs, and fell back against the toilet door as soon as she was inside. Two other girls were laughing and joking as they tried on each other's lipstick and pushed strands of hair back into place. Ruby closed her eyes and listened to their conversation, they definitely weren't from *her* estate. Life was easy for them. All they had to do was go to school, do their homework and hang out in the warm eating raspberry ripple and fluttering their eyelashes at boys. They approached Ruby and she peeled her body away from the door to let them pass, wishing she could swap her life as easy as they'd just swapped lip gloss.

She felt duped. Matthew had set her up, meeting her from work, getting her to agree to dinner and all so he could get her back to his house where she would spend the evening fighting with him over sex. She took a deep breath and made her way over to the mirror. She looked tired and pale and the place stunk of perfume. She needed air and opened the window. It was small and high and she had to use the sink to push herself up onto the ledge to get her head out. It led out into the alley and she looked back over her shoulder towards the toilet door. She'd left Matthew with half a pizza, hopefully he would still be eating it.

She pulled her body through head first and, using the lid of a huge metal rubbish bin to take her weight, she got her legs free. Just seconds later she could hear voices coming up from the metal staircase leading from the basement. She jumped from the ledge and squatted down behind the bin to keep from view. A group of men hung about just feet from her as they gathered in the alley to say their goodbyes.

The stench of stale tobacco and alcohol filled the air from the open door of the basement below and when Ruby dared to inch forward she could just see through the railings into the room. Tables were set out and covered with red and white chequered cloths. Pablo's basement looked nothing like a storage cellar! She turned her attention to the men gathered at the top of the stairs and she gasped for she now recognised one of them.

"Carlito!" she breathed in astonishment. He seemed to look right at her and she ducked out of the way and cringed, waiting for him to come and grab her out but instead he started talking.

"Sergio, chill out I'm dealing with it. Do you trust me?" he asked and the other man wiped his face with a handkerchief and snorted into it. Ruby clenched her eyes tightly shut, it sounded gross. She pulled her knees in to keep small and hidden.

"Yeah I trust you, Carlito, I just get tired of waiting."

"Well business takes time, Sergio! Look it won't be much longer. I have a plan and, unless I'm very much mistaken, things should get a lot easier from now on." The broken cobbles on which Ruby was perched were wet and slippery and as she leaned back against the wall, trying to alleviate the pins and needles creeping up from her feet, she slid onto her bottom and kicked the bin.

"What was that?" she heard Sergio ask. Footsteps slowly made their way towards her and she almost screamed she was so scared. Mr Alessi had told her that he offered services to the mafia and Carlito was one of his *very* private clients. She was petrified now. She had mistakenly gate crashed a private mafia conversation, what would it look like if she were found? They would think she was spying, probably torture her, and then leave her in the alley all alone. She huddled and waited, praying that Matthew wouldn't come looking for her. If he shouted her name from the open window above she would definitely be busted.

"Relax, Sergio, it's a rubbish bin and what do you get in rubbish bins? Dirty sewer rats, that what you get in rubbish bins. I don't think we need to concern ourselves." She heard the footsteps again, they were closer now, and she held her breath and shivered with fear. "Look, Sergio, I'm going. I didn't come here to carry out pest control on Pablo's behalf. Are you saying goodbye or not?" Carlito asked, shrugging inside his coat as if he were cold. Sergio turned and walked back and Ruby bit on her fist to keep from crying out with relief.

"So when, Carlito?" he asked as he held out his right hand to shake. His left hand swiped the handkerchief across his eye. Carlito took the hand and held it firmly, pulling Sergio in for a hug. "You have the love of a brother, the faith of a priest and the impatience of a child," he chuckled. "Soon, Sergio, soon!"

12
Special Delivery

"I've got the post," Ruby declared bright and early as she pushed her chair out with her foot. She dumped her coat over the arm whilst juggling a box in one hand and using her chin to keep it steady. Danny made an *uh huh* noise from the other room and then appeared suddenly in the doorway with a pen between his teeth. He narrowed his eyes on her suspiciously and she froze, wondering what the problem was.

"What? Am I late? What's the time?" she asked, trying to check her watch, but he shook his head and removed the pen. His eyes were concentrated on the box.

"Post's already been," he told her thoughtfully. "Where did you get that? Did someone hand it to you?"

"Yeah, a man outside, just as I was coming in. He called out to me and asked if I would pass this on to a *'Mr Alessi'*."

"Did he call you by your name?" he questioned and she shook her head.

"No. Danny, why what's the problem?" she was getting worried and it didn't help when all of a sudden his eyes widened and he entered the room swiftly, reaching out to take the box from her.

"Whoa, I think you should put the box down, like *right now!* Let me take that." He removed it from her hands and placed it carefully on Mr Alessi's morning newspaper, opening the window as he did so. Ruby was fixed to the spot feeling confused.

"It's cardboard, Danny, not anthrax!" she joked and he smiled nervously.

"Not anthrax, no, but in my limited experience with cardboard boxes they don't tend to bleed." He gestured towards the carpet and the trail of blood that had followed the box to the table. Ruby stepped away and gasped, holding her hands out in front of her and shaking them off like they were dirty. She felt properly grossed out. Danny poked the box with his pen and then ran the nib of it through the tape on the top, splitting it open. He looked up at her as he gingerly lifted one of the flaps and then peered inside before scrunching his nose up and letting it drop back down again.

"You OK?" he asked and she folded her arms tightly across her chest. "Want to go get some air while I deal with this?" he encouraged kindly and she did, desperately, but she shook her head just as Mr Alessi stepped into the room behind her.

"Problem?" he asked and Danny pointed his pen at the carpet and then the box, letting him make his own mind up.

"Ruby was handed it in the street and told to give it to you," he informed him and Mr Alessi looked her over as if assessing for damage.

"Ahhh, Ruby, are you OK? Did he call you by your name? Did you recognise him?" She shook her head. "You get a good look? Would you recognise him again?" he bombarded her with questions and she struggled to keep up.

"Yes. No. I mean maybe. I don't know," she stammered.

"Right let's get it over and done with shall we?" he asked walking up to the box and slipping his hands into a pair of black leather gloves. He pulled a handkerchief from his pocket and placed it over his mouth before lifting the flap to peer inside. He dropped the flap back down again raising his eyebrows. "Danny, can you get someone to dump this in the river please? Tell them to just chuck the whole lot off the bridge, let nature do its thing. Then call someone to come clean the carpet. I want it as good as new," he muffled into his square of material. He turned and looked at Ruby placing his hands on his hips.

"I think it might be nice if you stayed in at lunchtime today, Rubes, and that's an order if you're wondering," he clarified. "I'll have Amanda get you something in..."

"Like that's safer!" she snorted and both Mr Alessi and Danny laughed. She still hadn't hit it off with the difficult woman on reception. "So, what is it? What's in the box?" she asked unable to take her eyes off it. She felt both absolutely freaked and completely intrigued.

"Nothing," Mr Alessi declared flippantly. "It's not for me. I think they wanted next door," he lied not caring if she believed him or not. He expected that she would do as she was told and ask no questions.

"Truth you said," she surprised him and he laughed, having been caught off guard. Danny turned and looked at her in astonishment.

"I'm sorry, Ruby?" Mr Alessi asked her in disbelief while Danny's mouth struggled to keep from smirking.

"You said the truth. You need to be able to trust us you said. Well, after I've been handed a bleeding box, I think you owe me the truth in return. Unless of course you want me to take it next door and dump it on *their* reception desk like the idiot you obviously take me for?" She was defiant and also furious.

She'd been approached in the street, handed something gruesome, told to stay in over lunch and then spared the details like she couldn't handle it. Both Mr Alessi and Danny looked at the box and then at her. *Could she handle it?* With no answer from either of them she stepped forward, put her face in the crook of her arm and then lifted the flap to peer inside. She jumped back with a squeal looking at Mr Alessi in horror. "What?...What the..." she panted. "What *is* that?" She turned away and dropped to her knees grabbing the metal bin to gag into it. She was coughing so hard it made her stomach muscles hurt and Danny handed her a bottle of water from his desk.

"Drink," he ordered. She took it and did as she was told before turning and sitting on the floor feeling faint and looking *very* green. Alessi glanced at the box and then back to the crumpled mess on the floor.

"It's my cat," he told her flatly. It was matter-of-fact, like *file those, photocopy that, grab me a coffee, just check the pockets of my coat for me, find that file, oh and in that box there is my dead cat...go chuck it off the bridge!*

"How do you know...I mean..." she gritted her teeth and closed her eyes against the spinning as she thought about it all over again.

"One, it's wearing the collar I bought it and, two, it went missing a few days ago. I've been expecting its return...in various forms."

"Oh god, Mr Alessi, I'm *so* sorry," she looked into his eyes and he nodded at her, reaching out his hand and hoisting her up, against her better judgement.

"I'm not," he told her his eyes looking as sincere as his words sounded. "There's a point to everything, Ruby. So I lose my cat, people lose their cats all the time. Never get attached to things you can't afford to lose, Ruby, and you will never be too disappointed."

"So what's the point? You said there was always a point?" she badgered, sounding distressed.

"I've just discovered you aren't too scared to face the nasty stuff. You can do boring and mundane. That's great if all I want is a no seeing, no hearing puppet, there are millions of *those*. But someone who can deal with the down side of the job, and I'm talking so down dark is definitely the only way to describe it, well, that's gold dust. I just got myself another Danny, and you're feisty too, I like that. But don't start going against my advice too often, the world is a dangerous place, Ruby. When I say stay in over lunch I don't mean go out and get kidnapped for ransom. I'm sure your dad won't be very happy when I tell him you're not coming home because you're too busy getting your fingers chopped off, got it?"

Ruby nodded and paled again. "I think you should sit down," he advised and she tried not to laugh, *he* was the one that had made her stand up! "Danny, get her a chair and a coffee," he ordered and Danny glared at her playfully. He was being told to run around after *her*. She giggled and then quickly took the chair he offered and bowed her head, placing it between her knees to keep from passing out completely.

13
A birthday not to remember!

"*Danny*," Ruby cooed sweetly like she wanted something.

"*Ruby*," he cooed back mockingly, his face buried in a large and heavy directory as he searched for an address. She smirked. He was very funny.

"My friend Sasha is here. We're going out to celebrate my seventeenth. Do you think it would be OK if she came up? The front door is locked now and no more clients are due." She was leaning round the door, dragging her teeth over her bottom lip nervously.

"Yeah of course," he agreed glancing up at her. "Everything's locked away so there shouldn't be a problem. You haven't told her stuff have you because even best friends can get you into trouble you know?" he asked and she shook her head. Since Mr Alessi broke the news about what she was really dealing with, Danny had started to be *a lot* nicer. It was like she was *officially* part of the criminal department now and not just squatting like she had been up until that point.

Clearly Danny thought she wouldn't last but it was now September and she'd been with the firm for four months. He had definitely mellowed.

"Never!" she exclaimed sounding deadly serious. "I haven't told a soul." she promised and he grinned and nodded towards his phone. She nipped across the room and perched on the edge of his desk to ring straight down to reception. "Hi, Amanda, can you send Sasha up please, *thanks*." She slammed the phone down hard. "Love you!" she tacked on sarcastically.

"Ahhh I love you too," he replied and she swivelled slightly and grinned at him.

"I was *talking* to Amanda," she told him sternly and he grinned back cheekily.

"So was I!" Ruby laughed out loud and just like the last time the sound was so beautiful he just wanted to keep her going with a string of good jokes. "It'll be nice to meet someone you went to school with actually. Let's see if she has any dirt to dish on you," he teased, tapping his pen distractingly against his desk. Ruby gave him a cross look.

"Don't you dare go grilling my friends, Danny, or else I'll have to go out looking like this!"

"There's nothing wrong with how you look," he informed her. "Are you getting changed *here* then?" he asked seeming surprised and slightly delighted at the prospect.

"Yes she is!" Sasha replied as she entered the office looking about nosily. "Hey, you must be Danny? Ruby's told me *so* much about you." Danny stood to shake her hand and smirked.

"Has she now, Sasha? Pleased to meet you. So what's she told you then?"

"Well I can see it's definitely *all* true," she giggled giving him a sexy checking out look as she said it. He tried not to laugh as she went on to spill. "She said you were fit. She said you've got a gorgeous smile. You have very sexy style and she would definitely..." Sasha trailed off and he glanced at Ruby who was in the middle of a 'cut it out' mime with her hands. She stopped abruptly and gritted her teeth. He laughed out loud.

"Right, well, don't let me stop you. Do you need me to go away?" he asked. "I can make myself scarce for about twenty minutes or so but then I *must* get on."

"No it's fine, honest, I can use the coffee room to get ready," Ruby assured him, still blushing. She broke eye contact, feeling self conscious, and turned to Sasha. "So what have you dug me out to wear then?"

"Well I went round to yours with Marcus, that's one of my brothers, Danny," she filled him in and he nodded like he knew already. "We knocked but there was no answer. Your old man was flaked out face down on the sofa, not dead don't worry he was definitely breathing..."

"That's a shame..." Ruby interrupted checking out her nails idly. Sasha looked amused for a minute and then went on.

"It was so easy, Ruby. We thought up some big elaborate plan. Marcus was going to distract him with a can of Special Brew and I was going to slip up the stairs. Needn't have bothered, all I had to do was go straight up, rummage through your bedroom and get everything you need to make you look drop dead sexy and irresistible to *all* men!"

"Wow and you found all that in her bedroom did you?" Danny teased. Ruby slapped him with a ruler looking indignant. He was being incredibly engaging and flirty now that Sasha was around. Sasha always brought people out of themselves. Ruby's friend giggled and perched on the other side of Danny's desk making him blush slightly. She managed it so much more seductively than Ruby had.

"She doesn't need much to blow your mind Danny...or your wallet," she told him making her eyes go wide. He shook his head at her and slid his chair back so he could stand and get some space. Sasha laughed, liking the discomfort she was causing. "So are you going to come out and buy her a drink, *it is her birthday?*" she sang out and he smiled looking at Ruby.

"Maybe," he told her squinting cutely like he might just do that. Sasha clapped her hands to get their attention.

"Right, I got you some sexy heels, little black skirt and that gorge cream top that looks fab on you. It makes your boobs look great. I mean they are great...don't you think they're great, Danny?" she smirked cheekily and he chuckled nervously. Ruby covered her face in total humiliation but Sasha carried on like nothing had happened. "I think we might curl the hair, what do you think, Danny, straight or curly? Blokes love that don't they?" she asked whilst playing with a lock of Ruby's long dark hair. It reached right down to her middle.

"Yeah, straight or curly, blokes love that," he agreed highly amused by it all. "Hair is *always* good."

"Right, let's get started! Where's the coffee room?" Sasha asked bossily and Ruby slid off the desk feeling mortified. She was unable to look at Danny as Sasha followed her out onto the landing, giving him a cute little wave as she disappeared from view.

Ruby changed quickly, feeling uncomfortable about taking her clothes off at work. Danny was only in the other room and she was all too aware of Mr Alessi's passion for surveillance. Sasha ran a tong through her hair while Ruby applied some makeup. After nearly killing them both with hairspray Sasha opened the door so they could breathe and a few minutes later Danny was leaning in the doorway checking Ruby out.

"Wow you look *really* great! Where are you going?"

"Clubbing! You know The Lounge down the road?" Sasha declared bobbing up and down excitedly and he raised his eyebrows.

"What as in The Lounge *'eighteen and over'* down the road?" he queried.

"Err yeah! And I have a mission for Ruby."

"Sasha *please* no missions, OK? I always get dragged into them so just...*shhhh*." She didn't want Danny to know about the missions but Sasha wasn't one for containing herself.

"What's a mission?" Danny asked, ignoring Ruby's protests and Sasha was more than eager to tell.

"Oh she *always* gets a mission. She starts off all *'No, no, not a mission, Sasha. I'm not doing it. You can't make me. I don't want to'*, and then you try stopping her after a couple of drinks. It's hilarious! This time she has to find the first fit bloke and drink him under the table. She's good at that. Ruby *never* has to take money out. Blokes are always buying her drinks...aren't they babe?" Ruby kept her mouth shut looking guilty.

"Is that so, Ruby?" he asked her with surprise. "Can I just double check that you are *seventeen* today? I'm just a little bit confused because you look much older, you look great in fact, you're going clubbing in a place with age restrictions, which are there for a reason, and you clearly intend to get wasted. You're *seventeen*, right?"

"Uh huh," she confirmed applying more lipstick and then blotting it off again.

"So you work for a law firm and you're going out to break the law?" he smirked but his eyes were slightly serious.

"Uh huh," she confirmed again, checking her teeth for lipstick.

"I didn't know you drank, Ruby?" he sounded a little different now, concerned maybe.

"Ruby! Not drink?" Sasha burst into laughter. "How can you live with an alcoholic and *not* drink?"

"All the more reason not to I'd have thought," he shrugged. "Please be careful, Ruby," he urged and she turned away from the mirror to frown at him tiresomely.

"Yeah I've got it, don't walk the streets alone, don't get into cars with strangers blah, blah, blah."

"No I don't mean that. Just remember you don't have to follow in your dad's footsteps," he reminded her. She stopped what she was doing and looked at him blankly. She hadn't been expecting that. He smiled and tilted his head from side to side. "And of course don't walk the streets alone, don't get into cars with strangers blah, blah, blah." He gave one of her curls a tug and then left and went back to his work.

By midnight her mission was well and truly completed, despite her sober objections. Though she still managed to dance, joke, and laugh perfectly, her mind and body were really only slaves to the alcohol coursing through her body. She needed water and went to the bar where a man, nearly as drunk as she was, asked if he could get her something stronger. She declined with a shake of the head downing the water as quickly as she could. He slipped his hands around her middle nuzzling into her neck and making drinking very difficult. His hands moved to her bottom and she tried to keep him at bay with her free hand, leaning back and squirming. She was much more interested in diluting alcohol but didn't seem particularly bothered by the sudden attention either. He wasn't reading the signs and she pushed his face away from hers with the flat of her hand.

"Will...you...just...stop it!" she ordered but he wouldn't and she moved back as far as she could right into another man leaning at the bar. "I'm sorry," she apologised. "He just won't get the..." she looked up and was surprised to see the man she'd bumped into was Danny. He smiled and shook his head at her with disapproval.

"Message?" he asked raising his eyebrows but she was unable to answer before she was nuzzled into again and then groped. Danny scowled wanting to knock him out. The bloke was probably twice her age and less drunk, which made him mad. He looked about for Sasha but she was with her brother Marcus, Matthew and some of their other friends. All were completely unaware of Ruby's predicament.

Danny shook the hand of the man sitting on the other side of him and said his goodbyes, placed his phone in his inside pocket and took hold of Ruby. He uncoiled the man's arms from around her body and told him she was already taken. He then grabbed his glass and downed the contents as he walked her to the cloakroom, leaving it on a bar as he passed. He was forced to search her pockets for the ticket while she crumpled into hysterics at having his hands touch her waist. He was getting nowhere fast and resorted to trying to describe the coat to the cloakroom assistant. The woman, perched on a stool, was more than happy to help Danny out. When she eventually found what he was looking for he took it gratefully, along with the mobile number she offered him. He then placed the coat around Ruby's shoulders before taking her out into the fresh air and darkness.

"Ruby, you really are a liability do you know that?" he berated her and she tripped and giggled. He put an arm around her middle to help her keep balanced. "You're at work tomorrow I hope you remember that. Alessi would kill you if he knew you'd called in sick because of alcohol."

"Well then I won't call in sick because of alcohol. I wouldn't anyway, that would mean spending the day with my dad and *that* makes me feel more sick than the three vodka shots I just had." He rolled his eyes at her in disbelief.

"Ruby, you're seventeen! How often do you drink like this?"

"Only when life gets too much," she declared, feeling pleased with her response.

"And how often is that?"

"Every weekend!" she giggled and hiccupped.

"So you're a binge drinker then? That's just as bad as what your dad does, do you know that?"

"Yeah well I haven't roughed anyone up, called them a slut or trashed anything have I so I'm not as bad as him at all!" she clarified. He frowned and stopped, leaning her up against a wall to look into her eyes.

"Is that what he does to *you?*" he asked, sounding concerned, and she shook her head. It was an unconvincing shake which turned into a nod and then a giggle and then a hiccup. "It's not just about the impact it has on other people, Ruby. Just because you're not hurting anyone else it doesn't mean you're not destroying yourself. Not to mention just how vulnerable you are like this." He desperately tried to reason with her but she smirked cheekily at him.

"Are you going to take advantage of me, Danny?" she asked hopefully and he pulled her away from the wall and began moving again.

"Walk it off, Ruby!" he told her with frustration. "I don't like seeing you like this."

They got to his car and he helped her in but she refused to put her seatbelt on, choosing instead to play with the recline option on the chair. "How does this work? Oh, Danny, I think your car is broken? I'd take it back look the seat doesn't go...AGGGH...BACK!" she screamed and was now flat out.

"Ruby, for god sake sit up! And put your belt on!" he shouted at her, trying to make it go up again.

"There's enough room for two over here," she invited seductively but he chose to ignore her. "Can I come back to your place, *please?*" she'd resorted to begging. "I don't want to go home."

"No! Absolutely not! You're going home I'm afraid whether you like it or not," he told her sternly. She suddenly looked very sad, her dark curls over her face, her eyes wide as they peeked out from behind it. He felt bad for her. "Look, Ruby, I really like you but you're just seventeen and I've just turned twenty. That's a fairly big gap. You would have to be at least eighteen before I would even consider taking you back to my place...or sharing the recline option on my passenger side with you. Also you are very, very drunk and you don't know what you're talking about. You *really* need to sober up!"

"I do know what I'm talking about," she protested. "I really like you."

"No you don't know what you're talking about else you wouldn't have just propositioned me like that...or told me that you really liked me." He sighed deeply. "Look I really like you too but just not like that...well I suppose a bit like that but...no!" He was arguing with himself now and it made her giggle. "It would be wrong, not to mention the fact that Alessi would string me up for messing with you. He is very protective and he feels responsible for your safety. See how you feel in a year's time and throw yourself at me then. I'm sure I'll be more than happy to oblige."

He smiled kindly but she still looked sad and beautiful. He wanted her to feel better and so reached out and took a gentle hold of her chin, brushing her hair from her face and leaning in. He kissed her gently on the mouth, letting it stray slightly past the boundary of *just friends'* before pulling away and pushing the shiny locks of her hair behind her ears. "Happy birthday, Ruby," he whispered and then pulled her belt across and started the car to take her *straight* home.

14
The hangover from hell

The following day she climbed the stairs to the top floor, her head pounding harder with every step. She felt hot and *very* sick. The thought of having to face Danny was *not* helping. She hovered in the doorway and he checked his watch before looking up at her.

"Morning, Ruby. Thirty minutes late and I'm afraid he's not in the best of moods. You're going to have to take some flack for a bit," he warned her and she flopped down onto the chair opposite. His eyes grazed over her. The curls were still just holding from the night before, giving her a pretty waif and tousled look. It was dark and shiny against her very pale face and her eyes were dark too from a lack of sleep. Her mouth wore no lipstick but her lips were just as pretty without it. They were a lovely shape and colour and he suddenly realised he'd been fixated on them for longer than he'd intended, for longer than he had been on any of her other features. He broke away to shift the papers in front of him, hoping she hadn't noticed. She had and was in the middle of trying to work him out when she was startled.

"RUBY!" Mr Alessi bawled out and she jumped. Danny cringed for her.

"Come on just get it over and done with and try not to walk out, yeah. You can take it," he reminded her. He came round the desk and took her elbow gently, escorting her to the office door and leaning inside. "She's been here for a few minutes so she's not *that* late," he defended casually, trying to play down her tardiness. Danny closed the door behind her and listened from outside.

"Thirty minutes late! I should sack you do you know that?"

"What for being late *once* in four months?" she argued and Danny rolled his eyes. He knew she'd fight back.

"No, for spending the night drinking and then being too hung over to make it in the next day!"

"I *am* in and you can't sack me just because I went out and celebrated my birthday!"

"No but I can sack you for drinking, for lowering the tone of the firm! If you'd been spotted by a client doing drugs I'd be able to sack you on the spot and do you know why, because it's not only unprofessional but it's also illegal. We *are* a law firm in case you hadn't noticed. And also, in case you hadn't noticed, you are *not* old enough to drink and that means that last night you were breaking the law! A sackable offence!"

"Yeah but I never saw any of your clients because I still haven't met any of them, well not properly anyway, so that's just an excuse to have a go at me. You are *not* my dad and what I get up to in my own time is none of *your* business."

"No, I'm not your dad and it's a good job too because if I were I would ground you for the rest of your life! You want people to see the real Ruby, not the Ruby who's set to get bad grades, not the Ruby who lives on a bad estate in town, not the Ruby whose dad is a raging and abusive alcoholic. You want people to respect you for what you're capable of achieving, for what you are *more* than capable of being, but nobody is going to respect you if you don't respect yourself! If you were my child you would know the meaning of respect and self respect. It would have been the first thing I'd taught you."

"How do you know what you'd do? You don't even *have* children!" she bellowed back at him.

"Yes I do!" he objected. She was astonished, she had no idea he had family. It dampened the fire blazing inside her and she lowered her voice to a more acceptable level.

"But you're not married? Are you? I thought you lived alone?"

"I do, Ruby, but that doesn't mean that I've never *been* married and nor does it mean that I've never had children. You don't need to be married to have children. You should make a note of that because it's the way *you're* headed."

"How dare you! I can't believe you just said that! You are so rude sometimes and coming from the man who harps on about respect!"

"Stop changing the damn subject because you think it will get you off the hook. I'm not stupid. I'm not your dad that you can run rings round. I'm not your teacher who doesn't know how to control you or Amanda on reception who doesn't know when the wools being pulled over her eyes. The point is I *was* married once, *and now I'm not*, but that doesn't change the fact that I know what I'm talking about. Your father doesn't deserve the title because he does nothing to earn it. He fails to protect you time and again."

"Just back of, Mr Alessi, and leave my dad out of it!" she defended, but more for herself than for her father. She wasn't about to take a grilling for her dad. If he was failing her it wasn't *her* fault!

"OK, fine, you want to move on to how lucky you were that it was Danny who gave you a lift home last night? How else would you have got back? Accepted a lift from a stranger or maybe you're pushy little friend Matthew? I'm sure he would have loved to oblige given the state *you* were in. You need to be more careful or you're going to get hurt. Either way if you carry on drinking I will kick you out of these offices so hard your backside won't touch the tarmac, got it?" She stayed quiet. "RUBY! Are you even listening to me?"

"Shhhh, *please,* Mr Alessi, just stop shouting my head is killing me," she whispered placing a hand either side of it and trying to push against the splitting sensation in her skull.

"Is it?" he asked like he wasn't surprised. "That will be your brain cells dying and all thanks to the alcohol. With *your* grades coming up you can't afford to lose any more, Ruby." He placed his hands on his hips and looked her over with a sigh. "Right, what's the worst possible job you could do right now?"

"Why?"

"Well I need to know what you're up to and what you're not up to. I need to know what to do with you for the rest of the day," he told her and Danny prayed that she would see what was coming, but she didn't.

"Ugh probably shredding that would be hell. The noise, the sitting still, the box room with no window and the walls that are too white, not to mention the boredom, anything but that I can handle," she told him helpfully.

"Right in that case there are five boxes of paper in the box room and they *all* need shredding and putting into black sacks. Oh and, Ruby, I want it done by 1pm so crack on!" She buried her head in her hands realising now that he just wanted to establish the worst possible punishment for her. He was relentless as he grabbed the door and evicted her coldly. "Go, Ruby, *now!* If it isn't done by 1pm you're out of here."

She was unable to look at Danny as she passed and he was in the middle of talking to Mr Alessi when she came back into the office looking sheepish.

"There isn't any paper that needs shredding in the box room," she explained and Mr Alessi shoved the file he was holding at Danny and stormed right past her.

"Follow me," he ordered and she did as she was told. "What's that there?" he asked pointing to the boxes lined up against the back wall.

"Brand new unopened boxes of copier paper," she told him thinking that was obvious, which made his next order incomprehensible.

"Exactly and it all needs shredding by 1pm so get on with it!" he boomed, spinning round and slamming the door behind him. She sank into her chair, he was mad. Tears began to flow and she rested her cheek against the cool table.

"Hey," she heard a whisper and looked up. It was Danny and he was holding a cup of coffee. "Here this might help...and these." He placed a couple of white shiny tablets on the desk.

"Thank you," she snuffled, wiping her face and eyes with the back of her hands and fingers. She pointed at the unopened boxes of copier paper feeling helpless. "Does he really want me to shred all of that or is it a test? I don't know what to do. I'm scared of him, Danny. I think he's lost it," she sniffed and he chuckled and pulled up a chair in front of her desk so he could talk to her quietly.

"Yeah he wants you to do it. It's kind of a like a lesson. Get this right. I've been here for ages. I started working for the firm when I was fifteen running errands, all that kind of boring stuff. I gradually worked my way up as I studied. One day he caught me smoking out back and he hit the roof, just like he did with you. He took me to the deeds safe, no window, no contact, nothing. He placed a catering size box of teabags in front of me and a couple of bumper packets of yellow post-it notes and told me I was to roll the tea leaves into the post-it notes until every single one of them was done. They were to be neat, of equal diameter both ends and I wasn't to go home until I'd finished. It took me *eight* hours!" he told her looking hacked off at the memory and she gasped in shock. "I didn't get home until midnight."

"So why did you stay? Why didn't you just...I don't know...find another job?"

"Because what he was doing made sense...and because I didn't really have the guts to say no!" he cringed and she giggled. "It gave me time to sit and think about it. As pissed off as I was I have to admit I also felt happy knowing someone cared enough to try and do something about the mistakes I was making and the damage I might be doing to my health. I knew that he would support me as far as I wanted to go in the firm and he has. I have always had a job, though he does regularly threaten to fire me, that's just his way, Ruby. He would never actually do it. I've messed up over the years, everyone does, and he's never kicked me out. He only does stuff like this if he really cares about someone and he clearly has a soft spot for you. I think that's quite sweet." She scrunched her nose, not so sure about the sweet bit. "Strangely his lesson did have another outcome that he *hadn't* bargained for."

"What was that, repetitive strain injury?" she asked seriously and he laughed.

"How do you know about repetitive strain injury?"

"I picked up some things from Tom Marshall's files," she shrugged with a grin.

"Very good! But no it wasn't RSI. I became the best fifteen year old joint roller my school had ever seen!" he told her raising his eyebrows and making her giggle. Mr Alessi stepped into the doorway and from her reaction Danny knew he was there. He leaned in towards her and whispered loudly.

"And that's why you shouldn't drink you stupid girl!" Her eyes grew wide and she desperately tried not to show the amusement that was pulling at her mouth. He stood and turned to spot his boss in the doorway.

"Ahhh, Mr Alessi, I don't think she'll be any more trouble," he told him turning to give her a sly grin. Now both of them were facing her and she was expected to be serious. Nightmarishly impossible!

"She's not to have any distractions or visitors until she's completed her job," Mr Alessi told him firmly.

"No I couldn't agree more, Mr Alessi, and to make sure she's really bored I'm going to shut the door on her." He slammed the door hard making her head thump and her mouth grin. He was very, very, funny.

15
Life is full of lessons

At 11am she was still soldiering on and Mr Alessi popped his head in. She paused, mid shred, worried that he might be about to shout again.

"Sandwich? I'm popping into town," he asked her and she shook her head delicately.

"No, thank you." This man's mood swings were so changeable it made her dizzy. He could give the weather a run for its money. One minute he could be mean enough to sack her and the next he was feeding her or booking her in for GCSE resists!

"Ham?" he went on. If she hadn't thought it would kill her to do it she'd have rolled her eyes at him.

"No, really, I'm fine."

"Cheese?"

"Mr Alessi, I really couldn't manage..."

"Salad then. I'll get a salad roll. How about crisps?"

"If I eat I will definitely be sick everywhere so..."

"So I'll hold the chocolate bar and get you a juice to go with it. See you in a bit." He knocked against the door with his knuckle. "Crack on."

While he was out Danny snuck her another coffee and a grin and left her to it without a word. He was being *really* nice. By 12.45 she was done and she carried the black bags through to Mr Alessi's office. He asked her to place them in front of the mantelpiece and when she turned back he was stood facing her with his back to the doorway. She could see Danny behind him in the middle of his own office.

"So," he gestured towards the black sacks, "What do you see right there?"

"Black sa..." she began to reply but spotted Danny shaking his head vigorously and stopped herself. He mimed what looked like a huge circle and then jabbed his finger towards a framed painting on the wall. *Ahhh bigger picture,* she told herself and looked at the bags again. "A lot of waste, Mr Alessi. Perfectly good paper fit for nothing but the red bin now." Alessi nodded, encouraged. Danny held up a piece of paper and pointed at it before pointing at her. She smiled and tried to make it look like the smile was in recognition of what Mr Alessi was hoping to achieve. "I guess you could look at the paper like me really...well...my future," she corrected seeing Danny doing jumping gestures with his arms. "My future is unwritten." Danny was pretending to write backwards, from right to left. "You make it what it is don't you...by the choices you make and the paths you take and that?" Mr Alessi was still nodding and pinching his chin thoughtfully between thumb and forefinger. "I guess looking at your future tied up in rubbish bags is...well...a terrible waste and a terrible thing to do." He beamed and Danny did silent mock clapping.

"Very astute of you, Ruby," he commended looking over his shoulder at Danny who threw the piece of paper he'd been holding in an attempt to get rid of it. Being smooth and flat it simply fluttered to the ground close to his feet, making him look *very* guilty.

"She missed one, I'd punish her," he told Mr Alessi picking it up again and trying not to laugh.

"Do you want to spend tomorrow sticking all that shredded paper back together, Danny?" he asked seriously and Danny shook his head. "Well then *I suggest*..."

"Look, Mr Alessi," Ruby interrupted, saving Danny from a rollicking. "I just want to say that I really do get what you're saying and I really do appreciate what you've done today. I was an idiot last night. I hate my dad for doing the exact same thing I do every weekend. I told myself it was OK but it's not and I really don't want to make the same mistakes as him. Thank you for caring, not for shouting because that hurt, but giving me the time to reflect on where I've been heading has been really...helpful." She looked passed Mr Alessi's shoulder and through the doorway. "Also, Danny, I wanted to tell you something."

"Yes," he responded with a very handsome smile and not a clue as to what she was about to do.

"I would just like to say that I'm so sorry for hitting on you last night," Danny's eyes grew wide and he cringed before immediately ducking towards the filing cabinets and out of view.

"You did what?" Mr Alessi asked as he turned to glance at his young trainee lawyer who, of course, was no longer there. He turned back.

"He neglected to tell me that, Ruby. And did he reciprocate?"

"Did he what?" she asked, unsure what that meant.

"Did he *hit on you* back?" She tried not to laugh at his use of *her* words, realising that she'd just messed up *again!*

"No he was a perfect gentleman. I should never have done it and I will *never* put him in a position like that again. Could you tell him that when you see him because he seems to have disappeared?"

"Right, I will. Well I suppose I'm glad he at least behaved himself. I wouldn't want to have to sack *him* now would I for not promoting the integrity of the firm?" he asked sternly, a warning for Danny that he should continue to behave himself if he'd ever considered otherwise. Ruby acknowledged the threat on Danny's behalf before giving Mr Alessi her big blue pleading eyes.

"Am I done now?" she asked hopefully and he smiled warmly at her just as Danny plucked up the courage to come back into view.

"Yes, Ruby, we're nearly done here. I thought we might have a little game first to try and lighten the mood?" he invited and she nodded and smiled just to humour him. "So, word association. I say something and you tell me the first thing that comes into your head, right?" She nodded and braced herself. "You ready?"

"Yes."

"Perfection."

"Hmmmm...perfection...erm...Oh! Almond Blossoms by Vincent Van Gogh," she responded, trying not to think *too* much, and he smiled, looking both pleased and surprised by her response.

"Van Gogh?" he queried sounding impressed.

"We were asked to recreate a Van Gogh painting at school and I fell in love with Almond Blossoms. It's perfect with the blues, the delicate flowers and twisted branches. It's one of a kind. It's my favourite."

"I know the painting well. Thank you, Ruby." Danny shook his head like she was unbelievable. *What had she done now?* She frowned at him feeling distracted.

"So, Mr Alessi, are we done then?" she asked, eager to get away before she caused any more trouble, but he took her arm and walked her across the room.

"Sit down in my chair and eat the lunch I bought you. Here's the bin," he told her placing it by her feet. "I don't want any sick on my carpet do you understand me?" She nodded and turned her nose up at the salad roll and packet of crisps. She did instinctively reach out for the carton of juice and downed that pretty quick. "You need to eat at least half of what's here because it will make you feel better. You look like death warmed up," he told her before leaving the room.

"Thanks very much," she grumbled. He came back half an hour later smelling like he'd been drinking coffee and lots of it.

"Come with me," he ordered her and she stood and followed him into Danny's office. "I'm in court this afternoon. Danny, you're not going anywhere are you?" he asked him and Danny shook his head.

"Nope I'm here *all* day."

"Good, give me your blazer then."

"Sure," Danny agreed helpfully, pulling it from the back of his chair and handing it over. Mr Alessi led her to the coffee room and over to the sofa.

"Now lie down and get some sleep while you can. If you can't get it at home then you'll just have to start napping here. You can't go without sleep it isn't good for timing or judgement. You've accrued half a day's holiday so take it."

She smiled gratefully and settled onto the sofa. When she stopped fidgeting he placed Danny's blazer over her and pulled it right up to her chin. She buried her face into it. It smelled wonderful and the whole thing made her feel like she was being hugged...by Danny. No surprise then that the dream that followed was *all* about him.

She woke, dazed, and much more comfortable at 7pm. She made her way through the dim lit offices to find Danny working at Mr Alessi's desk. He grinned and spoke as he continued to fill in a form and cross reference it with some other piece of paper stapled inside the front cover of a file.

"I thought you might be here for the night. I checked on you a couple of times," he informed her and she cringed.

"Oh god I didn't talk in my sleep did I?" she asked desperately hoping after the dream she'd just had that she hadn't. He glanced up at her.

"No, why, what were you dreaming about?" he queried looking intrigued and her face immediately flushed. He chuckled and shook his head. "I won't ask forget I said anything." He put his pen down and stopped what he was doing. "How are you feeling now? You prepared to hate Almond Blossoms?"

"I'm feeling much better thank you. Why would I hate Almond Blossoms?" she asked suspiciously and he laughed at her.

"You'll see." He picked up his pen again and went back to his form. "You better get going it's dark already. Are you taking the bus?"

"Yeah I think I will. I'm still feeling fragile."

"Have you missed the next one?" he asked stopping to look at his watch. She pulled her mobile from her pocket and double checked the time.

"Maybe, sometimes it's late. Maybe I'll be lucky," she hoped. He clicked his pen and wrote a line of numbers on a scrap of paper.

"Here's my mobile number, any problems, if you miss the bus or feel unwell waiting for it, call me. I'll give you a lift. Don't go walking its dark, Ruby," he told her firmly.

"Thanks, Danny," she replied taking a look at the mobile number, *Danny Glover's* mobile number! She didn't have the concentration to put it into her new mobile phone. Mr Alessi had given it to her the day before, for her birthday, and she needed a bit more practice at saving new numbers. She slipped the note into her bag instead.

"Will you be OK tonight?" he asked, studying her intently.
"Yeah, Danny, I'll be fine," she lied. Going home was *never* fine.

16
Next stop

She climbed to the top deck of the bus and took the seat right at the front, sitting by the window so she could lean her warm head against the cool glass. It was very soothing. The bus began to move, swinging out from its bay. It bounced, shuddered and jumped as it joined a queue of traffic. The low rumble and hiss made her sleepy and she felt herself slipping away, losing contact with all the noise around her. She dozed and woke suddenly, feeling somebody sitting next to her. She didn't want to look right at him so she took advantage of the light in the bus against the darkness outside to study his reflection in the glass. He was tall, broad and dark.

    The bus was quiet, nobody was talking, no children shouting and running up and down the stairs and not a single baby was crying. She checked her mobile, it was 7.55! She'd missed the 6.45 bus and had to wait for the next one. She must have been asleep for at least thirty minutes. Her journey didn't even take thirty minutes but the bus was still moving. It didn't make sense and she felt confused and disorientated.

    The top deck was empty save for the figure sat next to her and also the two similarly dark dressed men in the seats behind. She felt intimidated and sick. The travelling hadn't fared well with her uneasy stomach and now she'd woken to find that these men had all chosen to sit and crowd her. With so many seats free why would one of them choose to sit right next to her? It felt so wrong but she braved a look up at her seat companion's face. He turned and smiled down at her. It was a face that she hadn't seen before. She looked away uncomfortably and concentrated on the houses passing outside the window. At least they were on her estate now and her stop was fast approaching.

    She tried to stay calm telling herself that they must have been caught in traffic, that would explain the delay...but try as she might it wouldn't explain the eerie men who'd all chosen to sit on the top deck. She needed to press the bell so she shuffled in her seat, getting her bag together and straightening her coat and skirt, hoping the man next to her would get the hint, but he stayed rooted. His legs were taking up the whole space to the front of him right up to the window. She stood and asked him to excuse her but he never moved and she glanced at the other two men who looked back at her with blank gut wrenching expressions. The atmosphere felt bad and it clung to them like rot.

"Excuse me please," she asked. "I need to press the bell. I'm not feeling very well."

"Oh I'm sorry to hear that," he told her coolly leaning right back into his seat.

"No, that's fine...it's just...your legs are in the way...I can't get by," she explained, feeling sure her stop was going to be missed if she didn't press the bell soon.

"Then why don't you climb over me?" he asked her and she froze. She glanced at the big round mirror mounted on the ceiling wondering whether the driver had noticed her predicament. The bus crawled to the top of the road. It would be making a right turn soon and then it would be approaching her stop. If she didn't press the bell and the driver kept going she would have to walk the estate in the dark. The bus hissed and slowed, waiting at the junction for a gap in the traffic.

"I need to press the bell. I need to get off," she told him more eagerly but he gestured for her to climb over his lap again. She felt faint. The brakes squeaked and hissed as the bus began to move again but it didn't turn right it turned left. She swung round to look out of the window. The bus was going the wrong way! "What..? Where's the bus going? It's supposed to go right!" she exclaimed desperately.

"Then why don't you take it up with the driver?" he asked her with a sinister laugh, shifting his legs so she could escape. She was full of apprehension as she moved in front of him and stepped into the aisle. She didn't like turning her back on him and it made her feel vulnerable not knowing if she was about to be grabbed from behind.

The bus was now trundling down the hill towards the industrial estate and one of the other men took the opportunity to put his legs across the gap as she neared. She was blocked again and she hadn't got very far. She stopped and grasped onto the rail above her head, pressing the bell desperately. It rung out but still the bus didn't stop. She pushed it again and again consumed by the fear. The man blocking her way snorted with amusement and then shifted his legs.

She didn't hesitate in rushing straight for the stairs but just before she reached them the third man stood and slipped in front of her. She followed, willing him to go faster, but he slowed and came to a stop. The man who'd sat next to her was right behind now and she was sandwiched between the two. They were so close she could feel their monstrous bodies as they jostled her in rhythm with the movement of the bus. She was certain she was about to die...or worse...while trying to hold herself steady using the walls of the staircase. She couldn't even see where the bus was going anymore.

The lights flickered then went out and the bus was plummeted into darkness. She screamed out and sunk down onto the step, placing her hands over her ears and closing her eyes tightly. She prayed that everything would go away in exactly the same way as she did when her father beat her, but she knew it wouldn't work. It never had. She began to cry and then she found her voice.

"Help me!" she shrieked out hoping the driver would do something, but he just kept going, turning, braking and speeding up again, while she tried to keep small and invisible on the stairs.

"I'm sorry, baby, did you want to get passed?" the man in front asked her, stepping aside. She stood and shoved him as she grabbed at the handrail and felt her way to the driver's booth.

"Please help me. You've gone passed my stop. I need to go back. You're going the wrong way," she begged but he paid no attention and just kept going.

She looked out of the front window at the dark looming shadows of the disused factories, the offices closed down for the night and the gravelly high gated lorry parks. The bus was empty, save for her and her captors, so it wasn't a difficult decision choosing between them and the emergency window at the back of the bus. She ran for it and reached the long seat, only to discover a mound there. She tried to work out what it was until her hands touched what felt like a pair of shoes. She screamed as a light outside illuminated the face of a bound and gagged man. He opened his eyes and started to wriggle and she broke into tears feeling just as helpless as *he* looked. What made matters worse was that she recognised him. It was the man who had taken her money when she boarded in town. It was the *real* bus driver. Her bus had been hijacked!

"What do you want from me?" she whispered turning to face the men standing at the front of the bus. They were now dark menacing silhouettes, watching her and waiting to see what she would do next.

"That depends on what you have to offer?" the man who had sat next to her asked.

"I don't have anything. I don't understand," she sobbed. "I just want to go home."

"Then why didn't you say so? Do you want to get out here and walk or do you want us to turn round and take you back?" he asked helpfully.

"I want to get off now, right now," she pleaded.

"Pete!" he called out to the driver and the bus immediately screeched and skidded. She fell forward banging her head on a metal bar bolted into the floor. The bus had finally stopped but she gasped out in pain, feeling dizzy as she held her palm to her head and checked to make sure it wasn't bleeding. It wasn't, but now she was on her hands and knees.

"You don't have to beg," a voice told her with a grin. "Well not just yet anyway," he added walking down the aisle towards her. "What's your name, sweetheart?" She shook her head in response and pushed herself backwards trying to get away from him quickly. He was quicker and reached down, grabbing her by the wrists and pulling her up. She thought it through at speed. What would be the point in lying about something he could prove easily? It would only mean trouble for her.

"Ruby, my name's Ruby," she told him.

"Ahhh we have a little gem on board and how she sparkles eh boys?" he observed, holding his hands out like he was offering her to them. They laughed together, a horrible raucous sound that twisted at her insides. He shoved her backwards into a seat and kneeled into the space so she was blocked in. One of the men from the top deck slid into the seat behind so he could lounge while watching her being harassed more closely. "Don't mind Nico," the man penning her in excused his companion. "He likes to get *hands on*, if you know what I'm saying?"

She turned her head to look at Nico and he grinned back, flashing a gold tooth at her. He looked capable of eating her alive and she couldn't help but squeal in fear as the tears began to roll down her face. The man in her seat reached out towards her and she clenched her eyes shut waiting to feel his hands on her but, instead, he yanked her bag from her lap. "Bobby, check and see if she's telling the truth. I want I.D," he ordered.

"Light, Pete!" Bobby shouted to the driver as he began to rummage through her bag. The lights came back on and Bobby pulled her bank card out.

"I don't have any money," she told them.

"It's a good job we don't want to go shopping then isn't it?" the man blocking her in grinned. She pushed herself back further. "Where do you work?" he continued to interrogate. She had a compliment slip in her bag that Mr Alessi had written a lunch order on. There was no point lying.

"Tangle and Alessi Solicitors, in town," she replied.

"What do you do there? What do you know about Tangle and Alessi?"

"Nothing, apart from how to work the copier and who likes sugar in their tea. I'm just the office junior."

"Where do you live?" he asked her with a chuckle, getting slightly more personal.

"On the estate."

"What *area* of the estate and what number?" he asked her more firmly. He already knew she lived on the estate she was on the god damn bus! She was being clever with him, buying herself time.

"Granville Lane, number 22," she told him.

"Lie," he declared loudly looking at her like she had a cheek. "Record it!" he bellowed out and she frowned. How did he know that was a lie she wondered and, more to the point, what was he going to do about it? He did nothing about it and Bobby suddenly spoke up.

"There's a mobile number in here, Mickey," he informed him and the man blocking her in narrowed his eyes on her.

"Who does the mobile number belong to? An admirer? A friend? A work colleague?" he pressed. She didn't know what to do. Were these people looking for information on Mr Alessi and his clients? They did seem interested in her work and colleagues but a mobile number was easy enough to trace.

"Just someone I know," she settled for.

"Really?" he asked raising his eyebrows in disbelief. "Usually people you know already have their number in your phone don't they? Does someone want a date my little gem?" he teased and she shook her head.

"No."

"WHAT'S HIS NAME?" he boomed making her jump and scream and then laughing when she did. He quietened to a whisper, "Whose mobile number is it, Ruby?"

"Danny, his name is Danny OK and I just know him...that's all."

"Danny Glover?" he asked sounding astonished.

"How do you know Danny Glover?" she asked.

"We *all* know Danny Glover. The question is how do *you* know Danny Glover? Why would he be giving someone who's only the office junior his mobile number? Does he want a date, a quick..."

"No!" she shouted at him fiercely cutting him off. She didn't like this man at all. Mickey was leery, creepy and unpredictable. "I was sick today at work and that's the reason I left late. He was worried that I might be too ill to get the bus or have to get off somewhere along the way to be sick. He said that he would come get me if I needed help. It's his work number. I hardly know him! He just brings me piles of boring stuff to do and tells me to get on with it. Today was the first day he's ever said anything remotely nice to me. No, he definitely doesn't want a date...and I don't want one either!"

"That'll be a first," he sniggered. "A girl that *doesn't* want a date with Danny Glover!" he declared and once again they all laughed out loud. He reached forward and she yelped out as he grabbed her wrists again and dragged her out of her little safe place. "Your stop!" he barked as he marched her to the front of the bus and shoved her down the stairs."

"But the driver? What about the driver?" she cried unable to get rid of the image of him being tortured while she got to walk free.

"*Not* his stop! Now keep this to yourself else next time you might get to ride for longer...just you and me," he threatened. "I like 'em young and pretty, Ruby, and I know where to find you so keep it shut, got it?" he demanded before practically throwing her into the dirt from the bottom step. The doors shut and the bus brakes hissed as it pulled away. She looked at the back window, imagining the driver still tied and gagged on the long seat beneath it. She burst into tears as the lights went out again.

She was petrified and promptly very sick. She didn't know what to do. She wanted to ring Danny but the mobile number had been taken from her bag so she curled into a ball and hid from view. She was so frightened that she stayed like that for two, long, cold hours.

17
Almond Blossoms

"Amanda, has the paper been delivered yet?" Ruby asked when she called in to reception the next day, forcing the loathing she had for the woman aside. She was desperate to get a glimpse of the day's headline.

"It isn't called the Evening Chronicle for nothing, Ruby. The time is 8.45am and the last time I checked that definitely *wasn't* evening" she mocked. Ruby rolled her eyes wanting to go and poke Amanda's out with a biro.

"Yeah funny that. I wonder how it managed to arrive at 10.30 yesterday. I really ought to go and telephone their office and put it to them that 10.30am isn't evening either! Clearly nobody told *them!*" She scowled and then left to make her way up to the top floor

The first thing she saw as she approached the top of the stairs was a copy of Almond Blossoms pinned to the door. She smiled at how beautiful the image was and that Mr Alessi had recognised her interest in it. She pushed open the door to find Almond Blossoms blue tacked to almost every inch of the landing. She was confused now. She went into the coffee room to fill and switch on the kettle and stuck to it, like every other thing on the draining board and shelf, was a copy of Almond Blossoms. The fridge was covered in them, the sugar, coffee and tea bag containers, the walls and even the milk. She frowned and turned to leave the room spotting that the sofa and the copier were also covered in the blue background images, pale flowers and gnarled branches.

"He's a nutter!" she whispered shaking her head and checking on her way passed to make sure the box room had also been redecorated. It had. She entered Danny's office and smirked seeing his desk had been covered in Almond Blossoms too. They were pinned all around the edge and it was most amusing that he hadn't even bothered to pull them off. He had simply sat down, started working, and gone along with the office's new image. There was even one on his phone.

"You seen the news by any chance?" she asked, perching on the seat in front of him and searching his face. She couldn't help but wonder what the guys last night would have to do with *him*. Why would people like that know *him...well?* Did he owe them money?"

"What? Ruby, why are you looking at me like that?" he asked her defensively and she shrugged and looked away.

"What's with the pictures?"

"Can't you work it out?" he smiled. "He'll be expecting you to. Think bigger picture, Ruby," he encouraged and she looked blankly at him.

"Do I have to?"

"Do you just want me to tell you? Not sure you learn anything that way, or that Mr Alessi would be best pleased, but I think you've had more than your fair share of trauma." He wasn't wrong there. He didn't know the half of it! She tried to manage a smile but the pressure was building and the result was something meek and only vaguely resembling a happy person.

Danny put his pen down and leaned forward onto his desk. God he was so handsome when he did that! "Word association," he reminded her. "Alessi says 'perfection' and you say 'Almond Blossoms by Vincent Van Gogh'. You then went on to explain that it's perfect because of the blue in the background against the colour of the flowers and the way the branches are all twisted. It's interesting and beautiful, yes?" She nodded trying to keep up. "His point, now pay attention because he will be grilling you on this later, all the things that make it special and perfect can become less special and perfect if you're bombarded with it *all* the time. He wants you to hate Almond Blossom by the end of the day."

"But why?" she asked sounding offended.

"He didn't like thinking that you had offered yourself to me. The way he sees it everything that makes you special and perfect is lost if you let just anyone enjoy them. If you don't respect your body then the people you offer it to aren't going to respect it either. That doesn't make it any less beautiful, you are still who you are, but it means that nobody appreciates it or looks upon it in the way that they should. You are supposed to be unique and powerful and your body is something to be valued. Sorry, Ruby, the point he's making kind of feels like a flowered up talk about the birds and the bees, which is a little bit uncomfortable for me, but please know that I played no part in this. *I* never told him about the *'room for two'* incident in the car or the *'take me back to your place'* demand you made. *You* told him that and he has ways of dealing with things that I think may well come from his father's side. It's all very dated I'm afraid but, once again, it's only because he cares."

She nodded. She understood, but closed her eyes feeling terminally embarrassed that Danny recalled vividly their time in his car together when she was a drunken, babbling idiot and he was Mr Cool, Calm and Collected. She also allowed herself to linger over the kiss he gave her, it was beautiful. Maybe she could have used that in Alessi's word association game. Perhaps today's lesson would have been *a lot* more enjoyable being forced to kiss Danny all day until she grew bored of him, which was unlikely. She grinned and when she opened her eyes again he was squinting at her suspiciously.

"Something funny?" he asked and she shook her head. "Why are you so keen to know what's going on in the news? You turned to journalism? Law not for you, Rubes?" he teased with a grin but she was finding it hard to see the lighter side. Last night had been traumatising and the memory was surreal. She couldn't believe something like that had really happened to her or that she'd *actually* survived it! The walk home had been awful and she was convinced that she would spot the bus on the side of the road and they would be waiting to pull her on board again.

She hadn't wanted to cut through the estate, where hooded figures lurked and people turned a blind eye, so she'd stuck to the road, hoping at least for the reassurance of traffic and maybe even a lift from someone she knew. Matthew had driven by and turned round to pick her up. He took her home and wanted to come in, wondering why she was walking so late at night and from the direction of the industrial estate. He also wanted to know what had upset her and caused her to shake so much but, of course, she wouldn't talk and *for once* he didn't hit on her.

Ruby now sat chewing on her bottom lip as she read through a Statement of Defence that Danny wanted a second opinion on. At 10.45 Mr Alessi walked in with a paper under his arm and it wasn't his usual broadsheet either.

"Morning, Ruby, how are you liking Almond Blossoms now?" he asked her, with a slight hint of antagonism to his tone that she didn't like the sound of.

"They're perfect and still just as beautiful and special...even if they are putting it about a bit," she commented with a tired smile but he didn't smile back. As he clenched his jaw in frustration she put her head down and continued, unable to help herself, "It's such a natural picture it's a shame Van Gogh didn't think to incorporate the birds and the bees." He narrowed his eyes on her and nodded slightly, acknowledging her little sarcastic comment. It had been duly recorded and she would pay for it, she was sure. The silence that followed was immense until finally, to everyone's relief, he broke first.

He started moaning to Danny about petrol prices, using the folded paper to gesticulate his point about social control, before slamming it down on Ruby's desk. She jumped and tilted her head to read the headline. It was the paper she was after, disproving Amanda's argument about it being an *evening* publication. The headline read; '*Bus driver found safe and well after hijack ordeal*'.

Ruby slipped the paper closer while Mr Alessi was still caught up trying to convince Danny that the hiking cost of fuel meant an increased divide between the rich and the poor. The best paid jobs and opportunities were going to those who could afford to travel the distance. Danny was sticking to the environmental argument that people couldn't continue to drain the world's resources and not expect to pay for it. He reminded him that he had only yesterday made Ruby shred a whole rainforest just to prove a point, a point that could have been made with a couple of hours of grilling. He also pointed out that the 'hair of the dog' could have been all that was needed to put her off alcohol forever and that he did own a massive gas guzzling 4x4, three very good points.

"That your bus, the No 47, Ruby? Mr Alessi asked and she was rattled.

"Oh...erm...no."

"The No 47 goes to your estate," Danny confirmed, looking perplexed.

"No. I mean, yes, it is my bus but I wasn't on it when *that* happened," she struggled turning the page quickly to make it look like she wasn't bothered about the report. She started to flick through carelessly. "The No 47 is always being targeted. They threatened to withdraw it a little while ago because the driver was robbed and kids kept throwing rocks at it from the bridges." Danny stood and made his way over to read the story. He turned the pages back again from over her shoulder.

"So you weren't on it then?" Mr Alessi asked her, his eyes searching. She didn't blink, she didn't flinch, she didn't turn away from his penetrating gaze she simply gave the illusion of an honest answer.

"No, I wasn't on it, Mr Alessi. I walked home," she confirmed and Danny frowned and nudged her.

"Isn't that a bit dangerous? You told *me* you were going to get the bus when you left here. It was dark, Ruby," he protested seeming unhappy.

"Yeah but...you know...I needed the air."

For the rest of that day she was bombarded with pictures of blossom, they were *everywhere!* For the first few hours she piled them neatly or pinned them, so she could enjoy them without them getting in her way, but after that they were just annoying and disruptive. She resisted the urge to chuck them in the bin until 5pm when the pressure suddenly started to mount. Mr Alessi began storming about declaring he'd lost a file and accusing Ruby of being the last one to touch it. She hadn't been! He was stroppy with her and shouted, *a lot!* He told her to find it or else she was fired. She wasn't to go home until she'd located it and if she did go home she wasn't to come back again. Sometimes she really hated Mr Alessi.

Danny was really lovely and at every opportunity he helped her search, pretending he wasn't whenever Mr Alessi walked in on them. Eventually she snapped, grabbing a pile of his little blossom pictures. She took them to the box room and shredded every single one, imagining it was Mr Alessi's tie with him still in it. She then went to his office and demanded to be listened to. He waved her off, told her to get out of his sight, but she wouldn't. She fronted his desk and refused to move. She even told him if he wanted her out he would have to take her out *he* was going to have to *make* her. Danny was stunned, she was unbelievably fiery and a real match for Mr Alessi who didn't quite know what to do with her when she bit back at him so fiercely.

"I've not had your god damn file! I wouldn't be surprised if it's in here under this...this...*mess!* I wouldn't be surprised if *you've* hidden it in here on purpose just so you can have a go at *me!* Danny seems to be safe, why aren't you bawling him out? Because he's a bloke? Because he's been here longer? Because it's some boys' network where you watch each other's backs but treat the women in the building like they're imbeciles? Well you can forget it, Mr Alessi. You keep threatening to sack me so do it go on, say it! You know you want to," she pushed and Danny tried to negotiate with her.

"Look I'll help you find it. Come with me, Ruby, *please,*" he begged but she pulled away from him and placed her hands on Mr Alessi's desk, leaning in as he sat and watched her.

"Why don't we look in here?" she asked staring straight into his green eyes and refusing to be the first to look away. It was a challenge and he knew it. She wasn't stupid. He leaned back in his chair but he wasn't going to break either. Danny fussed over them trying to split it up and quieten it all down.

"Why don't you come with me, Ruby? I'll make us all a coffee and then we can start again," he encouraged gently, but she clenched her jaw looking from one to the other.

"I've got a better idea, why don't *you* take Mr Alessi for a coffee while *I* make a start in here? Where is it, Mr Alessi? It's not out there, I've searched, and I know you don't take files out of this office so that just leaves in here," she told him pressing her finger to his desk. "Why have you accused *me* of taking it? I've not even seen it so how could I be the last one to have it? I've been copying and that's pretty much all I do. If you're going to set me up you need to make sure you know what my job is before you accuse me of something that I've had no involvement in. My job recently has been *all* about copying...oh yeah and some *shredding* too. It's in here isn't it? I say we start on your desk, then under your desk, then the floor and, if that fails, we check your drawers. And I'm not talking your filing cabinet drawers, Mr Alessi, I'm talking your *desk* drawers." His eyes flickered slightly and she caught it. She was looking for some indication that she was getting close and there it was. His poker face had finally let him down. "Perhaps we should try your desk drawers *first*," she proposed and he leaned forward.

"Try it, Ruby? Just you try it!" he growled at her and she wasn't sure what to do. Would he actually hit her or just sack her. She had taken blows before and she didn't want to lose her job, but he'd threatened so many times she was starting to think that maybe he wouldn't. They glared at each other. She stood and straightened her posture, hearing Danny sigh with relief. It spurred her on again. Why should she be the one to back down? He'd accused her of something she hadn't done. Why should she let him win just because his name was above the door...*and he paid her wages?*

She walked passed Danny but instead of walking out of the room, like they both thought she was going to, she walked round to Mr Alessi's side of the desk. She couldn't look him in the eye, she was too scared now. She could feel him, so close his arm brushed against her shoulder as she knelt by his chair to turn the key in his desk. He did nothing to stop her. She prayed she was right else she would look like such an idiot. She paused and he picked up on her hesitation, taking the opportunity to speak to her in a much calmer and cooler tone, offering her an easy way out.

"You don't have to do this, Ruby. You can stop now and we can go back to looking for the file in the *other* rooms."

"And accusing *me* of its reason for being missing? No thanks, Mr Alessi," she declined his offer as she pulled the largest of the three drawers open, the bottom one. She gingerly lifted the papers inside, his wallet, his car keys, an apple and what looked like a gun. She pulled her hands back with a gasp and her fingers reflexively curled into her palms like they'd just been burnt. He waited to see if she would crumble but no matter how shocked she felt she didn't want to appear rattled. "Is that one of your five a day?" she asked, sounding so cool she could have hugged herself. She wasn't going to go all girly and screamy in front of him *just* because he had a weapon of mass destruction in his bottom drawer. He didn't answer. She slid it shut and quickly pulled open the middle drawer. She lifted the plastic folders containing client interview forms out of the way and then she spotted a red file, a criminal file, the file he was looking for. She pulled it out and turned on him. "I think you owe me an..."

"Sorry, Ruby, my mistake," he interrupted, pulling the file from her hands brusquely and reaching in front of her to slam the drawer and turn the key. "Looks like you get to keep your job after all," he told her casually. She clenched her jaw at him and bit her tongue to keep from blowing up. She wanted to walk away from this with her head held high.

She turned and moved gracefully into Danny's office and grabbed her coat. It was only 5.30pm, the time everyone downstairs went home, but usually she stayed late. Not today, Ruby was making a stand. She slipped her bag from the back of the chair and left the top floor without so much as a goodbye to either of them.

18
Danny slips

The doorbell rang and usually he would have left it but this time he thought it could be Alessi come back to get some work done. To be fair they hadn't got much done that afternoon what with the huge argument and Ruby walking out. They had a big appeal coming up and Mr Alessi often came back into the office after he'd been home.

Danny switched to lamp light, slid the wooden shutter back and lifted the sash window enough to get his head through. He frowned, it was Ruby. He quickly made his way down the stairs and opened the front door. She wasn't there and he poked his head out. She'd started to walk.

"Ruby!" he called out into the dimly lit street and she turned looking very relieved to see him. He beckoned for her to come back and she slipped inside out of the cold. He could smell alcohol as he locked the door behind her. "What are you doing out at night on your own?" he whispered and she shrugged and looked about, trying to peer into the darkness.

"It's creepy here at night," she observed with a shudder and he smiled.

"Not as creepy as it is out there. Come on let's go upstairs its warm and light up there. I keep the place looking deserted because the last thing I want is clients turning up!" he told her and she giggled and climbed the stairs self consciously in front of him. She was so glad he couldn't see to check her out from behind. He passed her in the doorway on the top floor and took her coat, throwing it over the back of her chair as she followed him to his desk. She leaned against a wooden shelving unit stacked high with files and smiled. He shook his head at her. "You've been drinking, Ruby Palmer. Do you *want* to destroy another rainforest?" he enquired, getting all sensible on her. She crinkled her face like it was all so unfair.

"I don't think Alessi would care enough to be honest, not after earlier. I don't think I even have a job anymore. I walked out remember?" she grumbled and he laughed, still reeling over the whole incident.

"Ruby, walking out at home time is hardly a sackable offence," he smirked. "Though rifling through your bosses locked drawers when he's specifically told you not to probably is," he added turning his chair from side to side as he studied her with his deep dark eyes. She frowned and he went on with the teasing. "Discovering he keeps a gun in there is bordering on knowing way too much...but I clearly heard him say you get to keep your job, so I think you're safe." She let out a sigh of relief. "It was certainly entertaining seeing you challenge him to take you out. I bet you wouldn't have said that if you knew he had a gun," he laughed, teasing again.

"Oh god I never thought of that. I suppose I was kind of asking to be shot!" she exclaimed and he nodded.

"It did sound like it and I'm sure it actually crossed his mind for a second there. You're such a pain in the arse sometimes, Rubes. I bet he imagines pulling the trigger when you go up against him like you do, but to invite him to do it in the way that you did, well, *that* was hilarious!" She trembled recalling the whole horrible episode.

"But you think I still have my job then?" she asked insecurely and he nodded. "It's been a really bad day. I only had one drink, I swear," she confessed and he frowned, unconvinced.

"I can smell it, Ruby! By one do you mean one two litre bottle of vodka?" he asked sounding astonished and she glowered at him, pouting cutely.

"What does the size matter? Surely it's the quantity and I only had one!" she grumbled making him grin widely.

"Size, quantity, they're all volume. It's the same thing," he chuckled, feeling quite entertained by her. "Why have you been out drinking and, more to the point, why were you out drinking *alone?* Did your friends leave you? You look very nice by the way," he complimented and she glanced down at herself and smiled, feeling flattered that he'd noticed.

"I had an argument with my dad. It was big, *huge!*"

"Why?"

"He said I was cocky?"

"You are! But unlike your dad *I* quite like it," he confessed making her face flush.

"I was meant to be going out with Sasha. I was going to pay for myself and everything..."

"Well that'll be a first," he joked, pushing himself out of his chair and giving her a very lovely grin as he settled back against his desk to speak to her more closely. She huffed at him like he was being unreasonable.

"He stole my bank card and told me I couldn't go out. I wasn't going to stay in with him, especially with the mood he's in. I walked out on Mr Alessi and straight home to *him*. I've had enough, Danny!" she complained wearily. "I told him I would go without it and he made some disgusting comment about getting by some other way, which I'm not telling you so don't even ask because I'm not even saying. It. Was. Gross!" He half smiled. Her rambling was endearing but what she was saying was disturbing.

"I'm so sorry, Ruby, it must be really hard for you," he sympathised looking her over. "So, why are you on your own? I mean you said you would go out anyway and you're clearly *out*. I'm not being funny but you don't really *need* money. I've seen you in action remember..."

"You saw?" she interrupted, shocked.

"I saw *everything*," he nodded. She went all desperate and humpy, tilting her head back and groaning at the thought of Danny watching just how bad she'd been whilst clubbing at The Lounge on her seventeenth. "Don't worry, Rubes, some of your behaviour was quite enjoyable," he chuckled. "So, anyway, what's with your dad?" he changed the subject back again not wanting to make her too awkward.

"He put me in a bad mood. I didn't feel like pretending to like someone just so I could get a drink out of them so I grabbed one of his bottles on the way out. He shouted that he would call the police and tell them I was a thief. Can you imagine that? Talk about wasting police time! He's going to be furious when I get back. The last thing you should *ever* do is touch my dad's stash, he goes ballistic. I think he might *actually* kill me."

"Don't say that," he told her firmly. "You need a drink let me get you one," he offered and her eyes brightened. *That might help with the confidence* she told herself. He narrowed his eyes seeing the glimmer of hope. "A non alcoholic drink, Ruby," he clarified sternly. "I will get you a coffee...I could do with a break," he told her pushing his hands into his pockets as he stretched himself out. His shirt sleeves were rolled up untidily, his top button undone, his tie pulled skewiff and his shirt untucked. He looked amazing and she was melting like butter. She glanced over the avalanche of papers covering his desk.

"Yeah it's quite late I think you could *definitely* do with a break, Danny," she advised.

"Not from work, Ruby," he told her shaking his head slowly. "I can handle work. I meant from you." He smiled and then left her while he went to go and make coffee. She stood and frowned. *What did that mean? Did he really need a break from her? Was she a pain in the arse like he'd said and like her dad regularly told her?* She was still mulling it over when he came back in, hot cup in his hand. He passed it to her. "Drink," he ordered. "I don't want you stuck shredding all day tomorrow I need stuff done for this bloody appeal. I need you in here...with me. We're a team right, Rubes?" he asked her.

"So you don't think I'm a joke then?" she asked and he frowned and shook his head very slowly.

"Why on earth would I think you were a joke, Ruby?" She stayed silent waiting for an answer. "I think you're very funny but I certainly don't think you're a joke. Why would you even ask me that?"

"Just something Matthew said," she shrugged.

"Did he now?" He didn't sound very happy. "Shall I tell you what *I* think?" She nodded. "I think Matthew's a little insecure about who and what he is and he uses *you* to make himself feel better. You're not a joke, Ruby, far from it. If anyone's a joke, it's him." She contemplated his words as she took a sip. The coffee was very hot and come to think of it so was she. Coming out of the cold into a warm building, having downed a bottle of god knows what on the way into town and now being faced with the most handsome guy she had ever set eyes on made her ears burn.

She passed her cup into one hand and tried to shrug out of her thin cardigan but she got stuck. She struggled.

"Oh...uh...how hard can it be?" she despaired and he laughed, before sheepishly helping her to remove it. He held onto it like he didn't want to let it go and she wanted to kiss him so bad, to take their friendly kiss in his car to a whole new level. He smirked as if reading her mind and fidgeted uncomfortably, swallowing hard.

"Alessi's going to kill me," he told her, seeming worried, and she looked at him with wide amused eyes.

"Why, what have you done?" she laughed.

"Nothing...yet...it's what I'm about to do," he confessed, but before she could ask what that was he moved forward, dropped her cardigan to the floor and slid his hands into her hair, finding her lips with his. He kissed her slowly and perfectly before moving his hands to her back to hold her steady while he traced a line of kisses into the V neckline of her dress. She gasped out taken aback. The most gorgeous bloke she had ever set eyes on was kissing her, touching her, letting go...*with her!* She realised she was still holding the cup and tried to concentrate on getting it onto one of the shelves as his mouth continued to move over her expertly.

"God is there anything you can't do?" she breathed, feeling completely swept away by him.

"Algebra...and don't call me god," he breathed back making her giggle. She was still trying to place the cup somewhere and he mumbled from behind her ear.

"I couldn't give a toss about the carpet right now, Ruby, just put it anywhere." She got it safely on the shelf without spilling it and he took her now free hand and clasped it in his as he walked her backwards towards his desk. She felt anxious and her stomach had started twisting. Something was wrong but she wasn't sure what. This was what she'd wanted from the moment she set eyes on him, what she'd dreamt about so many times she found it hard to look into his eyes without blushing, but now it was happening, like *really* happening, and it was happening fast.

His hands moved across her back looking for a zip and then round to her side sliding it down when he found it. His palm moved into the space between the material and her skin and her heartbeat rocketed as his warm fingers ran over her. She tried to concentrate, tried to focus her mind which was racing as fast as her pulse, everything in competition with the adrenalin pumping so hard she thought she might actually run for it. He grabbed her thigh firmly, squeezing it hard, and she suddenly realised what the problem was. She wasn't ready. He would know exactly what to do and it would be clear that she didn't. She had to do something. It was what she thought she wanted until now. She still wanted *him* but she felt out of control and she didn't like it. She was scared.

"Danny," she whispered.

"Ruby," he replied in exactly the same way as he did when she called him while they were working. He would play games copying what she said and mimicking her, especially if she was stuck or moaning. Ugh he was still so cool, as cool as he always was, and that just made matters worse. He was right at home but she felt completely out of her depth. For her it felt like her first day all over again. She had to do something he would be able to tell, he would think she was awful, they would have to work with each other...*tomorrow!* She had to stop it before it went too far.

"Danny, I haven't done this before," she mumbled in a panic. There, it was out, and he immediately stopped moving.

"What?" he whispered, his lips still touching her neck, his hands poised mid squeeze on her thigh. She tried to catch her breath, feeling terminally embarrassed.

"I said...I haven't...done this...before." He moved back to look into her eyes, releasing his grip on her.

"What are you telling me, Ruby?"

"Ugh what do you think I'm telling you, Danny? I'm a...*you know?*" she cringed like it hurt to say it and he closed his eyes. His mouth opened but no words came as he shook his head in astonishment. He bit his lip over and over like he was desperately trying to think.

"Shit," he whispered as if he'd just done something very, very, wrong. He opened his eyes and straightened the skirt of her dress trying not to imagine how much higher it would have been had she declared her sexual status just a few seconds later. He grabbed the zip on the side and fumbled trying to pull it up. He was much smoother pulling it down. He clearly didn't *dress* women very often. "I had no idea," he told her. "Please tell me I didn't read the signs completely wrong? I really hope I haven't upset you? Are you OK?"

"No, listen," she tried to explain. "I really like you. I wanted to...I still do...I just kind of expected..."

"Your first time not to be on an office desk?" he helped her out and she nodded. "That's fair enough. Had I known I wouldn't have...not like that...I'd have been more...less...oh shit! I can't believe this. I guess I just thought...I don't know," he trailed off and she frowned.

"Thought what?" she asked bewildered. Most people at school and on her estate thought she'd already done it. Boys had taken her on dates and then lied, it being a big boost for their reputation, but she'd never bothered to argue about it. She couldn't care less what other people thought...until now. She cared what *he* thought.

"You just seem so full of yourself that's all. You're beautiful, seriously hot, confident, bolshie, feisty. You are frighteningly streetwise for your age. You can go out and get everything you want without parting with a penny, I've seen you do it. You get really drunk, you've got all the moves and the lines and the men can't get enough of it. I watched you kiss four different blokes on your birthday, Ruby...I guess I just thought..."

"I would sleep with them too!" She sounded mortified and she looked devastated.

"I'm so sorry," he cringed.

"I have standards, Danny! I'm not easy!"

"I never thought you were," he responded sounding shocked. "I never said that," he argued, moving to keep her from scrambling away.

"You just did!" she snapped at him slamming her hand against his chest in anger. "Everything you described about me was the absolute definition of easy! And *you* thought because everyone else had *apparently* had me what did it matter if you did too, even though you told me you wouldn't touch me until I was at least eighteen! God I'm such an idiot. I don't know why I told myself you might be different. Why did I think I could tell you that I hadn't done it before and you not be *completely* gobsmacked? Is it so hard to believe? Do I *look* that desperate?"

He shook his head while she ranted. "Alessi was right wasn't he, people don't see what's really there, what really matters? I wouldn't mind so much, Danny, if I at least had a history that was true! I've always said *no* but I liked you. I wanted you. The whole time I've wanted you, even when you were horrible to me. I wanted you just then but I felt frightened. It felt like you thought I knew what I was doing, that you assumed I could handle it like you, but I wasn't ready. I was worried that I would get it wrong!"

He stepped back and rubbed his face in his hands before running one of them around his neck stressfully.

"I've seriously messed up. I should never have touched you. I'm sorry. I...I need some air." He turned and walked away, moving quickly down the stairs. She heard the toilet door slam and buried her head in her hands. He wished he hadn't touched her, everything was ruined. There would never be a *'them'* he would never tell her that he loved her. Nobody ever would. She would have to leave work, her job. She would have to leave...*now*.

19
Running away

She slipped off Danny's desk quickly. She couldn't stay and wait for him to come back. She grabbed her coat from the chair and pulled it on whilst running silently down the stairs. She got out of the front door and ran, only slowing down when she felt sick.

Soon she was approaching her estate and she felt scared. Her phone began to ring and she dug it out of her pocket. It was Danny. He'd realised she'd gone missing but she wasn't in the mood for talking, especially to him. She turned it off and clutched it in her hand. She didn't care anymore, not about him, not about anything. She'd had enough of her cruel life and in a strange way she hoped that someone might just put an end to her misery. It was unlikely anybody would care or notice. However, as she approached the underpass to her estate her survival instincts kicked in telling her this was one of the most stupid things she had *ever* done. She was asking for trouble but she couldn't turn back now and she had nowhere else to go. Putting her head down she headed for the underground passage, petrified of who might be in there.

It was dimly lit and a couple of hooded figures were loitering. She pulled up her hood so they couldn't see her face and prayed they wouldn't try and stop her. They whistled and jibbed but to her relief they didn't try and touch her. She kept walking and after what felt like an eternity of concrete floor, walls, ceiling and strip lights, she was out of the tunnel and surrounded by the dark bushes, parks and playing fields that bordered the estate. She headed for the houses not looking forward to the little alleyways, green spaces, empty boarded up buildings and nooks and crannies where people hung out.

She hunched inside her coat as she approached another group of hooded figures, the red hot glow of their cigarettes growing brighter as they took deep drags on white sticks. They saw her coming and watched with interest, calling to her and offering her things she *definitely* didn't want.

Sliding off the bins and peeling themselves away from the walls they crowded her quickly. She put her head down, bravely trying to push through as they hustled her.

"Hang on a minute what's your name, baby?" one of them asked and she struggled to fight back the tears. She felt so intimidated and sick to her stomach she could hardly breathe. She was sure she was about to be attacked as she wrapped her arms around her body and moved away from the group as quickly as possible. She heard the same voice again. "Hey wait up. I asked you a question," he called after her, while the others laughed and whistled. He was following her now and she tried to move quicker. She thought about knocking on doors but she knew they would be left unanswered. The tears began to flow as she heard the footsteps closing in from behind. She wiped her wet face with the back of her hand and sniffed hard. "Why don't you just stop and talk to me?" he called her again and then, getting near enough, he reached out and pulled her hood back.

She spun round ready to fight for her life. He wouldn't get anything from her without having his eyes scratched out first. "Ruby! I thought it was you. What the hell are you doing walking the estate at this time by yourself?"

She couldn't focus through the panic and the tears but now her hood was down she recognised the voice. It was Sasha's oldest brother, Mario. "You're crying, what's happened? You want Mario to sort someone for you? No one messes with my little sister's best friend do you understand? I promised I would look after you, Ruby. Why the tears?" he demanded to know, itching for a fight, and she choked back the sobs.

"Mario! *You're* the bloody reason I'm crying. You scared the life out of me! You...you...*idiot!*" she stepped forward and hit him across the chest with the palm of her hand and he took a step back laughing at her.

"Whoa! Ruby. Ruby. Ruby. What are *you* like? Trouble just seems to follow you, but then you just handle it don't you? You're little and you handle it. It's what Ruby Palmer does. You're like a little...Jack Russell...that's it, a nasty little piece of work. Looks sweet and innocent but you wouldn't want to get too close or you *definitely* get bitten. You're cute do you know that?" he chuckled and she shook her head at him.

"Don't be hitting on me now, Mario! I've had a really bad night and I want to go home." She turned to walk away. "And I don't appreciate being compared to a small dog either!" she yelled back at him. He laughed as he called after her.

"I never meant it like that, babe!"

She made it out of the cluster of houses and greens and into *her* cluster of houses and greens. She could see her house and leaning against the fence was a figure, waiting for her. As she approached she began to cry, it was Danny. He caught her in his arms and held her tightly.

"Are you *trying* to get yourself killed?" he asked, sounding desperate, and she nodded honestly. He wouldn't let her go and she let herself be hugged as she sobbed. He squeezed her tighter. "I swear I never meant any of those things the way they sounded. Sex or no sex, history or no history, Ruby, you will *always* be Almond Blossoms to me. Please forgive me for losing control, for putting what I wanted first like that. I completely misread...*everything!* I will never do that again, I promise."

"You don't have to stay away from me forever, Danny, that's not what I want?" she told him looking pleadingly through her dark wet lashes.

"OK, well, how about we go back to at least eighteen? And next time, if there is a next time and if I haven't put you off completely, we do it properly. The way it should be, special?" She looked into his eyes and nodded as he wiped her face and brushed her nose with his finger affectionately. He then kissed her forehead and mouth once gently. "Weren't you scared walking home? Did you walk all the way through the town and the estate by yourself?" she nodded trying to dry off her tear soaked face a bit better. He rummaged through his pockets but to no avail and then opted for just using his jacket to dry her off. "I'll wear a different one tomorrow," he grinned after pulling a gross face at her.

"I don't want to go in," she began to cry again. "Please don't make me go back in there. I hate him, Danny. He's going to go mad. I touched his alcohol. Can I please come home with you, Danny, *please?* I swear I will be on my best behaviour. I won't ever drink again. I won't flirt or try it on. You won't even know I'm there." He held her at arm's length so he could look at her and sighed deeply.

"I wish I could, Ruby, I really do but it's just not possible. You live here, it's your home. If you don't come back here he will call the police and report you as missing. It will be messy and Alessi will kill me for getting involved with you like this. Talk to *him* if you're really unhappy. He will sort something for you, I know he will. He really likes you, hence the reason I know he would sack me if he knew how I overstepped the mark this evening. Look it's a well respected firm. The media would have a field day printing all about how I stole some innocent seventeen year old girl away from her devoted and desperate father for my own sick pleasure. Please, Ruby, just go in."

"No, Danny, I don't want to. He will punish me," she argued bitterly, wanting him to take her somewhere safer.

"Just get your head down and come into work in the morning. He might be asleep, you never know. If he's not, if he hurts you or scares you, just call Alessi and he will sort him out. You can always call me too, that hasn't changed, but Alessi is the one you need to speak to if you can't stay here. I can't...I'm not allowed to take you back to mine, all hell would let loose, believe me! Do you want me to call him now for you?" he asked her helpfully but she shrugged out of his arms feeling let down and walked away, locking the gate behind her and closing the back door quietly.

He stood and waited for shouting but nothing came. The bedroom light came on and then went off again. After two hours of loitering and watching the place from his car he eventually went home.

20
New shoes well worn

She thought that everything was going to be awkward when she arrived at the office in the morning. She was nervous about facing Danny but that soon went out of the window when he met her at the top of the stairs and pulled her eagerly into the box room, shutting the door behind them.

"How was last night, are you OK?" he asked in a smooth low voice.

"It was fine thank you," she sighed with relief. "He was asleep. I was lucky! So, anyway, what's going on?" she whispered. "Why are we in the box room, my most hated place in the world?"

"Because that makes it the last place Alessi will think of looking for *you*," he told her and she frowned not liking the sound of that. "I'm in court with him all morning, maybe all day depending on how it goes, so neither of us will be here."

"OK."

"That's good for you because he's still in a really bad mood. You've obviously done something to hack him off, Ruby, any ideas?" he asked and she shook her head solemnly.

"No nothing. Is it the argument yesterday, his drawers and the gun? Is that it?"

"I don't think so because he was off about you all day yesterday and it just got gradually worse. After you went home he calmed down for a while, talked about what a good worker you were, how he liked you and wanted to keep you. He said he felt protective of you but then he started getting all het up about honesty and loyalty. He gave me a big long lecture on trust and then decided that actually I shouldn't trust anyone...*ever*. I mean talk about lonely if *everyone's* your enemy!" he snorted.

"So I'm the enemy then? He set me up with that file and now *I'm* the enemy? It doesn't make sense! Maybe I should just ask him straight.

What do you think?" she sounded determined and she looked like she was preparing for a fight.

"I think whatever I say you will ignore me, Ruby, but if you're really asking me and you really care what I think then, no, don't ask him straight, not right now. He's in a *really* foul mood and now is *definitely* not a good time. Trust me."

"I thought we couldn't trust anyone?" she grinned cheekily.

"Well...you know...you can trust me," he told her sexily and she giggled.

"And you can trust *me* so the world's not *completely* lonely," she informed him and he smiled at her.

"There's something else, Ruby," he began cautiously. She didn't like the sound of that either.

"What *else* can I have done? I only just got here for god sake!" she moaned rolling her eyes.

"No, it's not what *you've* done it's what *we've* done. He came in first thing this morning and found your coffee cup still on the unit next to my desk. It had lipstick on it and he knew it was yours. He also found your cardigan on the floor by my desk and he knew that you'd been here *out of hours,* with me. Alessi being Alessi he conducted his own little investigation, starting with dusting for your fingerprints on my desk and finding them way too far back and facing forward for it have been caused by anything other than you sitting on it... *'seductively'*, his word not mine! He continued his investigation by interrogating me for a whole hour when I got in this morning at a decibel that could only be classed as a nuisance for the purposes of law and I'm assuming concludes with an interrogation of you. I wanted to get in first, sorry, it's like you're being bullied."

"No, Danny, it's not *like* I'm being bullied I *am* being bullied! What has it got to do with him anyway?"

"Oh it has a lot to do with him, Ruby, he's the boss."

"Well I don't understand if you're going to talk in riddles. I might just tell him we did it to wind him up," she threatened competitively, trying to think of other things she could do to aggravate him.

"Ahhh remember he has a gun, Ruby, *please* don't tell him that!" Danny actually looked scared.

"OK," she agreed less enthusiastically. "So, what do I do now then? You want me to protest my innocence, declare my virtue. Or maybe I should just tell him I'm a virgin and see how shocked he is to learn of it." Danny cringed, that one was for him and it hit hard.

"I'm still really sorry about all that. I really never meant that I thought you must be a..."

"Leave it, Danny, my head hurts!" she snapped putting her thumb nail to her mouth and biting at it anxiously. "He's making me grey do you know that? Did he really dust for fingerprints? The man's a nutter!" she exclaimed desperately and Danny nodded, agreeing on both counts.

"He told me that he wasn't finished with me and that he wanted me to start spending more time at uni and less time in the office. Get this, Rubes, he said that he wanted me to start *'dating'*."

"Doesn't he mean *courting?*" she corrected, her nose scrunching at how prehistoric it all was. "So the problem is me then isn't it? He doesn't like the thought of you, being the clever, perfect brown eyed boy that you are, mixing with someone like me! What's so wrong with *me?* I know I don't come from a great area but that doesn't make me a bad person, Danny."

"I know that and he knows that too. It's not that anyway. You've definitely done *something* to upset him but this obsession with me keeping my hands off of you stems right back to when you started. He was in two minds whether to leave you with Tom Marshall, but he liked you so much he wanted you up here with us so he could look after you. The afternoon you started up here was the first lecture I got on not mixing business with pleasure and maintaining the integrity of the firm. He liked your fight, determination, grit, all the things he also *doesn't* like about you. I think, honestly, it's more about him not wanting *you* to mix with *me*. I don't think he thinks I'm good enough for you. He wants someone to propose to you and then treat you right. He thinks I'm a try before you buy type."

"A what?" Ruby grinned making him smile.

"He told me earlier. He said *'Would you take a pair of shoes off the shop shelf and then ask to take them round the block a few times before committing? No, so don't do it with her then!'* See, it's not you."

Ruby perched on the desk leaning back tiredly and feeling completely baffled. What was it that she'd done to upset him *so* much? The door burst open and both of them jumped and fidgeted like they'd been up to no good, especially as Ruby had been leaning back on the desk in a way that he'd already described as 'seductive'. She imagined him dusting the box room for prints. He'd be dusting the photocopier next and she used that so much they would be *all* over it. She would look like a new pair of shoes completely worn in before anyone had parted with a penny. She smirked. Her brain really didn't help her out sometimes and now he was angry with her.

"So you think it's funny do you?" he boomed. She shook her head but she couldn't help smiling, the tension was just too much.

"No, it's just...I was thinking of something that's all. I'm sorry, no, Mr Alessi nothing is funny," she told him, forcing herself to straighten and drop the grin.

"Are you being clever?"

"No!"

"I'll deal with you later, young lady. Danny, get your blazer and the files, we're going," he ordered and Danny gave her a wink and went to get the files obediently. Mr Alessi stood in the doorway to the box room keeping an eye on her like she might try and run off with something, maybe his precious sidekick, Danny. She smiled again, oops!

"Mr Alessi, what would you like me to do while you're gone?" she asked, trying to be helpful and pleasant.

"Dust, Ruby! Your fingerprints are everywhere!" he shouted at her as he turned and stormed off. Danny cringed, gave her another wink and then left the building too.

The rest of the day was long and quiet and Ruby was glad of the peace. Alessi was seriously high maintenance! Danny came back at 5pm a little cagey. She could see he felt stressed and she knew he would have had

Alessi on his back all day. He was polite but cool with her, no more winking. She tried not to read too much into it. He had been nice to her earlier and maybe it was better that they stayed just friends, less complicated, less bloody noisy!

"See you in the morning then," she called softly leaning in to check on him at 6.30pm. He had a pile of papers in front of him, pen poised, but she knew he wasn't reading. He was just looking like he was reading to keep from having to talk. He placed the nib of his pen on the paper as if keeping his place as he spoke.

"You off then, Rubes?" he asked her softly and she smiled though he couldn't see it. He hadn't even lifted his eyes. She felt sorry for him. Working with Alessi was hard. He could be relentless sometimes.

"Yeah, I don't fancy being roped into any overtime. I might bump into Alessi so I'm going now. I worked through lunch so..."

"You don't have to explain to me, Ruby, I know you work hard. Make sure you get something to eat if you worked through lunch. You getting the bus, it's dark?" he asked still looking at the paper, nib keeping the same place. He was clearly not taking anything work-related in but he wasn't prepared to try and engage fully with her either. He was strange and distant but his questions still showed that he cared.

"Yeah don't worry about me, Danny, I'm fine." She narrowed her eyes on him wanting to get closer.

"Are *you* OK?" she asked shyly. He was the cool one, the one who could handle everything and she hoped that he wouldn't mind her asking him, her questioning his stamina. He looked up for the first time seeming touched as he smiled warmly at her. He placed his hand over his mouth like he was holding something in and nodded. He clearly didn't want to talk so she turned and disappeared out of the door and down the stairs.

21
The Demand

She had every plan to grab something to eat from the chip shop on the way home. She would tell her waster of a dad that she was sick and go straight to bed. Hopefully he would forget all about her after a couple of hours of drinking himself unconscious. She escaped through the firm's front door and right into a man on the High Street.

"Oh I'm so sorry I wasn't paying attention," she apologised, helping him to pick up his newspaper and cigarettes.

"Easily done, keen to get home from work eh?" he asked and she grinned.

"Is it that obvious?" she laughed and he nodded in amusement. "Well, anyway, I'm sorry, *again,*" she told him handing him the packet of cigarettes back. "These things will kill you," she smiled playfully.

"One thing's for sure something's going to. *Something's* going to kill all of us, some of us sooner rather than later," he told her raising his eyebrows as if he knew what her future held. She frowned. He'd just got way too heavy for *her* liking.

"Hmmm yeah...OK. Well. Bye then," she mumbled quickly and turned away hoping to leave Mr Happy behind her.

The temperature had dropped over the last few days and it was very cold. She pulled her coat around her body more tightly looking forward to the warmth of burning hot potato inside her and the pungent smell of vinegar on her fingertips. At the lights on the High Street she turned towards town, there was a good chip shop just opposite Jane's Jangles and she could watch people trying things on while she ate. Someone beeped at her and she turned as they passed, trying to work out if she knew who it was before waving. She was now facing the way she had come and Mr Happy, with the newspaper and cancer sticks, was still heading in the same direction as her.

She turned back quickly. She didn't want him catching her up. He was probably getting a bus on Grosvenor Street. He looked like a bus or train travelling type person with his long dark coat and black leather gloves. Something about that suddenly made her feel uneasy but she couldn't be sure why. She glanced back over her shoulder as she neared her turn for the town centre, but he was still there.

She ducked into a shop and spent ages browsing and trying to watch the door to see if he would come in. He didn't come in but he didn't pass either and she wondered where he'd gone. She could feel the shop assistant watching her, assuming she was planning her escape with an armful of his stock. She wasn't sure what to do. Maybe she should just make her way straight home, she was no longer hungry. She made her decision, save herself the stress of thinking she was being followed, she would turn left at the traffic lights and just go home. She bought some chewing gum, to prove the shop assistant wrong, and then checked both ways before leaving. She couldn't see him loitering outside but decided to stick to her plan and go home anyway.

At the lights she crossed over and turned left to make her way up the steep side street away from the town centre and the hustle and bustle of people. It was really cold now and she could see her breathe as it turned into white clouds in front of her. She liked it when that happened but she didn't like that her fingers and toes were starting to numb. She blew into her hands and shoved them under her arms, hugging herself tightly.

A car passed her, the only one since she'd turned onto Gladstone Road. The only other person walking had climbed some steps and let themselves into their apartment and now she was alone in the dark. She glanced back over her shoulder and her head began to rush, she felt dizzy and panic stricken. Mr Happy was behind her! If she stuck to the plan he would know where she lived, maybe that's what he was trying to find out. He might come and get her in the night. Maybe he had something to do with the men on the bus, maybe they were *all* waiting for her in the underpass to her estate.

She glanced back again, he was definitely still there. She unbuttoned her coat and reached inside digging frantically for her phone. She dialled Danny's number but despite her pleas to pick up it just kept ringing. She begged over and over, willing with everything she had for him to hear it and answer. She rang off and turned left. She was no longer heading towards home and she wasn't familiar with the layout of the next few roads and streets. They were part commercial and part residential and she'd never had to use them before. She had her known routes and she pretty much stuck to those, but she wasn't about to take her stalker home with her.

In this unfamiliar area she wasn't too sure where the dead ends and alleys might be, making it difficult to plan ahead. Certainly not many people lived in this part of town and it was due to be regenerated like the rest of the centre, with time. Right now it was just a lot of space and a strange mishmash of homes, offices and empty units. She looked back, he'd turned left too. It was official, she was being followed. She found the last dialled number and rang Danny again, her hands shaking the whole time. After six long rings he answered in a whisper.

"Ruby, what's up?"

"Oh god, Danny, thank you, *at last!* Where are you?"

"What? Erm..." he placed his hand loosely over his phone and mumbled, "I'm really sorry do you mind? It will only be quick. I wouldn't usually but it's kind of work stuff, some office junior." He then whispered even quieter. "I'll just chat quickly and get rid of her."

Now she couldn't concentrate and she was dithering. She'd slowed down, unsure which route to take, but when she looked back he'd maintained his distance, no closer, no further away. "Danny, come on stop explaining! Are you there or not?" she urged and at last he answered.

"Yes, Ruby, I'm here, what's up?" She could hear from the way he spoke he was walking and now the background was quieter.

"Jesus, Danny, about bloody time!" she panted, dithered and then took another left knowing she would at least be heading back towards town.

"I was in the middle of something, sorry. What's the urgency, why are you ringing me?"

"Because I'm being followed," she whispered. "Where are you, I need you?"

"Followed? Are you sure? You left over half an hour ago. You only live twenty minutes away by bus," he reminded her. "You said you were getting the bus..." He was working it out now. "It's dark, Ruby, why are you walking?" he demanded sounding angry. "I could have given you a bloody lift if you'd suddenly decided to stop taking the bus!" She glanced back over her shoulder. He was still there.

"Oh my god he's still behind me! Danny, stop telling me off, I'm definitely being followed. Please can you just come and meet me?"

"Well my cars in the car park. I'm in a restaurant. Where are you?"

"For god sake, Danny! Right forget it if you're too busy. I'll call Alessi instead." She was furious and verging on tears now. She needed someone, anyone, to at least tell her they were on their way.

"How do you know you're being followed? By car or on foot? Do you recognise him?"

"On foot. I bumped into him coming out of work and he's followed me the whole time. I'm not...I'm not sure where I am. Danny, have you even left yet?" She half shouted at him in desperation.

"I don't know where you are do I?" he bit back. "There's no point in me just walking out of here and wandering around. You tell me where you are and I will come straight away." She suddenly saw something she recognised.

"Oh, I think I'm behind...yes...I must be behind the old shoe factory. The one they plan on converting to flats. I've gone full circle. I can either take the road to get back to the High Street or...the alley...it will be quicker. It's not very long. If I take that I will be back in town in minutes. I can get a cab and you can..."

"Ruby, *no!*" he told her forcefully. "Don't take the alley, even if it's quicker! It's too isolated. I know where you are I will run up now. I'll call Alessi on the way. Is he still behind you?"

"Yes he's getting closer now, Danny, what do I do?"

"Take the road, Ruby, take the road!" he ordered.

"But the alley...I can see the road at the end and it's busy, there will be people I can..."

"Ruby, *not* the alley! The other way has flats on it just knock on the doors if you have to, walk up to the flats and push all the buttons he won't do anything if people are watching. Take the road do you hear me? I've already left the restaurant and I need to call Alessi. I will have to put you on hold for a few seconds but I'll still be here. Ruby, where are you now?" She didn't respond but he could hear her ragged breathing. "Ruby, answer me, where are you now?" he shouted at her.

"I'm in the alley," she whispered. "I know you said don't but I can see the road and he's getting closer, Danny. He started walking more quickly and I was scared he'd catch me up. The alley's shorter..." She gasped out. "Oh, god, no, please help me! This can't be happening!"

"What? Ruby, I'm not far away. What is it?"

"Someone's stepped into the alley at the other end," she cried out in desperation. "Danny there's two of them. I'm trapped! What do I do?" The phone went dead and Danny began to run, ringing Alessi at the same time.

Ruby stopped walking, her disconnected phone in one hand her other hand clasped to her chest trying to keep from screaming. She turned back and looked at the man who had followed her and then back the other way to see the tall dark figure that had entered the alley. He was pulling on a pair of black leather gloves and she began to shake, stepping back towards the damp slimy wall.

"Ruby," the man who had been following her called out and she turned towards him. As she did so she heard the ripping of tape from behind and a strip was placed over her eyes, just as a leather hand clasped her mouth. She heard ripping again and the taste of leather was replaced by the taste of glue as a strip of tape was placed over her mouth. She tried to struggle away but her hands were pulled together behind her back and the tape was wrapped tightly again and again around her wrists. She was now on her knees, having been pushed to the ground, and the cold wet mud soaked through her tights and onto her skirt and skin.

"Are you sure this is the one?" a gruff voice asked.

"Yeah, this is definitely the one. She's the easiest way to get what we need." She couldn't see his face but she recognised the voice as Mr Happy from outside the office.

"You know why you're here?" the gruff voiced asked, tugging on her hair so she was certain they were talking to her. She shook her head and squealed.

"Does she know?" he asked his companion.

"Maybe, maybe not, does it matter? Tell her what you want and she'll get it. She works there, for him. She's a little girl, all we have to do is put some pressure on and she'll give us *whatever* we want. Alessi just employed himself an easy target."

"Hey you," her hair was pulled again. "We want Johnny Giavani's file, got it? You get it here at midnight tonight else you won't live to see tomorrow. Come alone and I guarantee you will go home again, come with someone or get yourself followed, try anything clever and *none* of you go home. I don't give second chances do you understand me or do I need to clarify?" he asked her and she nodded her head quickly but then worried that he may think she wanted clarification and shook it. "Just so you know how little you mean in the big bad world you've got yourself caught up in. Just so you know how easy you are to dispose of..." he paused and she waited. It felt like an eternity before he spoke again. "Put Alessi's trashy little girl where she belongs," he ordered and she heard the slam of something heavy. She tried to wriggle away as a pair of strong hands lifted her from the floor and slung her like a piece of rubbish into a rancid metal container, bringing the lid down on top of her.

She was in an industrial sized rubbish bin. She curled up trying not to breathe in the stench. It was overpowering but with her mouth covered all she could do was breathe it in through her nose. She desperately didn't want to vomit because the tape would cause her to choke. She listened worried that something else was going to come next. If this were a film the metal bin would be emptied into the back of a lorry and she would be crushed by big teeth or taken to a landfill site and buried alive. She daren't move a muscle, risk reminding them that she was still there. As much as she wanted out she didn't want to be *out* with them.

She prayed that this was it and that they were done with their demands and then she heard shouting. She stayed quiet, desperately hoping they hadn't called others to come and finish her off. *No*, she reasoned, they couldn't have. They wanted the file. If they killed her now she would never be able to fulfil their orders. If she did get out what was she going to do? Would she do as they asked and go against Alessi, Danny and their scary clients or would she tell them what these people wanted? She felt desperate, torn and closer to petrified than she'd ever been before.

22
Who can you trust?

"Ruby! Ruby, are you here?" Mr Alessi called out.

"Just let us know where you are? Do anything you can and we'll find you," Danny shouted and she squealed and kicked at the inside of the bin. She wanted fresh air so bad now and sickness was close.

"Over here, Danny. She's in here, quick give us a hand." She heard the lid open and slam against the side of the container. The thick stench lifted slightly but it was still *very* bad. She couldn't see their faces but her hearing worked fine, if anything it worked better.

"Jesus, Ruby, what happened to you?" Danny fussed over her. "I'm so sorry. I had no idea until it was too late...I didn't think they'd go for you. Bloody hell, Alessi, are they targeting her or you? When they sent the parcel I definitely thought it was you, but what's *this* about? Why her?" Danny sounded furious as they gently lifted her out and onto the floor of the alley. Someone, she guessed Danny because his voice was coming from behind, was trying to remove the tape from her wrists. She reasoned it must be Mr Alessi trying to remove the tape from her mouth.

"There's no other way I'm going to have to pull it off but it's going to hurt, Ruby, so brace yourself," he told her and she squeezed her eyes and gritted her teeth as he yanked hard. The tape ripped across her skin and also pulled some strands of her hair from her head. She cried out before filling her lungs with air as quickly as she could, gagging and coughing as she doubled over on her knees.

"My hands, get my hands," she pleaded desperately, feeling vulnerable without them.

"I'm trying, Ruby, this stuffs a nightmare," Danny exclaimed. Mr Alessi began to peel the tape gently from her eyes, pulling downwards so that he wouldn't damage them. It took ages but eventually they got the tape off and she could see again. She struggled against the tape on her wrists. She was becoming hysterical and Danny tried to calm her. He used his door key like a saw against the thick plastic fabric until it began to split and then he unwound the tape from her wrists. As soon as she was free she stood and backed away from the both of them, trying to remove her red coat and escape the smell that was clinging to it. She threw it down onto the dirty floor of the alley. It was freezing but she would rather that than have any reminder of the inside of the bin, her putrid prison.

Danny quickly removed his coat and placed it around her shoulders. He looked furious.

"Alessi what's going on? Why Ruby?" he demanded but Mr Alessi just looked at her, his expression hard and impossible to decipher.

"What did they say, Ruby?" he asked her and now she was faced with a dilemma. If she told him he would want to follow her with the file. They had threatened to kill her and anyone she brought with her. If she didn't tell him she would be breaching his confidence, she would be sacked on the spot, not to mention what else he might do to her. Of course, neither did she know what *they* might do to her if she turned up on her own. Would they take the file and kill her? The internal struggle showed on her face and she looked like a cornered animal, ready to fight.

"Ruby?" Danny pushed gently but she wouldn't answer.

"Ruby," Mr Alessi spoke in a more soothing voice now. "You need to tell me exactly what was said. You need to trust me to know what to do. If you don't tell me, if you try to handle something or meet any demands on your own they *will* kill you...or torture you for more. If you co-operate with them they will see it as a sign of weakness. They will want more and more until the jobs, the risks, the breaches in confidence are so great you'll have moved to the other side and then, Ruby, you will be working against us and not with us. Do you understand what I'm saying?" She nodded.

"You think they've made demands then?" Danny asked him and he nodded, keeping his eye firmly on Ruby.

"That's why they've gone for her, Danny, because she's young, she's female and they think she will break easily. They're wrong because she won't." He sounded sure, more sure than *she* felt. "You need to tell me *everything,* Ruby" he told her. "Even if there's something you don't want me to hear." She didn't understand what he meant by that and shivered inside Danny's coat wiping at her face with the back of her hands. Everything smelled bad and she turned to spit on the floor, worried that something might have got into her mouth.

"They said they want the file," she told them, still bending over and unsure if she was about to be sick. She placed her hands against the wall for support feeling like she might pass out. They watched as she fought the nausea and then she started to gag and cough violently. She hadn't eaten all day and nothing came. Danny moved to place a reassuring hand on her back and as soon as she could she stood and turned to face them, looking very unwell. "They want me to get it and bring it to them here at midnight tonight...else...else...I won't live to see tomorrow. They told me not to bring anyone or they would kill us all!" She started to cry and shake. She was freezing and she felt terrible. "They told me if I didn't do it they would kill *me*. WHAT DO I DO NOW, ALESSI?" she shouted at him.

"First things first we take you to Danny's and get you cleaned up. You can't go home like that." Mr Alessi told her and she looked down at herself hopelessly.

"No one will notice," she half laughed even though nothing at all was funny, everything was such a mess. Maybe she was finally going mad, like him.

"That's not what I meant. I meant I don't want you dealing with putting yourself back together on your own. You're in shock and you need watching and looking after for a few hours. Danny will take you home in his car. We will take each day as it comes." He was so calm she could strangle him.

"I'm sorry, Mr Alessi, but I don't think you've quite understood. *Apparently* I don't have days I have *hours!* What are you going to do about the file? They will be here tonight and if I'm not they will be looking to kill me. They will come after *me!*" she told him jabbing her finger into her chest. "They know where I work! What if they know where I live?"

"Why would they know that?" he asked her suspiciously and she shrugged wearily.

"It feels like they know everything. The guy that followed me knew my name! What else do they know about me?"

"They're not going to kill you over some file, Ruby. As far as they're concerned you're just some office junior to me, dispensable, so what's the point? All this, the threats, the bullying, it was for *their* benefit, to get you to crack and do what they tell you. It makes their job so much easier if you just find it and bring it to them like a good little girl, rather than them having to find it themselves. You have more than a few hours, *trust me*."

"Trust *you!*" Ruby snorted under her breath and he shook his head at her before leaning in to the metal container to hook out her bag.

"Come on you need to get to Danny's place."

"Aren't you coming? Are you just going to leave now and disappear off to wherever you live?" she asked accusingly and he smiled at her.

"I'm coming too," he nodded. "I'll be following."

They walked through the alley and onto the High Street making their way to the car park. She climbed into the passenger side and grumbled as Danny got in behind the wheel.

"What took you so long anyway? I had to practically beg you to come and help me!" she complained hating him with as much passion as she loved him. Mr Alessi leaned in securing her seatbelt.

"He was on a date, Ruby," he told her slamming the door ruthlessly. She turned to Danny and glared at him wanting to burst into tears.

"On a date!" she repeated, stunned. "That's why you wouldn't come? I heard what you said on the phone. When *I* needed help you said that you'd get rid of me, that I was just some *office junior*. You're an idiot do you know that? Alessi was right you do *'try before you buy'*. You creep! Just take me home, Danny. I never want to see either of you again!" He had nothing in his defence and turned away from her deathly glare to start the car. "I hope she was worth it," she went on feeling sorry for herself and he pushed himself back into his seat with a sigh and took the car back out of gear.

"No, not really, Ruby, *nothing* could be worth how I felt when you told me you were trapped, when your phone went dead, when you weren't in the alley, when we found you in a bin disposed of like a piece of rubbish, taped up like...like they meant it," he stammered seeming really bothered. The date was Alessi's doing not mine, I can assure you. I didn't want to be there but *she* didn't know that. I didn't want to hurt her feelings or for her to be messed about so I went along with it. It's not her fault that Alessi is so desperate to stop me seeing you that he'll set up dates in the hopes that I'll get it out of my system and you'll be safe. I was just going through the motions for the sake of some peace and quiet. He's gone on at me *all* day, Ruby, and I couldn't take anymore."

"Then you should have said no," she told him flatly her eyes glistening with tears. He couldn't look at her, he felt too guilty.

"Yes I should have said no and I wanted to but I was tired and I thought maybe I could go out to keep him happy, be nice to keep her happy and then go home without *you* ever having to know. I'm not interested in dating, Ruby, not anymore, not since you came along. I couldn't get my head round it when you called. You *said* you were getting the bus. It didn't make sense and that's why I didn't come straight away because for all I knew you could have been on your estate, not still in town. I'm really sorry I let you down, Ruby, and, *no*, it wasn't worth it."

23
The set up

Danny let them into his apartment and then immediately went to the front window to look down on the street.

"Alessi's on the phone outside. Let's get started on sorting you out shall we?" he proposed.

"OK," she nodded shyly. He paused and smiled at her before disappearing off to the bathroom to get things setup. He moved about noisily while Ruby took in the size of the place. The main living area was huge, executive and immaculate. There were no pictures of him or anybody else, which she thought was quite strange. There was no sign of a girlfriend, no photos of a lad's holiday and no indication that he kept pets. All the doors running off the living area were open and she walked around the room so she could peer into each one. There were two bedrooms with beds made, both clean and tidy, curtains open, lamps already on. A spare room was set up with gym equipment, weights and a pull-up bar. The kitchen was white and open plan and, again, immaculate. There wasn't even a cup or bowl left in the sink from breakfast. She was starting to wonder if he might be a *little bit* obsessive.

"Bit unlived in eh?" he asked having walked up behind her silently. She was startled and spun around.

"Oh, no. I mean, *yes*. It's lovely though...just...very..." she was lost for something that sounded right.

"I spend a lot of time at work. I eat out a lot and sometimes...I sleep out a lot too," he told her and her eyes grew wide. At least he was honest about it!

"Not like that, Ruby," he exclaimed tiresomely. "I visit people, you know, family. I work so much during the week and over weekends I don't get to see them in the way I'd like to. I try to see them at night and often it's late so I stay over. I suppose I'm on the move a lot. This place is just a bit too quiet for me. I prefer noise, life, busy, you know. I don't like having too much thinking time on my hands."

"Why, what's bothering you?" she asked, sounding genuinely interested and not in the least bit teasing. "What don't you want to think about?" His eyes searched hers and then he smiled choosing not to tell.

"Shower's ready. Why don't you go and get cleaned up. I've put a shirt in there. I'm afraid I don't have much else that would suit you...or fit you for that matter," he smirked looking her up and down. "Bring your stuff out and we'll put it in the washing machine. I have a drier so it should only take about an hour or so. Is that OK?" She nodded and slipped into the bathroom.

When she emerged all flushed and smelling of soap, Danny let her put her things in the wash and the machine was all set up and ready to go. He then invited her to sit on the sofa in the living room with a cup of sweet strong tea and some biscuits. Neither of them knew what to say and she felt awkward wearing one of his shirts in front of him. Even though she was far from being naked she felt exposed and shy.

"See what I mean?" he suddenly asked her and she frowned, confused. "Too quiet," he cringed handsomely and she giggled, stiffening when suddenly the front door flew open. Danny put a calming hand on her knee and she relaxed for a moment.

Mr Alessi looked cold and hard as he walked over to face Ruby. He stopped on the deep dark rug in front of them and stared coldly, causing her to fidget. A slam on the coffee table next to her made her jump and she looked to her side to see the local newspaper. He'd thrown it down with *some* force.

"How was the bus journey home on Wednesday, Ruby?" he asked her sternly and she tensed.

"She didn't get the bus she walked, remember?" Danny defended but Mr Alessi shook his head at him.

"No you didn't walk though did you, Ruby? What do you know about that?" he pointed towards the paper but she didn't bother to look. She didn't need to she'd already read the story and she knew what it said.

"I don't..." Danny began softly.

"The No. 47 bus that was hijacked, Danny, she was on it. It *was* her bus, isn't that right, Ruby?" She nodded and glanced at Danny.

"I'm sorry, I lied," she told him before turning back to Mr Alessi, "I didn't know what to do!" she pleaded.

"So you thought you'd lie? You thought you'd lie to Danny? You thought you'd withhold vital information from *me?*" he demanded and she wrapped her arms around her body feeling frightened. "Why did you come to our firm, Ruby? What do you know?" he interrogated and she backed away from him.

"What? You know why! What do you mean, what do I know? I don't understand, Mr Alessi, please. I've had enough of this!" She sounded desperate.

"Oh I've only just started, Ruby," he warned her menacingly. "The day you came to our office you were told to go out for lunch..."

"We've been through this!" she cried out. "You didn't *tell* me, you *suggested!* I thought that was all dealt with!"

"You specifically went against my advice and as a result you saw my clients."

"Yes but..."

"I told you they would want to know who you were. I told them you were just a junior, you weren't important, you were dispensable, but they wanted to check you out for themselves. My clients had that bus hijacked because they knew that *you* would be on it. They wanted to press you to see what you would come up with."

"And you knew?" Danny was incensed.

"Yes I knew, Danny, I couldn't exactly say no could I? She works in *our* office!"

"So you sanctioned it?" he snorted in disbelief.

"Yes and they came back with *your* name."

"*My name?*" he sounded perplexed and slightly less defiant now. When he looked at Ruby she lowered her eyes guiltily.

"I'm sorry," she whispered. Mr Alessi began again while Danny was still trying to comprehend what he was saying.

"If that's not proof enough that she's willing to leak information then what about the fact that she chose *not* to tell *us* about it? She had no idea who those guys were but clearly they meant business. Our clients think she's working for someone else. She never told us because she didn't want to risk breaching who she *really* works for."

"What, *no!*" she protested. "I don't work for anyone else, they lied!"

"Alessi, hear her out," Danny tried to reason but he scooped up the paper and held it in her face.

"I brought this in to the office on purpose. I left it in clear view for you to read. You didn't think to bring it up? You had plenty of opportunity to share your ordeal with us but you stayed quiet. WHY?" he shouted and she bit her lip trying to hold back the tears.

"Maybe because she was petrified!" Danny argued for her.

"Or *maybe* because she doesn't want to blow her cover. She could be here for a rival. She could be here for the police, here to make Rossi's case unsafe by stealing from *our* client's file. She could be working for corrupt officers like Killen and that would mean expecting stuff like this to happen. So what other business do you get involved in, Ruby? police business? Another organisation perhaps? Are *you* the one leaking information, Ruby? Danny, you clearly can't keep your hands off her like you've been told. She has you well and truly hooked. Have you told her where the file is kept?"

"What, no!" he denied forcefully and Ruby shook her head and covered her ears, trying to block it all out as she cried out.

"No! I work for you and only you, I swear! I fell asleep on the bus and when I woke I was surrounded by three men. One was right next to me and the bus was empty. I knew there was something wrong, it didn't feel right." She looked up at Mr Alessi, her eyes wide. "They took a detour and I begged them to move out of my way but they blocked me in. They wouldn't let me leave my seat." She looked from Mr Alessi to Danny. "The one next to me suggested I climb over him. I thought they were going to attack me. I felt sick and I didn't know what to do." She pleaded with her boss now. "I had no idea who they were or what they wanted. I managed to get to the lower deck and begged the driver to turn back but he wouldn't listen to me, he wouldn't stop and they took me onto the industrial estate. I thought I was going to die, Mr Alessi! I never thought it was a set up. I never thought it was related to anything. I just thought I was unlucky."

She hung her head and placed her face in her hands as she explained what she really thought was happening. "I thought they'd decided to hijack the bus, it's *always* being targeted like I told you. I just thought I'd been caught up in it because I fell asleep, an unaccounted for bonus. I didn't think they wanted anything...not information...I just thought they wanted...*me*." The tears streamed down her face recalling her traumatic evening but Mr Alessi was heartless.

"Very touching, Ruby, but that doesn't explain the name. Why give Danny's name?"

"I didn't *give* Danny's name!" she yelled at him.

"So you're saying my clients are liars because I'm telling you now, Ruby, they're going to love that!"

"Yes! Yes I am!" she confirmed wiping her tears on the back of her hand and shifting up onto her knees to try and cover them. She didn't like being attacked by Mr Alessi and being inadequately clothed just made it worse. She worried that he might let his clients come and get her or that he would chuck her out on the street dressed like she was ready for bed? Danny pulled a throw from the side of the sofa and slung it around her shoulders, it was then that she noticed she was shivering uncontrollably. "I ran to the back of the bus and found a man tied up and gagged."

"Yeah one of their own, Dave Lazio, they can get quite into it sometimes," he informed her coldly. "They wanted you to think you were headed the same way. It wasn't the real driver of the bus he'd been knocked out and dumped in a shelter before the No 47 even arrived to pick *you* up. The man who took your money was one of our client's men. He was the man at the back of the bus." She shook her head feeling disorientated. That's why the news report didn't make sense. That's why there was no body and no account of intimidation from the driver when they found him.

"They asked me what my name was and that's when I thought about you guys, this place. I decided the last thing I should do was try to lie about anything they could clarify easily so I told them my name. I was glad I did because they grabbed my bag and searched for my bank card. I had a compliment slip in there too so there was no point trying to lie about where I worked. While they were there they found Danny's mobile number on a slip of paper and wanted to know who it belonged to. Again, I thought it would be possible to trace it and I didn't want to look like I had something to hide by lying so I said it was a friend's."

She pulled the blanket more tightly round her shoulders trying to stop her teeth from chattering, "They wanted the name so I said his name was Danny. *They* came up with his surname *I* didn't give it. I was shocked. I asked them how they knew him but they wouldn't tell, they just said they knew him well. They wanted to know if we were together...like...together, together, and I made it clear that I wouldn't touch him with a barge pole. I told them I was just some office runner but he said Danny wouldn't be giving his mobile number to some junior. They said I must be important. I explained that I was sick at work and Danny was just being nice, that he'd offered to give me a lift..." Mr Alessi turned to Danny interrupting her.

"And *is* that why she had your number?"

"Yes!" he boomed out seeming seriously angry. "I was worried about her and *you* had neglected to tell me that you had her all set up else I wouldn't have. She would never have looked suspicious. *You* caused this mess *not* her."

"You buy her stories too easily, Danny, I think you should keep your emotions in check. You can't afford to be soft, no matter how tempting she might be," Mr Alessi warned and Danny laughed like it *wasn't* funny.

"Don't you worry my judgement *isn't* compromised, how about yours, Alessi?" He ignored that comment and turned on Ruby again.

"So, why didn't you tell us what happened? Why keep something like that a secret?" he continued to badger but Danny jumped in, tired of her being bullied all the time.

"Maybe because people don't always do what you expect them to do when they've been scared or threatened. Maybe because they did more to her than she's letting on, more than they themselves are willing to confess to our client. Have you thought of that, Alessi?" he asked with his eyebrows raised. "So they work for Johnny Giavani but does that mean you trust them and everything they say because I sure as hell don't?" He then turned to Ruby. "Did they hurt you? Did they put their hands on you...*at all?*"

"No," she shook her head and whispered. "But the way they were talking and looking at me and the fact that they took me onto the industrial estate at night made me think they were going to. When one of them threw me off the bus he told me to keep quiet else I'd ride again, just him and me. He said he liked them young and he told me he knew where to find me. On the bus he knew when I gave a false address, which means he must know where I live. I haven't dared get on the bus since. I'm not going near it *ever* again. I don't *want* to ride with him. I didn't know what to do!" she exclaimed and Danny put his face in his hands and sighed before turning on Mr Alessi.

"If you knew she was being targeted and why, why the hell didn't you have her traced and tracked? How hard is it to do that? You could have had the whole story right from the horse's mouth rather than relying on what they say or she says. Surely that makes sense. They could have done anything to her and you could have been there to stop it if you knew where she was. She was on some old industrial estate with five of them. FIVE, Alessi! She didn't stand a chance, talk about intimidation!"

"I meant to have her traced," he explained, mellowing slightly. "But I was held up at court and then I got stuck in traffic. I thought I would be back sooner and that she would still be asleep. I was going to plant something on her before she left the building but when I called Johnny Giavani it was too late, she'd already been picked up."

"If you were going to be late you should have had them rearrange their little *test* or asked *me* to hook her up because, to be honest, your failing to do something so simple is *not* very reassuring. How long till I'm taking some nightmare journey with a few of our client's men and absolutely *no* backup?"

"It was an accident, Danny, and that's *not* going to happen."

"Why because she doesn't matter and I do? You're the one who needs to be more sure about your emotions and judgements because not long ago I was telling you to let her go and you were insisting that she would be OK with us. You *owe* her, Alessi! You owe her the same level of protection you owe me! Their games just aren't funny and it didn't need to take five of them to see if she would crack. One chair, one blindfold and one interrogator for one hour would have done just fine. They were in it for the thrill! It's not police or rivals you need to protect her from it's us, it's Johnny Giavani and the people *he* uses to do his dirty work for him!" He stood and put his hands on his hips, his jaw clenching like he might be about to fly at his boss. "I'm going to put her things in the drier," he declared walking out of the room and glad to get some distance.

He hardly said a word as he drove Ruby home. She gathered her things and opened the door, unsure if she should try and talk or just get out and go. He reached out and put his hand on her shoulder and she turned in her seat to look at him.

"I'm so sorry, Ruby. This is why I didn't want you working for us not because I thought you were rubbish or because I didn't like you. I didn't want you to get caught up in all of this. I'm sorry about what's happened. You've had it really tough but you've handled it *really* well. Thank you for being careful about the information you gave on the bus and even bothering to think about me, Alessi and our clients, when you must have been so scared. I really appreciate you watching my back for me and I swear I will do all I can to watch yours. Be careful OK and don't hesitate to call me if you need me. I will *always* be here for you, Ruby."

His eyes were deep, dark, and sincere and his face so handsome she couldn't imagine anything being so heavy that she wouldn't risk it to stay close to him. She was in and *in* was where she planned to stay.

"Thanks, Danny, I'll be careful," she promised.

24
A little bit of inside knowledge

Mr Alessi was out for the whole of the next day and although Danny messaged Ruby first thing to tell her to take the day off and recover, she refused. She messaged him right back to say it was more stressful at home than at work and begged him to let her come in. Within twenty minutes he was outside insisting that she wasn't to be walking anywhere. Mr Alessi was going to sort the dispute over her alleged breaches in confidence and reassure Johnny Giavani that she *could* be trusted.

They had a big appeal in a few weeks time, the appeal of one of Johnny's most valued men. Typically the day didn't go anywhere near according to plan. At 9.30am the police arrived with a warrant to seize and copy documents from a client's file. They were investigating a Mr McGregor for money laundering and any transactions, deals, purchases and sales needed to be examined with a fine toothcomb. The firm was edgy and, while Stephanie Tangle assisted two officers in locating all closed and open files on her arrested client, Ruby was roped into photocopying all the documents they wanted from the files.

She was watched the whole time like she might try and hide or steal something incriminating. The officer overseeing her was of medium height, dark haired and fairly broad. He made Ruby feel uncomfortable and he had an annoying nervous habit, clicking his pen over and over until Ruby thought she might go mad. He also blew his nose constantly and each time it was loud and forceful enough to startle Ruby and leave her with a headache. She was a nervous wreck by the time she was done and he'd *finally* released her from her copying duties.

It was 4.30pm and she went straight up to the top of the building to begin copying for the appeal file. Danny was stressed, having tried to fit some copying in while indexing heaps of information and preparing letters. At long last the bundles of evidence were almost ready to be distributed to all parties.

"Hey," Ruby greeted him as she leaned in the doorway feeling exhausted. When Danny looked up from his hands and knees with a pen between his teeth, his tie pulled skewiff and the most pleased expression anybody had ever given her she suddenly felt like she could go another seven and a half hours no problem. She smiled and he grinned and removed the pen.

"Ruby, you're a life saver! Please don't ever leave me, I can't cope!" he grinned wearily and she giggled.

"What's up?"

"Ugh it's this damn copier I can't get it to work properly. It keeps saying F1 error, what does that mean?" he asked, holding his hands out and desperately hoping for some great pearl of wisdom.

"Ahhh," she cringed painfully. "It means call the photocopier guy I'm afraid. It does it every now and then." He looked devastated and she felt sorry for him. "I'll go call him now," she told him helpfully and before he had a breakdown right in front of her. Within half an hour the engineer had arrived. While Ruby had been locating the engineer's telephone number Danny had popped out and he now came back up the stairs, greeted the copier man briefly and then took Ruby by the elbow to lead her into Mr Alessi's office. They kicked back on his floor and decided to skive. While the engineer tinkered and hummed – out of tune - Danny brought Ruby up to scratch. He'd been to get take-out coffees and two huge jam filled biscuits, it was a carpet picnic and Mr Alessi would have flipped. Danny was lovely to her, fussing over her and wanting to know how she was feeling after the night before. Clearly the rubbish bin incident had *really* shaken him.

"So what's so special about *the file?*" she asked eventually, making it sound spooky.

"Hmmm," he responded trying to finish his mouthful of biscuit. "Well, one of Johnny's main men, Rossi, was sent to prison five years ago. A police officer was held hostage and tortured and Rossi stood trial for it. He protests his innocence, which of course most people do, but he is protesting his innocence to Johnny and he doesn't really have to do that. It was a bungled drug deal and it was *big!* The main man responsible for trafficking into this country was a police officer, Officer Killen, nasty piece of work too. Killen is as corrupt as they come, he's brutal and dangerous and he's still policing our streets as a free man. He had the connections across the forces to see that the goods made their way from Columbia and Peru without too many heads turning."

"Other than to look the other way?" Ruby guessed and Danny grinned and nodded.

"The goods went missing in transit and everyone was pointing the finger at each other. Rossi was involved in bringing it into this geographical area and the heist happened just before it reached him. Killen had made a deal to share the profits and *he* was the one who accused our clients. Needless to say that never went down very well. An officer turned up in the boot of a car that had been pushed off a cliff, lucky in some ways but not in others. He'd endured twenty-four hours of the most heinous crimes you could imagine, before being thrown from the cliff to drown."

"And he was lucky *how?*" Ruby cringed.

"He was alive," Danny responded as if that was obvious but then he thought about it. "I don't know maybe that's not so lucky. Anyway, the officer pointed the finger, said it was our client's man, named names, and so Rossi went down for it. We believe Killen tortured one of his own men and then *made* him accuse Rossi. Killen had no intention of sharing the profits from the drug trafficking, he was just using people to get the drugs across the borders and into the area that his own force covers. He was using our client's people to do it. He just wanted it here so he could push it on the streets himself and keep one hundred percent of the street value. All this time we've been preparing an appeal. Names of corrupt officers have been gathered along with enough evidence to hazard a shot at challenging the 'beyond reasonable doubt' principle that saw Rossi go down.

"Beyond reasonable doubt?" Ruby repeated softly and Danny explained.

"To find someone guilty of murder you have to believe that they did it 'beyond reasonable doubt'. The jury that Rossi was tried in front of reached a unanimously guilty verdict, that is to say *every* single member of that jury found him guilty..."

"Beyond reasonable doubt," Ruby confirmed and Danny nodded.

"That's right. The jury, which is made up of twelve members of the public, are supposed to be impartial, you know, unbiased? In the Rossi case they weren't even allowed to see their families for the duration of the trial. They were accommodated by the tax payer in hotels and ferried to and from court under secure transit. But we have evidence to suggest that the jury was nobbled..."

"They were what?" Ruby looked horrified. "Isn't that breaking someone's ankles or something?" Danny chuckled and nudged her.

"No, plonker, that's hobbled but it *is* a technique that's come up in some of my cases and it's not very pleasant, I must say. No, nobbling is where the jury are threatened and intimidated either outside of the court or from the docks by interested parties. Because of the nature of the trial, the severity of the crimes committed and the kind of people involved - as well as the underlying theme of institutional corruption - the jury were understandably edgy. Add to that a bit of intimidation and suddenly you're looking at a unanimously guilty verdict. So, the file they were hassling *you* for, it's important. It has names, police officers names, *Killen's* name, as well as evidence to suggest that the jury were pressed for a guilty vote.

Every time our client comes in new information is shared and placed on the file, which is locked in a safe...somewhere in this building. When Alessi's clients are coming in it goes with him to his office."

"So that's why you guys were so stressed because Alessi is responsible for keeping the file safe and the information on it secure?"

"Uh huh," Danny agreed taking another bite of his biscuit.

"But it's been leaked and used to go against our client's appeal?"

"Bingo, you're a clever girl, Ruby. Your teachers were so wrong about you," he teased and she giggled and rolled her eyes at him.

"No they weren't," she grumbled insecurely. "So who wants the file, the police?" she asked and he nodded.

"I'm afraid so which means, Ruby, trust no one. Killen could be using anybody to get it for him. Threaten or pay people enough and they will do anything for anyone, unfortunately." She shuddered and the room fell silent until a knock at the door startled them both.

"Copier's ready!" the engineer shouted and Danny glanced at his watch, whispering quietly.

"Brilliant and it's only 6pm!"

Ruby twisted round on her bottom, draining her coffee and placing a hand on his raised knee.

"I'll stay and help. I have no plans, *no life*. I'll stay till late with you. We're a team remember so we can crack on with it together. We'll get through, over, round the mountain, even if it kills us," she promised and he grinned and ruffled her hair, tapping her on the nose.

"Let's do it!"

"Oh," Ruby suddenly stopped. "I just need to pop home first. I left my mobile under my pillow this morning by accident. Someone was texting me *early!*"

It was him and he held his hands up.

"Guilty!" he declared and she giggled.

"It's fine, I won't be more than an hour tops and then I'll be back. You'll definitely still be here, right?"

"No way, lady, you're not going anywhere on your own. I'll take you home," he insisted, standing and taking her hand to pull her up.

"You're not coming in," she told him defiantly.

"OK then I'll take you home...and wait for you outside," he corrected.

25
A secret shared is a problem halved

They locked up and left the building, making their way to the car park. It was Autumn and, although the day had been relatively warm and sunny, the evenings and night times were very cold. The sky was clear and the air crisp and fresh compared to the stuffiness of the building.

"Alessi is *really* sorry, you know, about how he's treated you these last few days," Danny explained. "He didn't want to believe you were working for someone else. He said he will be in tomorrow but he's had quite a bit of private business to attend to today. He gave me permission to enlighten you about the trial and he said he will apologise personally to you as soon as he sees you. You've had it pretty rough but you've stuck with it. It's amazing, Ruby, you haven't changed a bit," he laughed, kicking his feet through some leaves.

"What?" she asked stopping and staring at him. "Why would I have changed? Since when?"

"Since school, Ruby," he smiled at her.

"School?" She was baffled.

"Yeah, school. I went to St Mary's too, Rubes. I was going into Year 12, the lower sixth, when you started straight into Year 9. You would have been thirteen. Rumour had it you'd been expelled from your last school." She nodded like that was an uncomfortable memory.

"Yeah, I have my dad to thank for that. It seems they don't appreciate abusive parents threatening teachers and they moved *me* like it was *my* fault. They came up with some excuse to get rid of me and said I was trouble. They said I lowered the tone. Apparently, I was bringing my classmates down with me, what a great friend eh?" she shrugged seeming disappointed. "I mean what does *'down'* mean? And what's *'my level'* anyway? They should have just told me I belonged in the gutter because that's how they made me feel. I wasn't worthy and I rubbed off on people. I was *'bad, rotten, a waste of time and energy'* and so much more. God, teachers can say some really nasty things sometimes and it sticks too. A defiant face, a mouthful of abuse, some disruptive behaviour and they think that means you have no feelings, no conscience, no pride, but it doesn't mean that at all. I was glad to be out of that place, Danny, it was a rubbish school anyway," she grumbled resentfully.

"Ruby, you're a great friend and I don't believe you were trouble at all, well, not without good reason anyway. If the school couldn't handle you then that's their failure not yours. At the end of the day it's your job as a teenager to test the boundaries and it's their job to teach you an appropriate way of doing so. It's also their job to notice that things aren't great at home and to recognise that one of their students might need some help and support. If you're looking to blame someone don't go looking in the mirror because you won't find the right person," he told her with the most sincere smile she'd ever seen. She smiled back feeling herself melting. He was *so* lovely.

"I don't remember you at all, Danny. I'd have thought I would. I mean if you looked anything like you do now I'd *definitely* have noticed!" He pressed his lips together shyly and turned his face away to watch the traffic.

"I think you had bigger things to worry about. It must have been pretty tough. We kind of kept ourselves to ourselves anyway in the sixth form. We didn't want to be mixing with the kiddies," he teased and she hit him playfully. He glanced at her before going on. "Do you remember a John Billingham?" he asked her cautiously and her reaction shocked him. She crossed her arms and moved away like he was the epitome of all evil. "What? Ruby, what?" he pleaded.

"Please tell me you're not friends with John Billingham? If you are, Danny, you can copy all by yourself tonight and I'm *never* coming back to work. What do you know? What's he told you?"

"Hey relax. I don't know anything that's why I'm asking *you*. For the record, and I'd shout it if I had a megaphone, I'm absolutely and never have been friends with John Billingham. He's weird! He used to pick out kids when the first years started and bully them, he made their lives hell.

He picked you out too didn't he, Ruby? You stood out with your waist length dark wavy hair, big blue eyes and gorgeous little figure. He took a shine to you...*unfortunately*."

"Yeah that's an understatement," she told him with a troubled frown.

"We found you really entertaining and that's why I remember you. We used to talk about how impossible you were going to be when you were older. How a man would need oven gloves to handle you and we joked about who would be brave enough to go there," he grinned at her and she cringed.

"Great, so I'm a monster?"

"Hardly, Ruby, but you were a little wild child. Billingham definitely couldn't handle you could he? All the other kids bent over backwards for him. They did as they were told but you were different, Rubes. Every time he did something to you, you got your own back. He barged you in the corridor so you threw hot chocolate in his face. He whispered some comment to you in the dining hall and you poured yoghurt in his lap. He stole your bag and emptied the contents into the river so you pushed him off the bridge and broke his leg."

"Yeah OK I remember! Are you going to list them all?" she asked tiresomely.

"No but there is one thing that threw everyone, the day you got him expelled. It was you who got him expelled wasn't it, that was the rumour? No one ever found out what he'd done to you first..."

"And they're not going to either, Danny, so leave it where it is yeah?" she warned.

"Why, I told you about the firm, about our clients. Why can't you trust me enough to tell me what happened with Billingham? What did he do to deserve being expelled like that?" She'd started walking again.

"Can we just get in the car please?" she requested impatiently and he unlocked the doors. They climbed in and he locked them again, turning the engine over so he could heat up the space around them. "It's not a nice story, Danny," she told him looking into her lap and twisting her fingers.

"Was mine?"

"That's different *you* weren't hurt, *I* was," she told him shaking her head. He looked unhappy as he frowned back at her. "Look, he was furious with me over the trouble I'd caused him. He said I should behave like all of his other little victims. One day in hockey I belted Emily Carrington round the ankles and Mrs Rodgers called me a thug. I mean *me*, a thug?" she looked indignant and he snorted in amusement. "As punishment, public humiliation, while everyone else went in to get changed I had to put the equipment away in the sports shed. You know the one?"

"I remember it well, but why was that public humiliation?"

"Did you see the stupidly girly PE kit we had to wear, with the pleated slip, tight white t-shirt and gym pants?"

"Hmmm, yeah, it was nice," he reminisced, imagining Ruby in it.

"Shut up you fool! It was *not* nice, not if you were wearing it and especially as everyone else was breaking for lunch and could see me in it." He was stunned into silence and she continued. "Anyway, I was in the shed and the door slammed shut. I turned round and he was behind me. He wanted me to do as I was told but I told him to take a running jump. All the other stuff leading up to that day wasn't bullying, I could handle that. I could react and do something to retaliate, something that made *me* feel better. That day in the sports shed *that* was bullying. I felt intimidated, sick and threatened. He kept me in there for like half an hour."

"Doing what? What did he do?" Danny was tightly wound and she could see he was ready to snap.

"That I'm not telling you but let's just say it got pretty heavy and I told him I'd tell if he touched me. He said Ruby Palmer wasn't a grass and that I wouldn't want people to know but I *had* to do something. I told him that I didn't want to tell, people would say I'd asked for it, but I told him I *would* tell, the teachers, the police, everyone. I told him it would be awful for me but after I'd done it I could hide myself away in a cupboard for the rest of my life if I wanted to. He, on the other hand, would *never* be able to hide. I told him there were places for people like him, for men that hurt girls and women. I told him he would be quite popular in prison for all the *wrong* reasons.

I scared the crap out of him basically and he wasn't willing to take the risk...thankfully. He backed off and then completely ignored me after that. The harassment stopped and he wouldn't even look at me as he laughed and joked with his stupid friends without a care in the world. But I couldn't let it go. I would have to walk right past him like his little secret was safe with me and I'd just had enough."

"So you came up with a plan to get rid of him?" he asked and she nodded.

"Yeah I stole a bottle of vodka from my dad. I knew I'd pay for it that evening but I didn't care. I got a couple of roll ups from some dodgy bloke on our estate and then I got hold of a really dirty magazine to show him up for the pervert that he was. I followed him, smuggled the stuff into his bag in the library and then came to one of your classes, I think it was sociology..."

"Yes it was I remember well. We watched you come in and talked about how hot and gorgeous you were going to be when you were older...and we were right." She narrowed her eyes on him.

"Did you ever do any work, Danny?" she queried and he laughed and shrugged.

"I've not done too badly," he defended. She shook her head at him disapprovingly.

"I'd soaked a bit of sponge with the vodka and I squeezed it into his hood as I passed. I told the teacher that Mr Manning wanted to see Mario, Sasha's brother?"

"Yeah I know Mario. He was furious because he hadn't done anything wrong."

"He was fuming and he was about to storm off when I burst into tears outside the class. He came rushing back and he was lovely to me. I told him he didn't have to see Mr Manning at all but that I was scared. Of course I couldn't tell him *why* I was scared but he assured me he would watch my back and he always has. So what happened after I left the class, Danny?" she asked him and he blew out a whistle and grinned at her.

"Well, Mrs Spint got a whiff of the alcohol on John and ordered a bag search there and then. The whole class had to empty out their bags and pockets. John emptied his and low and behold there was a bottle of vodka, two joints and a magazine so nasty that it made Mrs Spint scream the place down. He was marched off to Mr Manning and *apparently* he never denied a thing. He just took the rollicking and walked." She nodded, her face defiant. She'd got rid of him once and for all.

"And good riddance too!" she declared proudly.

"Wow so you planted all that stuff on him then? We figured it had something to do with you as you'd just been in to our class. It seemed like too much of a coincidence that only minutes later all hell had let loose and we were all being searched.

"Yeah sorry about that," she cringed. "It wasn't just vodka in the bottle either, there was enough to make it smell of vodka but it was topped up. I poured half into another bottle and stashed it, knowing the place would be teaming with teachers, checking lockers and bags. On the way home I retrieved it and hid. I drank the whole lot."

"And that's when you started drinking? You'd have been what fourteen."

"Yeah and I knew it was bad for me and I knew it was horrible for a young girl to behave like that but it took away the big knot that constantly pulled in my stomach. It eased my memories and fears. Even though he didn't get what he wanted, the torment of waiting and dreading while he kept me there drove me mad. That's what he'd left me with, this feeling of being helpless, at someone's mercy, *my* destiny, *my* quality of life, all determined by *him*. The alcohol drowned it all out and it felt so good. I was a mess though and Mario found me unconscious in the park. He carried me back to his house. Sasha's parents were really good about it."

"They're a nice family," Danny agreed and Ruby nodded.

"After quite a few hours of being sick they took me home where my dad went off on one because I stole his drink." She sighed deeply. "And that's the story of John Billingham. You're the only person who knows. I didn't tell anybody, not even Sasha or her freaked out parents. So, Danny Glover, if it comes back to me you are dead meat do you understand?" she threatened and he nodded sadly.

"Ruby, honey, what exactly did he do?"

"That memory was flushed down the toilet with half a bottle of vodka, Danny, and as far as I'm concerned that's where it's staying. I drowned it, flushed it out and now it's gone. Please don't ask me again because I'm not prepared to go there. He didn't get what he wanted and that's all that matters."

"Are you OK now?" he asked and she nodded.

"It's made me stronger and more determined. I wasn't going to bow down to him. I wasn't going to bow down to anyone. I wasn't going to say yes sir, no sir, three bags full sir and I never will. I won't be bullied without a fight, Danny. He never broke me. That's what he wanted to do, scare me into submission, but I wouldn't and his nasty little plan backfired, *big time.*" Danny pulled up outside her rundown house.

"But your dad still bullies you?"

"Yes he does but he doesn't put his hands on me so I'm just grateful. He's never done anything like that. He says nasty stuff to me when he's mad and sometimes it's disgusting but I can live with that...apart from the other day when I begged you to take me home. I'm sorry for doing that, I was emotional and too tired to deal with it."

"No worries, Ruby," Danny looked at her sadly. "Please *don't* apologise. You're the last person who should be apologising."

26
With family like this who needs enemies?

"OK, I'll just pop in and grab my phone and then I'll be right back, wait here OK?" she ordered looking at him suspiciously. "Please, Danny, you will wait here won't you? I will only be a minute."

"What have you got to hide? You running a cannabis factory in there?" he wanted to know as he leaned back and forth giving the ugly council terrace the once over. She moved to get back into his line of vision.

"*Promise* you will wait for me here!" she demanded.

"OK. OK, I'll wait here...for *five* minutes," he agreed and she noticed that he'd cleverly attached conditions. She shook her head at him and narrowed her eyes.

"Well that's fine because five minutes is all it will take. I only need to grab my phone."

He lounged back into his seat and watched as she slipped through the tall wooden back gate and out of his view. He waited for two minutes, which felt like an eternity, and then climbed out of the car. He hung about for another minute and then locked it and made his way to the gate. He followed the short path through the overgrown garden and heard raised voices coming from inside. The glass in the door was smashed like there'd been a break-in and it was easy to listen to what was being said. He could see into the kitchen but the occupants were just out of his view.

"I *said* where have you been, it's dark?" a man's voice demanded to know and Danny guessed he was listening to Ruby's father.

"It's nearly Winter, dad, it's always dark. It's not late and I've come straight from work. That's where I've been all day and that's where I'm going back to as soon as I've picked up my phone."

"Think you're so clever don't you? Jumped up teenagers bagging cushy little jobs where they don't even have to get their hands dirty. Making their parents look bad just because they're out of work. I have a skill you know a trade, Ruby! What can *you* do? I got my hands dirty for years, worked my fingers to the bone and for what, nothing, that's what!"

"Dad you haven't worked in over sixteen years. That's probably why mum left you, tired of trying to raise a baby without any money. You lost your job and that's really sad but you weren't the only one made redundant and there were *other* jobs."

"Where Ruby? Where are the other jobs? I don't see anyone breaking my door down to offer me one, do you?"

"Because that's not how it works. *You* have to go to *them*," she snorted like he was unbelievable.

"I'm nearly fifty years old! Who's going to employ a fifty year old, you tell me that, smart arse?"

"You weren't fifty years old sixteen years ago," she pointed out. "If you'd hunted you would have found a job by now. Maybe not the first one you went for but you would have got one...*eventually*. You just have to put yourself out there."

"What like you I suppose?" he scoffed sniggering like a dirty old man at a joke she hadn't yet worked out.

"Yeah I put myself out there. I wasn't handed my job walking down the street. I went in, nervous as hell, and ignored the snotty woman on reception who looked down her nose at me. I answered the questions I was asked and then I turned up and worked my arse off *every* day. I haven't missed *one*!"

"Yeah you put yourself out there alright, just like your mother!" he snarled and now she knew where he was going.

"Right, I'm not getting into this. I'm not going to let you make me feel like I'm dirty because I'm really not. I have a decent job and I work hard to keep it. I don't *sell* myself. I don't *put myself out* like *you* think. I get paid for doing a decent day's work. You can think what you like." She started to leave, pushing herself away from the kitchen sideboard and into Danny's view, but her dad blocked the door to the hallway.

"Think you're so clever don't you? Well let me tell you something *you're* not going anywhere. You got your exam results through ages ago. I kept hold of them. They're right here. Want to take a look, Ruby?" he tempted waving a brown envelope in front of her face. She snatched it off him.

"You opened it? It was addressed to me!" she sounded betrayed.

"You're my daughter *I was taking an interest!*" he slurred leaning against the frame and chuckling to himself. He lifted a clear glass bottle and drained what was left of it with one swig before slinging the bottle in the direction of the sink. It missed and he watched as it shattered all over the floor. He shrugged and looked back to Ruby who was clutching her grades in her hand and looking about the room in disbelief.

"This place is a tip. I cleaned and tidied all of this before I left this morning. Have you been out and bought food with the money I left on the table?"

"I had a liquid lunch, sweetheart."

"Dad, come on! I left that for food. There is alcohol everywhere you don't need to buy any more. That's *all* the cupboards have in them. Look!" She opened one of the low level doors which fell off its hinges. She sighed and placed it against another cupboard door. Inside the unit could be seen two similar clear glass bottles and some cans of lager. "Have you eaten anything at all today?" she asked sounding more sympathetic.

"Liquid diet like I say darling. I hope you're going to fix that cupboard door you clumsy heavy handed little cow, throwing your weight around, slamming doors, breaking them off their hinges. I tell you what, I don't have time for a job you're a handful, Ruby. Raising you has been hell. You drove me to this, do you know that?"

"Raising me?" she queried with a nod but she never went on, swallowing down all the nasty words she wanted to throw back at him. "Can I fix you something to eat?" she asked more kindly, desperately trying with him. Her attempt was admirable and it just made the cruelty seem even worse.

"YOU CAN FIX THAT SODDING CUPBOARD DOOR!" he shouted at her and she sighed feeling defeated and trapped. She looked down at the envelope and opened it, reading through the grades and fighting to withhold her disappointment.

"Clever girl eh? You think you're better than all of this, better than me and this place. Well I'm telling you you're not. I'm Michael Aspel darling and this, my dear girl, is *your* life," he told her spreading his arms wide as if offering her the whole depressed heap of mess. He pulled out a chair and fell into it laughing at his own joke until he couldn't stop coughing, then he stubbed his cigarette out right on the surface of the table. Ruby turned her nose up in disgust, threw the envelope and white slip down and walked straight passed him.

"And where the hell do you think you're going? Walking off like that. Bloody rude you are!" he shouted after her.

"I can't do this now!" she shouted back as she ran up the stairs and locked her bedroom door. He hoisted himself out of the chair and followed her, slurring obscenities the whole way.

Danny slipped in through the back door and looked over the place, taking a glance into the living room and raising his eyebrows at just how trashed a place could look. Did she really live here...with him? He went back to the kitchen table and picked up the white slip of paper before sliding it back into the envelope and placing it in his inside pocket. He made for the stairs where he could hear her dad still shouting.

"Bloody unlock this door or I'll break it down!"

"Just go away and leave me alone!" she cried out.

"Right!" He slammed his shoulder against it and the splintering of wood made Ruby call out to stop him.

"OK. OK. Just pack it in. I'll open it." She slid the lock and opened the door. He pushed it open so hard it slammed against the bedroom wall. Danny looked about him. Spindles were missing from the banister, some were cracked in half like a foot had been put through them and some were missing completely. There were numerous foot holes in the plaster of the wall running up the stairs and in all of the doors. Ruby's bedroom door had a fist hole and a foot hole in it. Danny ran his hand over his face and mouth feeling sick and angry. He could hear Ruby rummaging around in her bedroom.

"Have you seen it? My mobile phone, I left it here this morning. I need it. Dad, have you seen it?" she asked him.

"Yes I have and it got me a good price too."

"What? No! You sold it? I will have nothing left at this rate! That was mine! It had all my numbers on, my messages, my photos!" she exclaimed sounding really hurt.

"Yeah I'll bet it had photos. Is that how you make your money, Ruby?"

"Oh just stop it!" she yelled at him. "Who did you give it to? I want it back! How could you? I left you money! Why would you do that to me?"

"It was stolen anyway, how would *you* get a phone like that?"

"It wasn't stolen my boss gave it to me!" she argued.

"In return for what?"

"In return for my trust, dad," she told him wearily. "It was a birthday present because, while you were busy drinking, *I* turned seventeen. God I don't believe you, is *nothing* sacred?" There was silence and then she spoke up again. "Oh god...no...please tell me you didn't..." Danny couldn't see but he heard a drawer being slid open. "You took my necklace too! That was the only thing I had left of my mum! I *hate* you! Who did you give it to? I will get it back myself!"

"No can do I'm afraid. Sentimental crap! Baggage holds you back, Ruby, let it go," he laughed at her and she screamed in frustration.

"One day you're going to be on your own because one day *I'm* walking and when I do I won't look back!" she threatened.

"Not so fast," he ordered and Danny could now see that her dad had stepped into the doorway and was blocking her way again.

"I'm going back to work. Someone's waiting for me. I don't have time for this now. Excuse me please."

"You're not going anywhere. *You* are *my* daughter and you're grounded. You can stay in and tidy up this place. It's a pigsty and you're a lazy cow."

"Please move out of my way," he heard Ruby's voice cracking and she sounded close to tears.

Danny wasn't sure what to do. He desperately wanted to help Ruby but she'd made it clear she didn't want him in the house and now he could see why. She was a proud and private young woman who had never really complained about her dad or asked for help. He knew she wouldn't thank him for being there but he couldn't leave her to handle it alone and he couldn't muscle in without humiliating her either. He waited hoping it would calm down. Then he could slip away and pretend it had never happened. He could wait for her in the car and leave her pride intact.

27
A step too far

"I told you you're grounded!" Her father snapped at her shoving her backwards. He kept walking towards her and she kept moving away, losing her balance and falling back onto the bed. She turned, trying to scramble to the other side before he could reach her, but he grabbed her legs and pulled her back, flipping her over in one effortless move. She tried to fight him off but he pinned her down and looked her over.

"Please don't do this now," she begged. "Please, dad, someone's waiting. They might come looking for me."

"I know you're a bit stupid but you do know what working late means don't you, Ruby?" he asked her in a low sinister whisper.

"Why are you so horrible? Things could be different it doesn't have to be like this. You could be nice and I could be..."

"What could you be, Ruby, good?" he laughed like that was impossible.

"I *am* good!" she protested. "I try so hard with you but you always want to be nasty. You always want to hurt me and make me cry."

"That's life I'm afraid, sweetheart. I'd have thought you'd have grown out of fairy stories by now."

"Life doesn't have to be like that! Not everyone lives like *this!*"

"You think it's different in other homes? You think other people don't argue and fight?"

"Not like this they don't. I've seen dad! Sasha's parents don't fight. Her dad doesn't hit *any* of them, *ever!*"

"Well maybe he should and then maybe his oldest son would stop dealing on street corners and his wife would know her place," he slurred.

"Mario doesn't deal. Mario's nice. He's nicer than you! He's looked out for me and that's more than you've ever done!"

"Yeah I'll bet he has and I bet he loved turning you from my sweet little school girl into a woman over night." His eyes were roaming again and she squirmed.

"No!" she sobbed. "I didn't turn into a woman over night and I didn't turn into a woman because of Mario. I just grew up that's all, it's what people do! I *am* a woman, you just don't like that I am. I can't do anything about it. It's not my fault. I'd rather be little at least when I was you didn't look at me like...like...*that!*"

"Do you know how hard it is to have a woman in the house again?" he asked in a low menacing whisper. "You look like you're mother, just like her, especially trying to wriggle away like you are now," he sniggered watching her futile efforts. "She was cold too!" he mumbled under his breath.

"Cold! What are you talking about?" she sounded panicked. "I'm your daughter you shouldn't even be saying things like that to me! I'm not your wife and I'm *nothing* like her."

"Yes you are, Ruby, you're exactly like her. All the men looked at her too and it drove me mad but she knew her place I made sure of that. *I* was the only one who ever touched her. Perhaps you need to be shown who the boss is around here, perhaps *you* need to be put in your place too," he threatened.

"Stop looking at me like that! I hate it when you look at me. Leave me alone. Don't you *dare* lay a finger on me else I'm walking, I swear. I don't care whether I have anything to take with me. I don't care if I end up on the streets. I'm not staying here if you put your hands on me. You do it and you're on your own," she promised him.

"See just like your mother. You're a walker, Ruby. When things get hot you'll walk, just like she did. You're the same and you will end up working the streets to survive just like she did too. I wouldn't have had her back even if she'd begged me, not after where she'd been. You're going the same way, Ruby Palmer. You walk out that door and I give you two weeks before you're begging to come back. It's scary out there, Ruby. You think it's hard in here, well this is nothing compared to what will happen to you out there. You ask your mum...oh no you can't because she's not here is she?" he tormented and she began to cry and fight hysterically.

"I'm not like her! I'm not! I would never walk out on my child and leave her with someone like *you!*" she bellowed hitting out at him. He laughed ignoring her arms and fists as he grabbed her face with one hand and slapped it with the other. He then brought the back of his hand down against her other cheek. He raised his fist to thump her but she turned her head out of the way and he collapsed in a heap on the pillow. He was unconscious, the drink and exertion had finally taken over.

She struggled to push him off, gasping for air under the weight. It was impossible and she was stuck. Suddenly he was lifted from her and Danny was pulling the sleeping bully off. As soon as there was space she wriggled herself free and began to kick the corpselike lump away with her feet. She hugged her knees and buried her face while she tried to steady her breath, rocking back and forth as she sobbed.

"Hey," Danny's voice was soft. "Come, Rubes, let's get out of here." She looked up to see him glancing around the room. It was now trashed like the rest of the place. She wiped her tears on the back of her hand feeling terminally embarrassed at him seeing where she lived, him seeing *how* she lived.

"It didn't look like this earlier, not when I left. I tidied this morning. I clean and tidy constantly but when I get home it always looks like this again," she tried to explain, worried he would think she was a disgusting slob. He nodded like he already knew and his eyes were sad. "He spends every day drinking and trashing, that's all he does!" she sobbed and Danny reached forward and wiped a tear from her cheek.

"And hits you?" he asked and she looked away feeling ashamed. "Come let's go."

"What's the point? This is how it's always going to be. Who am I trying to kid? This is my life, Danny. I'm not going anywhere. You may as well go without me. Tell Alessi I said thanks for the break but law...well...it's not for me."

"You wouldn't happen to be saying that because of these would you?" he asked opening his jacket and giving her a glimpse of the brown envelope poking out of his inside pocket.

"Oh man! What are you doing with that? Please tell me you haven't read them, they're useless!"

"Not useless," he told her with a smirk "You can spell FUDGE with them. I think that's pretty cool." She gave him a really sweet teary giggle. "To be fair you can't spell much with the other grades, too many consonants and no vowels," he went on.

"Why have you picked them up? I was going to burn them."

"Well, because Alessi will want to see them. He takes an interest in his employees, especially his favourites. Also because when you go back to school to retake them they will want to see this and you have to pay for copies. I'm saving you money by keeping them safe for you," he informed her, formally patting his jacket. "Now let's get out of here before Shrek wakes up," he advised. She frowned wondering whether she should be offended but then took the hand he was offering and shuffled off the bed.

In the car he locked the doors and drove them to a quiet spot before pulling over. "What are you doing?" she asked looking wary. He reached down towards her legs and she gasped and looked at him through stunned eyes.

"Relax," he told her grasping the bar beneath her seat to slide it back. She felt like an idiot.

"Sorry, I thought..." she began and he laughed and nodded holding up his hand to stop her.

"I know what you thought, Ruby. He turned in his seat to get a better look at her and then reached towards the foot well again, stopping briefly to clarify, "Glove box." She nodded shyly and shifted her knees so he could open it. He took out a bottle of unopened water and then dug a handkerchief from his pocket. He twisted the top off the bottle and spilt the water onto the white material. He looked up at her with a grin, "Clean," he told her lifting the handkerchief and then soaking it some more. "Right, if you could just..." he suddenly looked nervous and unsure what to do.

Gently putting one hand under her chin he tilted her head back into the headrest. He held the cold compress to her cheekbone and she cringed, sucking in air as it made contact with the split flesh.

"Ouch! What did you do?" she demanded accusingly grabbing his hand to pull it away. As he did she saw that the white material had been dyed red. "Am I bleeding?" she asked surprised, instinctively putting her fingers to her face to touch the wound. "Ugh," she gasped out in pain quickly flipping down the visor to look in the mirror. "Oh, jeez, look at the state of me. Usually I get my hands or my arms in front of my face in time. I must have been slow this evening, probably worrying about you coming to look for me." He sighed and found a clean corner to soak and press against her again. He pushed locks of her hair out of her eyes and hooked the dark waves behind her ears as he continued to clean the blood from her face. "Much better," he finally declared as he reached into the glove compartment again. He pulled out a small green bag.

"Cross stitch?" she asked with a giggle.

"No," he laughed as he pulled out some steri-strips and peeled them off, placing them gently over her cut to hold the gap closed.

"Steri-strips. Are you serious?"

"In our line of work you never know when someone's going to break your nose or blow your head off," he smirked. "I've had to use these, *a lot!*"

"Do steri-strips hold heads on? Wow that's seriously sticky stuff," she observed, sounding amused, and he stopped and smiled at her before playfully nudging her on the chin with his fist.

"I was pretty mean when you started working with us wasn't I?" he asked her and she raised her eyebrows in surprise.

"If putting it like that makes you feel any better then, yes, you were *pretty* mean."

"That bad eh?"

"If you don't like someone you don't like someone, Danny, simple as," she concluded.

"No not '*simple as*'. I *did* like you..."

"But you don't anymore?" she asked, teasing him, and he quickly corrected.

"No, I do. Oh you know what I mean," he grumbled seeing the smile creep onto her face. "I've always liked you, Ruby, right from that first day I spotted you at school. You were giving that loser, Billingham, a run for his money. I thought to myself that's the kind of girl I want to end up with, one that isn't scared to stand up for herself, one that will put me in my place if I'm rubbish. I just didn't want to think of you being corrupted by all of this that's all. I thought you'd been through enough with John and you looked so young, pretty and innocent. I just didn't want you to get hurt but you already knew pain didn't you? You were older than you looked and not as innocent as I thought. You've not been sheltered, Ruby, and protected your whole life. You've fought all the way, and you're strong, determined..."

"And still pretty?" she asked hopefully. "I mean not taking the face as it is now into account of course." He grinned at her and ran a delicate finger over the steri-stripped gashes.

"I was wrong about that too, you weren't pretty at all, that doesn't come close to describing what you are. You're stunning, Ruby. You're beautiful. You're...Almond Blossoms. Will you let me take you for a coffee?" he invited and she laughed at him.

"Hmmm you're forgetting that we have lots of work to do. I could just make coffee when we get to the office?"

"Dedicated as that would be I think I would rather buy you a coffee and enjoy your full attention. I'd like to get to know you better, Ruby. You've been through a lot this evening, work can wait while we have a coffee, what do you say? Are you going to blow me out?" he frowned like he seriously hoped not. She smiled and fidgeted in her seat.

"One coffee then straight back to work," she negotiated. "After what you told me earlier I think I have something I should to tell you."

28
Brother or informer?

"So what's the gossip then?" Danny asked when they eventually arrived back at work. He led her into Tom Marshall's office dropping Johnny Giavani's file on the floor with a thump. Mr Alessi had asked him to check through it and make sure it was all in order. Ruby was looking about the familiar room.

"What are we doing in here?" she asked. He shook his head at her and turned the light back off that she'd just turned on. "Erm, Danny, what are you...I mean how are we supposed to work in the...Right, we have come here to work haven't we?" she asked accusingly just as the lamp flicked on. He was already reclining in Tom's chair with his feet on the desk.

"Ruby, do you mind? If I wanted to try and make out with you I would take you home. I wouldn't bring you in *here!* This place doesn't scream romantic and it doesn't make me hot. It makes me feel nervous, under pressure and over worked, not the best ingredients for passion. Yes, we're here to work," he reassured. "Like I told you before, *before* you ran off and left me, that I don't want it to look from the outside like somebody is inside. Lamplight and closed shutters are always best."

She lowered herself into one of the leather armchairs and glared at the lamp like it was to blame for not switching on sooner. It could have saved her from jumping to conclusions.

"Why are we in here?" she asked flatly wishing the ground would open up and swallow her whole, him too so he couldn't remember what an idiot she'd just made of herself.

"Well if you were one of Alessi's clients and you wanted to know every little thing that was being said about your file where would you place a bug?"

"Ahhh upstairs in Alessi's offices. I get it."

"Correct. I can't see any reason why they would think of bugging Marshall's office. I'm not even sure what he does to be honest!" he told her and she giggled at him.

"He's a trainee civil litigation lawyer, Danny, now don't be bitchy," she chastised sweetly and he smirked, taking his feet off the table and sliding a couple of drawers open just to be nosey.

"Want one?" he asked offering her a fruit bon bon from an open pack. She scrunched her nose and shook her head. He copied her, "Nah don't think I will either he's a bit weird isn't he and look, why kill the packet like that? Just pull it open carefully like a bag of crisps. You don't need to rip it apart like you're a half starved lion and the packet of sweets is a dead antelope! They do eat antelope, right?"

"What half starved lions or trainee civil litigation lawyers?" she asked with a cheeky smirk.

"Either," he shrugged throwing the obliterated bag back in the drawer and pushing it shut like it contained a dirty secret.

"So, Danny," she called for his attention and he looked at her and grinned.

"So, *Ruby*," he toyed sexily knowing this was leading to something uncomfortable.

"What's the deal with Alessi? I mean why would the mafia be using *his* services? It's not like we're the metropolis here is it? Why would the likes of Johnny Giavani stumble across a general law firm in the middle of a medium sized town and say *'Hey, Carlito, that looks like a pretty good firm to take our highly confidential matters to'?"* Danny stopped scrolling through his phone and looked up at her without moving his head. It made his eyes look dark and sinister, like he was scowling at her.

"I'm loving the Godfather accent are you sure you don't want the bon bons? You could shove them in the sides of your mouth, like jowls"

"No, will you shut up about the bloody bon bons and anyway that would probably split the steri-strips and make my face bleed again..."

"Good point, don't do it," he advised professionally.

"I'm not going to and will you stop changing the subject! What's the deal with Alessi?"

"How would I know, Ruby?" he asked huffing at her like she was annoying.

"Err because if *I've* thought to ask him then I'm damn sure you have. So?"

"So?"

"Ugh, Danny! So, did you ask him?"

"Yes as it happens I did?" he told her tossing one of Tom's files on the floor and grabbing up another one to flick through. "How's this for a case title, *Re: Claim against neighbour – plant pots!* What's that? I mean we have Re: Attempted Murder, Re: GBH, Re: Taken without owners consent. Marshall is sitting down here dealing with nuisance plant pots!"

"Are you jealous of Tom, Danny?" she asked narrowing her eyes on him suspiciously.

"Jealous? Me?" he snorted cutely pulling the pin of papers out and flicking through the correspondence absentmindedly.

"Well he is very good looking, and young, and already in the first year of his training contract," she teased and he looked up.

"Do you think he's good looking?" he dropped his feet to the floor and leaned forward onto his elbows to study her more closely.

"Not my type but..."

"But what?" he asked so quickly she couldn't help but laugh. "What's your type?" he interrogated seeming fascinated.

"Danny, I'm really into clever men." She leaned forward and put her elbows on the table looking confidently into his eyes. He leaned back in his chair as she continued to edge herself forward. "Guys that are young and fit." He smiled at her. "Guys that know how to look after themselves and aren't afraid of the darker side of life." He dragged his teeth nervously across his bottom lip and raised his eyebrows at her like he might just laugh under the pressure. She ran her hand through the length of her hair and twiddled with one of the curls causing him to fidget. "Guys that look damn hot in a suit and know how to make me laugh." He ran his hand around his collar, suddenly feeling very hot as she left the seat of her chair to lean further onto the desk. She was now all he could focus on. "Guys that don't try and change the bloody subject like I'm some idiot that won't notice they've done it! Now spill! What do you know about Alessi?" she demanded firmly and he rolled his eyes and fanned himself with the empty folder.

"Whoa, Ruby, you're *good!*" he told her leaning under the desk to turn on the computer. "But I'm afraid to say I know about as much as you do on that one. I asked, yes, and do you know what he told me?" She pressed her lips into a hard line. "OK, obviously you don't know and that's why you're asking me. He told me to mind my own business, keep my nose out and keep my head down. He told me knowledge isn't always a good thing. If you possess it and someone wants it you might give it to them by accident. It can make you a target. If you don't know anything they can't get it out of you."

"Doesn't stop you being a target!" she pointed out. "All that means is they can torture you all night but you're guaranteed not to breach his confidence. That's *very* reassuring!" she exclaimed with a shudder. Danny laughed and then sighed as he placed a framed picture of Tom Marshall and his girlfriend face down on the desk, leaning onto his arms.

"So? What's the news?" he asked again and she suddenly became nervous, unsure if he would believe her, unsure whether she should even confide in him.

"It's Carlito, I saw him...with officers."

"What, police officers?" he frowned at her.

"Yeah. Isn't that like one of their ten commandments, 'Though shalt not be seen with cops?" Danny shook his head.

"No. I mean, *yes*, but...it can't have been him."

"I'm telling you, Danny, I know what I saw. It was in an alley out back of Pablo's restaurant, you know the one?" He nodded. "The ladies toilet window leads out into the alley."

"Were you seen?"

"What? No way! I hid behind some huge metal bin thing as soon as I realised there were other people in the alley. It stunk, it was gross, it brings back memories of last night. I recognised his voice straight away. I didn't realise it was the police he was with at the time else I'd have said something sooner but earlier it suddenly dawned on me. The officer that was posted to watch me all day today had this funny nervous habit. He kept clicking his pen and it made me really uptight. I felt like I couldn't hit the green button fast enough. In the end I couldn't help but turn and look at him, he drew attention to himself," she told him fidgeting in her chair fully aware that Danny hadn't taken his eyes off her once. When she was asking him questions about Alessi he kept busy and distracted but now he was watching her intently while she spoke.

"Go on," he encouraged and she took a deep breath.

"He had a scar running right across his eye, it was all misty like he was blind and he kept wiping tears away with a handkerchief, sniffing and blowing his nose loudly. He saw me look at his injury. I never meant to but it was quite shocking. He told me it was an air rifle accident when he was five. His older brother shot him messing about. He said his brother had spent his entire life trying to make up for it. He was lucky to get into the police at all because of his poor vision. Carlito called him Sergio. He was the guy from the alley I'm telling you, Danny, the scar, the handkerchief, the constant sniffing and blowing it was *all* there."

"In the alley?" he clarified and she nodded, her eyes wide.

"Yes, in the alley."

"Ruby, honey, what were you doing climbing out of Pablo's toilet window?"

"Long story, don't ask. It involved Matthew, dinner and a reference to his place straight after dessert. I had no choice."

"Erm how about *NO*? Or, stick your invitation where the sun don't shine! Would you like me to stick it there for you, *Matthew*? Come on isn't that what Ruby Palmer does, threaten people?"

"Yeah OK so maybe I had a choice but I wasn't thinking straight and he was getting heavy. I went to the toilet, saw the window, thought *air*, opened it, realised I could actually *fit* through it and then wham bam I was in the alley without a second thought." He laughed, opened the drawer and threw a bon bon at her.

"Next time just say no, right?" he ordered like a chewy sweet across the head was a suitable punishment for not standing up for herself against some creep. She nodded.

"There won't be a next time, believe me," she told him. "Anyway what do we do now?"

"*You* keep your mouth shut that's what we do now!" he told her, turning his chair slightly on its pivot and keeping his eyes fixed on hers.

"What? We can't he's an informer!"

"*And* he's been Johnny's right hand man for five years, Ruby."

"So what does that prove? That's he's had the ability to inform for five years, that's what that proves!"

"I agree but it's none of our business. I've tried to convince Alessi that Carlito can't be trusted but he says Johnny won't buy it. What can I do? You can't force the man he's as stubborn as Alessi!"

"But they're expecting Alessi to find something that will explain why Rossi's appeal keeps being jeopardised. We've found the answer. His right hand man has been leaking information the whole time. That's a pretty big find, Danny."

"Yeah but are you prepared to stand in front of them, point him out and say Johnny your right hand man there, you know, your friend, ally, someone you've trusted like a brother, well he's been telling the police everything, right down to the size of your socks? There will be a price on your head, Ruby. Even if Johnny does believe you, which he probably won't, Carlito and whoever else he works for is going to want *you* sorted. We don't know anything for certain and it might just be a coincidence. It's too risky." He ran his hand over his mouth looking uneasy as he whispered under his breath. "It makes sense."

"What does?" she was eager to know and he sighed.

"The fact that he has always been in the meetings when information is leaked and..."

"And what?"

"Nothing it doesn't matter. I don't want to scare you."

"No way, Danny, just tell me! What?"

"Well when you first came up to our department, Ruby, you saw our clients by accident, not a great result but it was something that could have been sorted by sacking you. However, Carlito went and told you their names. He didn't have to do that and, more to the point, he *shouldn't* have done that. By giving you their names he ensured that *you* were made permanent. I thought at the time it was dodgy and now, if what you say about the alley is correct, it makes perfect sense. He wanted you to be made permanent so he could have you pressed for the file, Ruby. He saw *you* as an easy target. You've been set up, Ruby Palmer, which means it's safer to keep this to yourself. *You* have been through enough already."

"But it's Alessi's job. Every time they have a meeting in those offices upstairs Carlito is there too and he's taking that information *straight* back to the police. If he's that corrupt there's nothing to stop him making those breaches in confidence look like they're coming from us. We could already be in dan..." Suddenly a crash from the bottom of the stairs made them both jump. Ruby had been pacing the room, trying to get her argument across to Danny, but now she spun round to look at him with fear in her eyes. "What was that?" she whispered. He shook his head and put his finger to his lips.

"There's someone in the building. Someone's broken in," he told her as he briefly scanned the room, trying to formulate a plan. "Move it, Ruby," he ordered grabbing her arm firmly and snapping her out of her paralysed daze.

29
Family values

"Grab the file and get on the other side of the desk," Danny ordered quietly. Ruby scooped the notoriously sought after file from the floor. It wasn't the only file relevant to the case and their client but it was the most confidential, hence it's being placed in a pink colour coded folder like all the matrimonial files. It had also been given a dud name and account number. This file was a shadow file and to all intents and purposes it *didn't* exist. She held it to her chest and rushed back to the desk just as Danny finished pulling the plug on the lamp and the computer. The hard drive made a funny *giving up* noise as it unexpectedly powered down and she hoped that it hadn't been as loud as it seemed. They were plummeted into darkness and Danny put his arm around her, guiding her under the table and out of view. They sat opposite each other, knees hunched, the toes of their shoes touching, waiting.

"Do you think they heard the computer? Do you think they know we're here?" Ruby whispered.

"No but the lamp and the monitor will still be hot. I'm praying they won't notice." He could feel Ruby tapping her toes against his nervously. "You need to keep quiet, whatever happens, do you think you can do that?" he asked her and all he got in response was silence. "I'm taking that as a yes, Ruby," he whispered.

The intruder *wasn't* being quiet as he made his way through the offices and up the stairs. The doors crashed open one at a time. First Howard's door, then Trudy's, then Sarah's then Lottie's, then Caroline's and that made their door next. Ruby squeezed the file and tightened into a ball preparing, but for what she wasn't quite sure. The place went quiet and Ruby couldn't decide what was worse, the noise of doors being thrown open or the deadly sound of nothingness...and a ticking clock. The longer she waited the more she wanted to be sick until suddenly the door flew open and Ruby clenched her eyes tightly shut, grasping the file to her chest and pulling in her knees.

A stream of light from the landing followed the intruder in and they watched as a pair of dark boots moved along the length of the desk. They could see through the gap just beneath the modesty panel, the panel that was thankfully keeping Danny and Ruby out his sight. The steel toe cap boots stopped and turned so that they were now only inches from Ruby's shoes. He stayed still and silent and Ruby looked up at Danny.

"This computers still hot!" he shouted out and Ruby scrunched her face trying to keep from screaming. "Oi, Bazza, you hear me?" the feet turned on the spot so that he was now facing back towards the door as he whispered to himself. "Stuck up little money grabbing gits there's someone still in the building." Ruby stared at Danny absolutely petrified. "Hey little office people I know you're in here somewhere," he sung out in an eager voice. "Come to daddy," he urged, his tone clearly happy now that he had victims. "I'm hoping I've got myself a pretty little secretary hiding somewhere here, maybe under the table. Is that where you are? Want to come and get friendly before I lift all the equipment in your precious little office. What *will* you tell the boss in the morning?" Danny moved silently, stretching over her knees and cupping the back of her head with one hand. He held the other over her mouth firmly. She began to shake uncontrollably and he pressed his mouth to her forehead gently and then moved his lips to her ear.

"He doesn't know you're here so stay calm and stay down." She tried to nod but it was slight, he was holding her too tightly.

"Here kitty kitty. Come out, come out wherever you are. Don't be shy *I* won't hurt you...my mate Bazza might though," he laughed and then slammed his hands down hard on the surface just above their heads, making Ruby squeal. "I knew it!" he boomed reaching over to try and grab her from under the desk. She slipped as flat against the back panel as she could while his hands groped around in the darkness trying to find her. "Working late sweetheart? I hope you're getting paid overtime because you're about to earn it!" he told her and she began to cry, desperately trying to dodge his plump leather gloved hands. Suddenly there was a loud crack and Ruby covered her ears as Danny dragged her into his arms. He held her tightly as he whispered almost inaudibly.

"Whatever you do *don't* scream!" The body slumped with a final grunt and the arm and gloved hand hung over the edge of the desk lifelessly. Blood ran down the leather fingers dripping onto the carpet with a gentle and regular patter. His open eyes stared at them blankly and the chair, which was pushed out from the desk, was covered in dark wet liquid and mess. Gradually Ruby realised it was blood and other disgusting things. The gunman turned and left the room, silently climbing the stairs to the top of the building.

Danny grabbed Ruby and pulled her out from her hiding place. "We don't have time to try and reach the front door and there might be others in the building. They are looking for that," he pointed to the file that Ruby was still clutching in her arms. "He," he jabbed a finger towards the man slumped over the desk, "He was just in the wrong place at the wrong time. He was after the equipment, the computers..." He looked Ruby up and down, "Whatever *else* he could lay his hands on." She shivered, she couldn't stop it. They heard another bang and Ruby's eyes streamed with tears. "That'll be Bazza I'm guessing," Danny told her. "We're going to have to stay in the building while they search it I'm afraid."

He reached for the heavy wooden shutters covering the window. It was stiff and awkward but Danny got it open just enough. He took the file from Ruby's hands, laying it on the window ledge and shoving it along out of the way. He then turned to Ruby. "Right you next," he told her and placed his hands around her middle, lifting her into the space between the glass and the wood. He then pulled himself up and slid the shutter back into place. There wasn't much room but he managed to get in behind so he could put his arms around Ruby, desperate to keep her warm, quiet and calm. The stairs creaked as someone came down from the top floor and the gunman entered the room again. Danny placed his hand over her mouth. "If you scream they *will* kill us," he told her. As they sat silently others joined the gunman.

"All the rooms have been checked and nobody's here. I've taken out two men, got more than they bargained for. They'd started lifting the equipment. Pretty sure they were just after the electricals and *not* the file. So, where do we look now? I've just been through Alessi's offices but I never expected to find anything up there anyway."

"It's like a needle in a haystack!" another voice complained. "It's probably with the closed files. I doubt it's even up here." He sounded defeated already. Each room had over three cabinets full of files and there were eight solicitors and three trainees all with their own caseloads. "Any ideas? You never seen which room he goes to when he locates it?" he asked in an irritated tone and Ruby tilted her head back to look into Danny's eyes. He frowned uncomfortably. Whoever it was informing they had to have been in the building *with* Alessi when he had the file.

"No, either he already has it when he meets us at the back door or he leaves us in his room while he goes to get it. Last time he already had it on him, you know, the time I told you the new girl was here, his precious little Ruby?" Ruby stiffened. They were listening to Carlito's voice. She was right, it *was* him. "But the time before that he left us in his office to get it. He wasn't long so I'm assuming it must be on this floor. If he'd gone to the basement or the ground floor he'd have been ages but it took him all of ten minutes. It must be in one of these offices. I say we just blow them all to pieces until we find it." The room went quiet while they contemplated that plan and then someone started clicking over and over. Ruby looked at Danny again and he nodded. He'd heard too and it was looking more like her theory was spot on.

"Let's get a couple of our men to visit that little girl's house see whether they've planted *her* with it," he sniffed. "That's the last place they think we'll look. Get Alessi's place checked out too. It's late just storm it and take him out." It was the police officer with the bad eye and he was sounding blood thirsty.

"Look calm it, Sergio," Carlito tried to reason with his edgy companion. "I've said we will get the file and we will get the file. I know I owe you big time and I intend to help you keep Killen's name clear. We will get the file, Rossi will stay down because they won't have a leg to stand on and Killen will continue to police the streets. You think I don't know what opportunities you've missed out on since the accident, that this glass ceiling you face every day of your life is my fault? I will help you get recognised OK. This will do it. If I know Killen he will see you fly through the ranks once his name has been protected. I'm telling you, bad eye or no bad eye, you'll be calling *all* the shots before you know it."

Now they knew everything, it fell into place like the last pieces of a jigsaw puzzle. Carlito and the wounded officer were in on it together. Carlito was the older brother that had taken away his sight, the brother that owed him and who had tried to make up for it ever since. Ruby was shaking, she'd held his hand and she knew he was bad then. He'd ordered the bus journey from hell. His brother, Sergio, had ordered her to be set upon in the alley and pushed for the file. She had been in the middle of it all and *now* they were going straight for her dad and Alessi.

30
Bang, bang, you're dead

They listened to Marshall's office being ripped apart as Carlito suddenly broke the silence with an order.

"We'll start in here and work our way along." The monitor smashed to the floor. Every file was pulled from the cabinet and then it was overturned with a crash. They were destroying *everything*. Ruby was leaning back against Danny and he held her firmly in his arms as they prepared to wait it out. It *could* take all night if they were going to do just as much damage to *every* single room. She felt something strange, a sensation through her shirt, vibrating against her body and coming from him, his chest, his breast pocket, his phone! She swung round just as he realised it too. It always vibrated three times first and then rang, *loudly!*

She grabbed at his chest in a panic at the same time as he did but they couldn't get it out fast enough. By the third vibration Danny had managed to retrieve it but before he could push the button and shut it up it was already too late, they looked up into each other eyes knowing they were in serious trouble. Within seconds the shutter had slid open and Ruby was grabbed roughly, pulled off the ledge, and dragged into the room to face the gang of armed men.

"Ahhh, Office Junior, how sweet. I was hoping to see you again," Carlito cooed as he walked over to take her shaking hand in his. She'd shoved the file at Danny before being yanked into the bright room. He'd immediately slid it up into the gap between the ceiling and the top edge of the shutter out of sight.

"Yo, Carlito, we have two for the price of one here, Alessi's prodigy," one of the men declared loudly as Danny was presented and held tightly by two pumped up men in dark suits. Ruby tried to see what was happening to him, worried that he would be hurt or killed, but Carlito's brother stepped up to her and stroked his fingers along the cuts on her face.

"Dear me, someone's been in the wars haven't they?" he observed, wiping his eye on a handkerchief and then sniffing and snorting like he had a heavy cold. Ruby couldn't help but turn her nose up, it sounded disgusting. "There's never a policeman when you need one is there, poppet?" he asked before gripping her face tightly and forcing her to look back at him. She heard Danny struggle but as she tried to catch another glimpse of him her face was struck from the side. She screamed out. She was bleeding again and Sergio was rubbing the back of his hand as if it stung. "No manners!" he bawled at her. "The youth of today have no god damn manners. I was speaking to you now *look* at me!" he demanded gripping her chin again. She cowered fearing he was going to strike her again but instead he spoke to her in a snarl. "Where's the file?" he asked shoving her backwards. She shook her head, refusing to speak and picked herself up off the floor. He was coming at her again and she moved away, trying to keep some distance between them. "You ignored strict instructions to get the file. It seems your spell in the rubbish bin did nothing for your level of obedience, Ruby. Do you even know where it is or are you wasting my bloody time because if *you* don't know then *you* don't need to be here"

"She doesn't know!" Danny declared trying to protect her. "She's helping me. She just copies that's all. We don't tell her stuff because it would be too easy to bully it out of her. Don't you think if she knew she'd have told you as soon as you dragged her out here? You don't need her so let her go. *We* told her to ignore your instructions it wasn't her fault. This has nothing to do with her," Danny begged trying to pull free and getting a fist in the stomach from Carlito for his efforts. Sergio laughed out loud.

"When I said she doesn't need to be here I didn't mean lock her away somewhere safely or, heaven forbid, let her go. If we don't need her then I may as well get *rid* of her," he grinned pulling a gun from his inside pocket. Ruby gasped out and clambered over the toppled filing cabinet. He pointed the gun at her as she backed up to the fireplace on the far side of Tom Marshall's office, but there was nowhere to hide.

"No, Carlito, please, stop him!" she heard Danny shout out from behind Sergio.

Her eyes were big and scared as questions bombarded her mind. Would it be over quickly? Would it hurt? What would they do to Danny? Would he tell them? Would they kill him? For a second an image of her mother flicked in front of her eyes, she was holding the gun and smiling, she looked just like Ruby. Mr Manning, her head teacher, took it and pointed it at her only to be replaced by Matthew. His eyes were grazing over her, checking her out one last time before he handed the gun to John Billingham. He told her to kneel down and beg him not to do it. She shook her head refusing to bow down to him and he handed the gun to Sasha. She scrunched her nose sweetly like she didn't want to but they were *making* her do it. Sasha finally handed the gun to Ruby's dad and he blew her a kiss and mouthed goodbye.

She heard a scream and it sounded like her. She was the only girl in the room but she couldn't recall forming the noise in her throat and neither did she feel it leave her lips. Then she heard a bang so distant she wondered if it had come from the room next door. She didn't feel alarmed she was merely a spectator now. Danny was still being held and she could see him clearly. He looked desperate and shocked. All the other people in her life had disappeared and the two men who had been so keen to keep a hold on him now let Danny go. He fell to his knees like he'd given up already and she couldn't understand why. Why did he look so distraught?

The door to the office flew open and more men pushed their way in. She didn't recognise any of them. People seemed to be turning on each other and the room was filled with the sound of cracking. It rang through the air but, strangely, Ruby wasn't scared. The gun shots were just angry wasps outside a closed window, they couldn't touch her and nothing was getting through. While everyone else battled it out Sergio stared at her, one eye misty and streaming and the other burning so full of hatred it made her feel like throwing up.

Danny kept low to the ground as he attempted to make his way towards her, picking through the carnage and mess. She now noticed that her stomach hurt and suddenly, without warning, the pains were cramping like a vice inside her. Was she sick? She looked down and placed her hands on her body, slowly. Were they even her hands? Was it even her body? Nothing seemed certain anymore, everything so far away and surreal.

"You've...," she trailed off, slipping her hand inside her shirt to her aching shoulder before pulling it out covered in blood. "You've shot me!" she began to panic. The pain suddenly registered and it crippled her. She screamed out and slid down onto the floor arching her back and gritting her teeth against the searing heat inside the wound. Suddenly all she could focus on was her and the noise around her. Someone had turned up the volume and it was petrifying, as intimidating as the gun that Sergio had just pointed at her. She tried to concentrate and push herself out of the way using her feet but she didn't get very far. The hunk of metal embedded in her body was holding her prisoner.

The shouting, swearing, shooting, crashing, all died down to a hum while she battled now with her excruciating pain. For a second the pain would lull only to be replaced with the feeling of red hot knives being stabbed again and again into her open and bleeding wound. The blood was pumping out of her at sickening speed. She grabbed at her arm wanting to rip it right off and she kicked her feet against the agonising torture, trying to escape it. She screamed out but it didn't help, she wasn't sure how long she could go on, she wasn't sure how much longer she *wanted* to go on.

Her body was wracked with exhaustion as she began to shake uncontrollably. She could hear her breath rattling in her chest and the sweat was pouring from her face. Now she was freezing cold and her fingers and toes had started to numb. All she wanted was to be warm, to fall asleep, to slip away from it all. If only somebody could turn the lights off, if only they could silence the din, she could sleep then. Her lids were heavy, her eyes rolling, her breathing so slow that on the next intake it would stop just like the pain, just like the noise around her. She felt lighter as her eyes closed and stayed that way, she was sliding, chasing a dream that teased her. It allowed her a glimpse and let her touch the edges just enough that she knew that it felt right in every conceivable way. She just needed to get a better hold, grasp it more securely and hang on, *make* it take her.

Try as she might the dream wouldn't form properly and, though she knew she wasn't alone, she couldn't see who was there with her. It was too bright and so stark that she had to shield her eyes and blink to keep them open. If only she could fall asleep fully, relax and let herself drift then she could leave this limbo place and pin down that dream that had tempted her. It would be better when she was asleep and, though nobody had told her so, she knew in her slowly beating heart that it was true. Suddenly the white gave way to darkness, slipping like a sheet from a washing line.

She didn't like the tunnel that she found herself in with its concrete walls, floors and ceilings and the strip lights that flashed overhead. She'd take the glaring white and blindness over the grey concrete tunnel any day. Why was she in the underpass to her estate and who were the hooded figures loitering with their backs to her? Getting close enough she reached out and touched one of them and they turned. It was Carlito and Sergio holding a black plastic sack between them. They pulled it open and encouraged her to take a look inside and there was Alessi's cat, alive and well.

Ruby smiled as she watched it happily turning in circles, sniffing its little pink nose up at her and meowing softly. She reached out to touch it, to take it with her, but a hand grabbed her shoulder and pulled her back roughly. It yanked over and over, pulling her further away, while Carlito and Sergio closed the bag and tied it, trapping the kitten inside.

"No it'll die," she screamed at them but Sergio just smiled while Carlito laughed and reached out his hand as if he wanted to shake.

"It's already dead, Ruby, we all are," he explained simply before pointing his finger at her and snarling. "Including *you!*" She shook her head and let her guard down just as the hand yanked at her shoulder once more. This time it pulled her off her feet and she fell back onto the floor swallowed up by the darkness.

"RUBY! RUBY! Baby, open your eyes, please open your eyes. You're going to be OK, I promise. Just listen to me, just stay with me.

Ruby, come on look at me. It's Danny. I'm here. You're not on your own. Don't go to sleep, don't go, please don't go. I love you, Ruby. Please stay with me. Listen to me. If you can hear me let me know. In any way you can just let me know," he begged and she screamed so loud he jumped back in shock. Quickly he slipped back alongside her and cradled her head, trying desperately to stem the flow of blood with his balled up shirt. He pushed hard trying to maintain the pressure but she wanted him off her. "You're back, Ruby. Thank god...you're back."

Danny pressed his lips against her forehead, her cheeks, her eyes and then her mouth. He whispered into her ear that she was going to be fine but she didn't feel fine she felt angry. She was nearly asleep but he'd dragged her back. All she needed to do was rescue Alessi's poor innocent cat from Carlito and Sergio, before *they* went to hell, and catch that damn dream. But Danny had awakened her and ruined her plan and now the pain was even worse, searing through her body again and again. She tried to fight him off, she hated him so much, she hated everything so much.

"Why couldn't you just let me die?" she screamed out, surprising herself. *Did she want to sleep or did she want to die?* Danny looked distraught as he frowned down at her.

"I think you already did, Ruby," he told her flatly and then shook his head like he couldn't handle it and changed the subject quickly. "Ruby it's OK the ambulance has just arrived. The paramedics are coming and they will be able to help with the pain honey. Just hold in there."

A group of men in green overalls surrounded her, stepping over her writhing body and pulling things out of their way so they could get closer. "OK, what are we looking at here? Ahhh gunshot wound and a hell of a lot of blood, we're going to need fluids and something for the pain..." They continued to talk but she couldn't keep still, she couldn't understand what they were saying. She tried to fight them and begged them to leave her alone as she arched her back on the floor, gritting her teeth and then giving in and screaming. "OK then let's try and make her more comfortable shall we?"

"We need to get her moving as soon as possible, time is of the essence guys," somebody advised seriously. She continued to hear voices, the click and fuzz of handheld radios and the sound of sirens. People stepped over her, shifted her, pulled at her clothes, pressed against her body, placed something over her mouth and bombarded her with questions. She closed her eyes against it all. Why would she tell them her name when they knew it already? They had used it enough. *Ruby, it's going to be OK. Ruby, it's the paramedic here. Ruby, can you tell us your name?*

"Ruby, you need to talk to us honey," someone urged. "Let us know you're with us, let us know you can hear. Do you know who you are? Do you know *where* you are? Do you know what's happened to you, Ruby?" She wouldn't communicate. She was determined to fall asleep even if it killed her. She knew what she needed and to shut her eyes, block it out and drift off to somewhere warm and sunny was pulling much harder than they were. She was sure that if she tried again this time she could reach that dream she wanted so desperately.

"JUST SHUT UP AND LET ME DIE!" she finally screamed out, her rage as intense as her suffering. She heard muffled laughter.

"Well I guess that's our answer. I think she's OK don't you?" one of the male voices declared with a chuckle. "I'm pretty sure we have some determination on our side, that's *always* a good thing."

"Yeah she has enough fight for all of us. She doesn't just shout like that when she's been shot," she heard Danny reply and they laughed again.

"SHHHH! Please just be quiet and let me sleep. It hurts," she pleaded and then she felt another sharp prick in her arm.

"OK I've just given you something, Ruby. That should help with the pain but it will also make you feel drowsy and groggy. It's OK if you sleep but I'd rather you talked to us for as long as you can. You're in safe hands and everything's going to be OK. We're going to move you in a minute. We'll be taking you to St Marys."

"SCHOOL?" she blurted out seeming just as unhappy about that as she had been about the questions. She heard laughter again and it was starting to annoy her. She still couldn't open her eyes. They kept asking her to but she didn't want to see what was happening or to let go of that inkling of hope that she might just leave them all behind. It was all so frightening and she felt dizzy and sick.

"We'll be going to St Marys Hospital, Ruby. Don't worry we're not taking you back to school, honey," someone told her sounding amused. "The hospital will be better equipped to check your injuries. You know, Ruby, I do usually try to give my patients what they want but on this occasion, although you've specifically asked us to let you die, I'm not going to. It's *not* happening, got it? So get it out of your head right now," he ordered and with that option suddenly taken away she opened her eyes.

She spotted four men in green overalls wearing green plastic gloves and Danny on the sidelines. It was what they had been begging her to do but as soon as she spotted the needle in one of the men's hands she scrunched her eyes tightly shut again, pressed her mouth together to keep from screaming and shook her head in protest.

"You might feel some discomfort, Ruby," he warned her and then he began to talk to someone else, she could tell because his voice was now more informative...*and less bloody patronising!* "We're setting up a cannula in the back of her hand. I don't want to waste any time." The voice then spoke to her again, loud and clear, like she was foreign. "I've put a cannula in the back of your hand, Ruby, it's so a drip can be put in. We want you to be all ready for theatre," he told her as the morphine finally started to kick in.

"But I don't have anything to wear!" she protested before drifting off to the combined laughter of the paramedics and Danny.

31
Counting the losses

"Hey, how you feeling?" she heard a whisper but her eyes still hadn't focused. Everything seemed strangely white and blurry.

"Where..." she croaked feeling disorientated and then she tried to sit, having sudden urge to get moving.

"Whoa! Slow down there. I think you need to take it easy. Don't make me push any buttons. The nurse gave me one and I'm not afraid to use it!" the voice warned her. She turned her attention to the gentle sound of his words, they were familiar and soothing. She blinked a few more times and then coughed. Her throat had never been so sore and dry. "Here take a drink, small sips they said," he advised. She felt him put the plastic tube to her lips and sucked gently. The liquid was room temperature but enough to moisten her mouth. Her eyes slowly started to clear and she could see him, Danny, sitting on the bed with a beautiful smile on his tired looking face. He was holding her hand, she hadn't even realised.

"I don't..." she began, trying to swallow against the rough pain in her throat.

"Don't speak if it hurts. It's the tube they put down your throat when they operate," he explained and she put her hand to her neck. He took hold of it and gently placed it back against the covers. "It's not there anymore they took it out just before you came round. It leaves your throat a bit sore. Do you remember what happened, Ruby?" he asked softly and she shook her head, her eyes so heavy all she wanted to do was sleep. His words were processing slowly but one stuck out in particular.

"Operate?" she asked huskily. It didn't make sense.

"You were shot, Ruby," he told her in a whisper and she was suddenly swamped by a tsunami sized wave of sickness. Her eyes closed and she began to panic. She heard an alarm sound, someone took her hand, there was a strange sensation running up her arm and then nothing. She was gone again.

When she came round later Mr Alessi was there with two police officers by his side. He smiled at her and then looked discreetly to one side of him and then the other. She nodded in understanding but to the officers it looked like acknowledgement at seeing her boss. She groaned and tried to shift her weight. Mr Alessi moved forward taking her under the arm and helping her to slide back so she could sit.

"How are you feeling now? You had a funny turn earlier but the anaesthetic can do that apparently. They gave you something for the sickness. Do you remember why you're here?" he asked and she closed her eyes to buy herself time. It was all coming back to her now but what was she going to say to the officers? They would want statements. What had she been doing in the office so late? Why was there a dead body on Marshall's desk? Why had Mr Alessi's place been done over, and her house too..." Her eyes opened wide and she sat forward quickly only to be forced back again by the agonising pain. "Ruby, take it easy," Mr Alessi told her firmly as he placed his hands on her shoulders gently and pushed the alarm. "Hello, I think she needs something in here, please!" he called out. The door opened and people rushed in surrounding the bed. A doctor tried to get a needle into the cannula in the back of her hand but she fought him and pushed the nurses away, gritting her teeth against the pain.

"My dad!" she blurted out and Mr Alessi looked worried as he stepped back slightly and allowed the officers to move forward. They took their place either side of the bed but her eyes were still on Mr Alessi as one of them spoke.

"Danny said your dad attacked you. It looked like there'd been a struggle in your bedroom," he informed her and she thought quickly. She had to be careful not to give away names or anything that would make her, Danny or Mr Alessi seem like targets. She looked back at the officer standing and waiting patiently for her to respond. She would play dumb.

"Is that why you're here, because he attacked me?"

"Ruby, you've been through a lot. If you feel up to it we *would* like to ask you some questions? Is that OK?" he asked. She allowed the doctor to take her hand and push the liquid drug into her vein. She tilted her head back as it began its journey around her body.

"What do you want to know?" she asked allowing the effects of the drug to numb her emotions and responses as well as her pain.

"Tell us about your father?"

"He's a bully," she confessed feeling embarrassed having to admit that in front of Mr Alessi. "He always has been. He drinks, steals for money and pawns everything to buy alcohol. He's an alcoholic and, yes, he attacked me last night." She looked up feeling disorientated. "It was last night wasn't it? What's the time? What day is it?"

"Its Saturday, 10.30am and, yes, it was last night," the officer informed her with an understanding smile.

"Right," she accepted, feeling a little less out of the loop. "Last night I went home to get my mobile phone. I left it behind by mistake and I felt lost all day without it. Danny and I..." She never usually referred to people in the grammatically correct form but she thought, given the circumstances, it was the most appropriate thing to do.

She remembered her English teacher telling her once, after splitting up an argument between Ruby and another girl, that the best way for her to get her point across, to be listened to and respected was to be polite, professional and to drop the 'f' word. "Well we have a lot of work on at the moment," she explained. "We're trying to prepare files for an appeal that we've got coming up. The police had me copying for hours yesterday on an old case being investigated for money laundering. You know, standard stuff?" she shrugged and then wished she hadn't when a searing pain made her pay for it. She gritted her teeth.

The officers nodded and so did Mr Alessi, but his nod wasn't in agreement his was in approval. She was handling them well.

"Are you OK to go on?" Mr Alessi asked her kindly and she nodded, but she wasn't in any rush to continue taking her time to breathe through the discomfort.

"Being tied up copying on the McGregor files meant I wasn't able to help Danny get the evidence files sorted for our appeal so I promised to stay late. I wanted to go home and get my mobile first and let my dad know where I was so Danny took me. He waited in the car but my dad flew into a rage. He said all sorts of awful things. He told me I couldn't leave the house and that I was grounded. He even pulled the cupboard door off its hinges looking for more alcohol," she lied. "I ran upstairs to hide but he forced his way in. He accused me of sleeping around...*which I don't!*" she defended fiercely just in case they got the wrong impression of her. All three men shook their heads as if they never would have thought such a thing. She glared at them suspiciously, her lips pressed into a hard line waiting for one of them to crack. Mr Alessi couldn't help but smile she could be very fiery, even willing to take on two officers and her boss from her sick bed.

"Go on, Ruby," he encouraged. "What happened next?"

"My dad told me he'd pawned my mobile phone and the only thing I had left of my mum; a necklace. He was awful. We argued and he threw me onto the bed and attacked me. He beat me around the face and head and then he just...collapsed. I never did anything to him. I tried to protect myself but I couldn't. He's heavy, he's big..." She looked to the officers with sad eyes and they both nodded back.

"Did he do anything else to you?"

"What? No! He passed out and I couldn't get out from under him. That's when Danny came looking for me. He found me upstairs and pulled him off. We left him there. Danny and I went for a coffee because he wanted to cheer me up, he was really supportive. Danny's a good friend. We chatted and then went in to work. Last night was a *bad* night."

She put her hand to her shoulder while the officer weighed up her statement and then glanced across the bed at his companion who spoke next.

"Ruby, did your dad hit you regularly?" he asked and she bit her lip and hung her head in shame, all eyes on her, waiting for her to recall the pathetic details of her pathetic existence. She nodded.

"Whenever he's drunk he does, yes, which is most of the time. He gets mad and lashes out at me. I didn't manage to cover my face last night, he had me pinned. I thought he'd broken my cheekbone it hurt so bad...wait..." she trailed off looking from one officer to the other, "You said *'did he'*," she frowned. "What does that mean? Why did you say that? You should have said 'does he', surely. What's happened?"

"Ruby," the first officer called for her attention as he took a deep breath and steadied himself to break bad news. "I'm afraid your dad died last night. I'm very sorry." Her eyes welled up and she allowed the fear, pain, and suffering of the last twenty-four hours, of all the things that she had been through in the last few months and every year of her life, to overwhelm her. The tears began to spill.

"But I...I never hurt him. He can't be. I swear. Danny pulled him off me and I pushed him away with my feet. He was alive, he was breathing, he was snoring. He's only passed out. He can't be...dead! No, he's not! You need to check again!" she protested beginning to sob and wiping her bandaged hand across her face. One of the officers pulled a pack of tissues from his pocket and tried to get his big fingers to separate the thin sheets. Her nose was running and she grabbed the packet impatiently pulling it apart and pressing a tissue to her nose as she squeezed her eyes shut. She pulled her knees up and rocked back and forth, burying her face into the starched white hospital linen.

"I think that's enough gentlemen if you don't mind. Ruby has been through major surgery and she's still in shock. We don't want to put too much of a strain on her now do we?" the doctor asked tactfully. "Maybe we could come back to this later?"

"Yes, of course, no problem," the officers agreed and then one of them spoke to Ruby again. "You are not to blame for your father's death please try and accept that. This is *not* your fault, Ruby."

"How do *you* know? I left him unconscious! How do you know it's not my fault? I should have stayed at home like he told me, maybe then he'd be OK."

"No, maybe then you would both be dead," he told her. "Your father, Ruby, he was shot too. The place was trashed and it was clear that someone had been looking for something."

"Shot? Where did you find him? Did they hurt him?"

"No he wouldn't have felt a thing. He was where you left him and he wouldn't have had a clue. You say your dad owed money, do you know who to?" he queried and she shrugged sadly, glad this time the morphine was working.

"To everyone and anyone who lent it. I don't know who exactly. I tried to stay out of it. Men would come up to me on my way home from school and stop me. They'd ask where my dad was but I would keep my head down and tell them I didn't know what they were talking about. Do you think that's why?" she asked, knowing full well that Sergio had given the order for her house to be visited. Their men must have killed her dad. Fortunately they didn't seem to have made it as far as Mr Alessi's place, at least *he* was still alive and well.

"It was probably over money, Ruby," the officer guessed and both nodded like they believed that to be true. She looked to Mr Alessi who nodded also. She'd done very well and he was proud of her.

"Ruby, we will need to speak to you again about last night, about being shot," the second officer explained. "We need whatever you can remember. No pressure just whatever comes. If you recall anything write it down, names, motives anything at all," he suggested and she nodded helpfully.

"Do you have any family?" the other officer asked her affectionately feeling really sorry for her now. She seemed so small and broken, so battered and bruised and he was saddened when she shook her head wearily in response.

"No, it was just me and my dad," she whispered realising she was now homeless and completely alone in the world too.

"What about your mum?" he tried hopefully.

"She left when I was a baby. She walked out and left me with *him*. I don't know where she is."

"That's fine we can trace her. If you give us her name..."

"No!" she snapped. "I don't know her name and I don't want her here either do you understand? Don't go finding her. I don't want her in here! I don't want her anywhere near me! She left me, please don't go bringing her back now, please!" She was desperate and the last thing she wanted was her mother.

"It's OK I will look after Ruby. She can stay with me. I feel responsible for her. She's my employee and she was injured in *my* building. She will be safe with me," a voice came from the foot of her bed. Ruby looked up at Mr Alessi stunned. He smiled at her warmly. "Is that OK with you, Ruby, are you happy to come home with me?" he asked gently and she nodded. "Then that's settled. Perhaps, officers, you could come back a bit later and we will see if we can jog her memory then? I want the people who did this to her found and I want them put away for a *very* long time."

"From what we found last night, Sir, I don't think there were very many people left. It looks like a gang, maybe two separate gangs, and everyone just seemed to turn on each other," one of the officers informed him. "It was complete carnage, lots of bodies. We are thinking drugs and we found drugs when searching the bodies. Computing equipment had been removed from the downstairs offices and the reception area too so clearly stealing for money was the motive for one gang."

"For the other gang..." the second officer cut in, "probably money owed for the drugs we found. One of our officers had obviously found the building open and gone in to investigate. We sadly suffered our own loss last night, a good man too. I'm sure all of this can be pieced together fairly quickly. I don't think it was personal but your offices *will* need some serious cleaners and builders to put the place back together," he prepared him. Mr Alessi nodded thoughtfully his hand over his mouth as he spoke through his fingers.

"Well I'm glad to hear it's not personal, every cloud has a silver lining eh?" he raised his eyebrows and Ruby detected the sarcasm, both of them knowing full well, it couldn't get any more personal!

32
Home sweet...mansion!

It was two weeks before the hospital allowed Ruby to leave. Mr Alessi helped her to the car and they made the journey back to his house. She felt nervous. She would be staying in a stranger's house, not that she was scared of him but she was concerned about being surrounded by *his* things, living in *his* space, by *his* rules, whatever *they* might be. He was hard enough to deal with at work. What would he be like when she was under his roof?

"Not far now," he reassured her giving a brief and awkward smile. She turned to look out of the window at the trees flashing by. The winter sun was warm on her face and she closed her eyes.

"Mr Alessi, why hasn't Danny been to see me?" she asked shyly. "I mean...is everything OK? He visited me when I first came out from under the anaesthetic and he was there when I was shot but then...nothing."

"Everything's fine. If you want to see him I can arrange it. We just needed to keep things low while we waited for the hospital to discharge you. There were police everywhere and after finding out Carlito had been informing suddenly everyone was jumpy. Do you know what I'm saying?" He took his eyes briefly from the road to read her expression.

"Yeah that makes sense."

"Listen, Danny visits here a lot so you can expect to see him as much here as you do in the office," he smiled and she looked surprised.

"What? Really? I had no idea you two spent time together *outside* of the office!"

"He's a good boy and I like his company, Ruby. We work from home sometimes when things are busy and my place is a *tad* bigger than his. It's just easier that's all. The office needs some major repair work and so *our* business, our criminal cases, they will have to be conducted from home until we can move back into the building. By the time we're moved back in you will be sick of the sight of him," he joked but she seriously doubted that. "Right, anyway, here we are. Let's get you settled in shall we?" he announced as they pulled onto a drive and waited for the big gates to open.

"Whoa, and you work *because?*" she asked in disbelief. The place was huge with its sweeping gravel drive and immaculately tended front garden, complete with cherub water fountain, pool and huge conifers. There were climbing roses everywhere and the place was beautiful. She counted eight windows to the second floor of the house and then gave up, wondering why she was counting windows anyway.

"I work because I love my job. It's my life, Ruby. I live it, breathe it, sleep it. It's kind of in my veins."

"Do you live here alone?" she asked suddenly worried that she might be intruding. He snorted in amusement.

"Yes, Ruby, it's just you and me rattling about here I'm afraid. I hope that's OK with you?" She nodded and he smiled. "You will have all the space you need." He pulled to a stop just outside the big wooden front doors and released his seatbelt. "Come on let's get you inside you look tired." She climbed out of the car with some help and he led her up the front steps to the porch.

Once inside he took her into the living room and made her comfortable on a sofa by the window. The sun was streaming through and she nestled into the cushions and closed her eyes.

"Do you know I feel like I'm home for the first time in my life?" she sighed. "I always imagined homes, real homes, to be warm, with cushions and throws and sunny places to sit and birds in trees outside the window." She smiled and looked up at him, feeling self conscious, and he pulled up a large footrest and sat in front of her. Her eyes were still puffy and red and the cuts and bruises on her face looked sore and blue against the pale white of her partially drained body.

"Do you know they had to transfuse you because you lost so much blood?" he asked her softly and she shook her head. It was all such a blur and bits, like the ambulance ride and her arrival at hospital, were completely missing from her memory. "It was very scary for everyone,

Ruby, don't go getting yourself shot again!" he berated her gently. "I'm meant to be dark haired not grey. I'm not old enough for grey."

"I'm sorry," she grinned. "I'll try harder in future." She suddenly became more serious and shifted painfully. "Look Mr Alessi..."

"Just Alessi will do when we're out of the office, Ruby," he corrected and she nodded. He must have given Danny permission too and that's why he got away with dropping his title when they thought nobody else was listening. "I know you and Danny call me Alessi when you talk about me, probably usually to tell each other what a monster I am," he guessed raising his eyebrows and she smirked but said nothing. She wasn't about to lie but she wasn't going to agree either. He chuckled. "I like to think I'm more than just your boss, Ruby, especially when you're not at work. You live here now and I care about you. This is your home too as far as I'm concerned so please, treat it as such. I don't expect you to see me as your boss outside of the office do you understand?"

"I understand...and...thank you. You don't have to worry it won't be forever. I'll get myself up and about and then I'll be out of your way. I swear I won't be a burden. You don't have to worry about your life being taken over by some annoying teenage..."

"Err no you won't!" he cut her off. "I'm expecting you to stay. I know I've been cruel, harsh, and stroppy sometimes but I have a lot of time for you, Ruby Palmer. You are like the daughter I never had," he confessed and she looked back at him in astonishment, her mouth open. He smirked at her. "By the way Danny showed me the results of your exams. He also pointed out that you can spell FUDGE with them. He was quite pleased about that." She giggled, Danny was funny and she could imagine him trying to convince Alessi that spelling FUDGE was a good thing. "I intend to get you back to school. If you're going to work with us you need to go to university, young lady. I expect you to work hard and turn your life around do you understand me?"

She nodded, determined to get back to normal as quickly as possible. "I'm going to arrange for some private tuition for you straight away. A tutor can come here in the evenings and you will retake your exams. Then we'll do A' Levels and then we'll get you into Danny's university, it's close by..."

"Yeah and apparently the tuition fees are £9,000 a year!" she exclaimed interrupting him mid flow and trying to make him see sense.

"Doesn't matter, I'll pay it," he told her just like that. It was as easy as *I'll stick a pizza in, I'll pop to the shop and I'll pay your £27,000 tuition fees in full.*

"I...I couldn't..." she stammered.

"OK then, if you're going to be proud about it, I'll freeze your annual pay rise in return for your promise to work hard, call it quits?" he proposed. She smiled looking uncertain and he held out his hand. "Shake, Ruby," he ordered firmly, pushing her into it. "I always shake on a deal," he continued professionally. She reached out gingerly and he gripped her hand and shook hard before she could back out. "That's a legally binding contract," he informed her.

"A what? What does *that* mean?" she asked sounding concerned.

"It means don't go breaching it or I'll sue your arse!"

Alessi was right and soon the place was buzzing as files were ferried from the office to his house. Danny was around a lot and though she wasn't up to much for at least a month he spent every break by her side making her laugh, though she begged him not to. Even a slight giggle hurt like hell but he was always so cute she couldn't help but give in. It always ended in tears and Alessi kept telling him off. She slowly began to get up and about and the work on the building was coming to a close.

Files were ferried back to their cabinets and Ruby went along for the journey. It was strange being in the building again. She stood looking at the front door for a while until Danny took her hand, squeezed it, and whispered that she would be fine. He took her on a tour of the place showing her where people had been found and what had been replaced, ripped out or blown to smithereens. When they arrived at Tom Marshall's room panic set in, her heart rate increased and she felt sick and sweaty. Danny knocked and tugged her inside gently.

Tom was lovely as usual and pulled a client chair out for her to sit down. Danny asked if he had any fruit bon bons but Tom didn't get the joke. Ruby tried desperately not to giggle. Tom suddenly remembered that he *did* have humbugs and pulled a bag from his drawer. When Ruby saw the devastated bag all torn and ripped apart she couldn't help breaking into hysterics. She was so glad that laughing no longer hurt.

By spring they were *all* back in the building. The evenings were lighter and the days warmer. It felt so good to be outside and Ruby loved breathing the fresh air more than she ever had done before. Nearly never seeing another spring day again was too much to comprehend.

The appeal had been adjourned to the summer, because the triplicate copying Ruby had done for court had been blown to bits. As a result it had been another day of copying, hole punching and numbering. Finally, bored out of her mind, she went to find Danny at his desk. She perched on the corner crossing her bare legs and pointing her flip flops towards the carpet. The breeze from his window was good and she tilted her head back and swung her long dark wavy hair. He'd been engrossed in a defence statement but now her eyes were closed he stopped circling to watch her. It would only be four months until her eighteenth birthday and he'd promised himself he wouldn't lay a finger on her until she was at *least* eighteen. That promise, especially at times like this, was very hard to stick to.

"You're not hitting on me are you, Ruby, because I'm very busy you know?" he teased with a cheeky grin. She opened her eyes and scowled at him playfully.

"As if I'd *be* interested in someone your age anyway, that's pervy!" she argued. He laughed and tapped his pen on her knee.

"Come on let's go grab a coffee and catch Alessi at home. We could take him one too. He said he was working on personal stuff today and to come by later and see him. What do you say, we could sit in the garden and chat about how much older I am than you and how I don't like you hitting on me?" She giggled and nodded sliding off of his desk to turn everything off and grab her things.

They went for a walk by the river and then grabbed three coffees to take home. When they pulled up outside Alessi's and waited for the gates to open Ruby noticed there was a big black car outside. She frowned and Danny looked uneasy.

"Shall we go for another walk?" he asked eagerly, looking over his shoulder like he might reverse back out of the drive, but she grabbed his arm.

"No I want to go in, Danny, please." He paused, unsure what to do. "Danny, please, I live here. Alessi is in there." He agreed begrudgingly and drove through the gates, pulling up alongside the long black vehicle.

"I think that's one of Johnny Giavani's cars," Danny told her and she was desperate to get out and see what was going on. She wanted to make sure Alessi was OK and eagerly unlocked the front door so they could get inside. Six men were lounging about at the bottom of the stairs and Ruby gasped, her eyes widening in horror.

"You! What the hell are *you* doing here?" She glanced over all of them immediately recognising Bardo, one of Alessi's good acquaintances, but she concentrated her attention on just one. He stepped forward with a sleazy grin.

"Hello again and what a pleasure," he told her sounding pleased. He glanced passed Ruby to briefly acknowledge her companion.

"Danny," the man greeted him and Danny nodded back not liking Ruby's reaction to him at all.

"Mickey. What brings you here?" he asked.

"I'm here with Johnny. We brought him along for a house meeting with Mr Alessi. They had some private stuff to talk about. We've been told to wait out here. Don't mind us," he grinned at Ruby and she made no attempt to try and hide her disgust.

"Why would he ask *you?*" she demanded and he laughed and checked her over slowly, lingering for long enough that she felt he'd completely undressed her.

"Because, baby, since Carlito sadly passed over to the other side I've been made his temporary right hand man. He trusts me. We go a long way back," he chuckled.

"No! He trusts *you?*" she virtually spat the words out at him and Danny slipped his arm around her.

"What's the matter, Ruby? How do you know Mickey?"

"How do *you* know Mickey?" she asked sounding like she'd been betrayed.

"He works for our clients *and* it seems he's been promoted too. Why what's wrong?"

"He's the one who sat next to me on the bus! He was there too," she pointed out Bobby. "He was the one who searched my bag. *He* watched the whole thing from the seat behind," she told him pointing out Nico. "*He* was the one driving and *he* was the one pretending to be held hostage," she concluded pointing out Pete and Dave Lazio. "But *he*," she jabbed her finger at Mickey like she could spit in his face she hated him so much. "He's the one who scared the hell out of me!" She confronted him now. "You threatened me and then made it look like I gave information you could *actually* use. You made *me* look like a traitor! I thought I was going to die you idiot!" She stepped forward and threw her coffee in his face.

"Whoa, Danny, control your girlfriend because if you can't *I* will," he threatened.

"I'm *not* his girlfriend!" she protested. "Do you like threatening women, Mickey? You're sick do you know that? What's the problem are men not scared of you? Do you have to pick on women to make yourself feel more like a man?" He wiped the hot liquid away with a handkerchief looking seriously hacked off.

"You'd better watch your mouth, Ruby. You might be looked after by Mr Alessi but that doesn't mean that people above him can't give orders to see you put in your place. Right now under the ground seems the best place for you." He put his hands on his hips purposely letting his jacket open so he could flash the gun in his waistband. Her blood ran cold. "I hear you've been close once already. Sergio always *was* a bad shot. I suppose only having one eye can do that," he laughed at his sick joke. "Now *I'd* have got it right first time, made sure you were dealt with properly." Danny stepped forward but the other men stepped forward too and Bardo tried to cool it.

"Come on, Mickey, chill yeah. We're not going to be here long and Ruby lives here. It's her home and Alessi isn't going to be happy if he hears you've been winding her up or getting into a fight with Danny so...please," he spoke tactfully, his voice deep and persuasive. Bardo was a big man and Ruby guessed he was the type that people usually listened to. Still, she wasn't taking any chances and pushed herself between Mickey and Danny placing her hands on his chest.

"Danny, I'll leave it now," she promised and he stepped back looking ready to snap. He wanted to rip Mickey apart for bullying Ruby the way he had.

"Where's Alessi now?" she demanded looking about.

"In the dining room and he's *not* to be disturbed," Mickey told her like she was a child. She nodded in agreement backing ever so slightly away from everyone. He watched her as she made her way to the fruit bowl and turned an apple in her hands. Then she ran her finger along the wooden unit as if checking for dust and *then* she turned and looked at Mickey who was still stupidly standing by the stairs.

"Like I'm going to listen to *you*," she told him rushing the double doors to the dining room as soon as she had a decent enough chance of getting there.

"Don't make me..." he snarled rushing forward but she was already there and pushed the doors wide open. Johnny and Alessi had been interrupted mid conversation and were looking at her as she turned her back on them to face Mickey.

"Don't make you what, Mickey? Go on, you were saying? What are you going to do to me?" He said nothing seeing the frowns that crossed the faces of his boss and Alessi. "What, so you *don't* want to threaten to put me under the ground again then?" she asked, goading him. "Not while you've got witnesses eh?" Alessi went to stand looking seriously unhappy but she grabbed the handle on both doors and swung them shut in Mickey's face. She then turned to yell at Alessi.

33
The truth hurts

"What are *they* doing here?" Ruby shouted throwing her hands into the air in despair. "Are you completely mad, Alessi? Do you know what he did to me? I know he was following orders but he could have got the same result some other way." She turned to Johnny, the first time she'd ever spoken to him. He was scary, straight faced, serious. "He's sick, is that what you want for your right hand man, someone who takes unnecessary risks, stealing buses, knocking innocent people out, getting all over the front pages of the news, just to see whether a teenage girl is taking information back to someone else?" He moved in his chair not liking being spoken to so directly.

"He's a good boy. I've known him a long time and his father too. We go a long way back and I trust him. I don't have to answer to you, young lady."

"He lied!" she argued back and Alessi tried to calm the situation but she wouldn't listen to him, wouldn't let him take her arm and pull her away. "He made it sound like I gave Danny's name, just like that, and I didn't. He set me up! You can't trust him. First Carlito and then him! I can't believe it!" she told herself. Alessi leaned forward to get her attention.

"Ruby, please, you need to think about who you're talking to." He didn't want to offend his guest further and tried to soothe Ruby's temper. "You really shouldn't be involving yourself like this. You shouldn't be talking to my client like that. In fact, Ruby, *you* shouldn't be talking to my client at all. Go to your room please," he ordered softly but she raised her eyebrows and scoffed at him.

"What with Mickey at the bottom of the stairs? No thanks! He threatened to take me on another ride, he likes them young by all accounts and I'm not sure I like the sound of that! Apparently *Nico* likes to get hands on, forget it Alessi I am *not* going back out there!" she told him defiantly and moved to sit on the sofa like she had no intention of leaving. "Who the hell are you anyway? Why would these guys be coming to you, a professional and respectable firm in some normal town? Why you? It doesn't make sense." He sighed and looked at his client who raised his eyebrows.

"It's your call. I think I quite like her. She's not afraid to stand her ground and make her point. Perhaps she could do with toning it down a bit but she's young, and clearly willing to take a bullet for a file she knows nothing about and a colleague she's never even met. Rossi was seriously grateful to hear about Ruby and Danny's bravery in your building. I'm sure once she's had her fingers burnt, probably the type that learns the hard way, she could be very...useful." Alessi stood and walked over to the sofa, sitting down beside her cautiously.

"Look I don't quite know how to tell you this," he paused and thought about it first pinching the space under his nose while he contemplated his next words. "Ruby, please, remember that whatever happens, whatever you learn or find out about I *am* really sorry about your dad. I want to give you all the things he failed to give you." She shook her head.

"It's OK, Alessi. It's sad that his life is over but he stopped living it years ago. He dragged me along with him. He's the reason I did so badly at school, trying to earn money with part time jobs, cooking, cleaning, managing the bills, there just wasn't the time for studying. The constant shouting and beatings meant there was nowhere to study when I got home and he just made everything so impossible and painful. Eleven years of school and what do I have to show for it? I'm old enough to survive on my own now. Forget about my dad I want to know about the mafia, why you?"

"Didn't you ask Danny?" he queried and she nodded suspiciously. "And what did he say?"

"He told me you told him to keep his nose out and mind his own business."

"Hmmm," he acknowledged and she could see he was trying not to smile.

"What? Are you telling me he's lying? Does he know?"

"I'm not saying any..."

"Yes you are! He lied to me?"

"Only because it's not his secret to tell. I'd bugged you that night you were shot, Ruby, that's how the place got cleared so quickly. After the rubbish bin incident I wasn't taking any chances with you and I placed a bug and tracker on you before you left Danny's apartment. As soon as we heard Sergio's order to visit your house and mine we were on it like a shot. I was able to pass the information on about Carlito and have our people go in and deal with him and his brother. That's how I saved my own home from coming under attack and how I got you two out of there. That's how Carlito and Sergio were taken care of."

He ran his right hand over his face and then used it to cover his mouth while he paused for what felt like an eternity. He sighed and smiled at her. "I heard it all, Ruby, from the fight with your dad, to the cosy little chats and flirting with Danny and your questions about me. He did admirably trying to change the subject but *my* you're a persistent young lady," he told her blowing out a whistle and raising his eyebrows. "When you set your mind to something you won't let up will you? I could hear he wanted to tell you but he never did and I'm pleased with both of you. I'm pleased with him for resisting *you* and his urge to share something that he shouldn't and you for not being afraid to push for more."

"Great, so Danny bare face lied to me, brownie point to him," she huffed folding her arms and shoving herself backwards into the sofa. She was clearly put out by the secrecy between them and it made both Alessi and Johnny laugh.

"Listen, that doesn't matter, let it go," Alessi chuckled but she kept the defiant face and clenched jaw. "You want to know why the mafia chose me?" he asked and she nodded stiffly. "Well stop complaining and listen then. They didn't choose me...I chose them."

"What? How does that work?" she asked sceptically. "They ask you at university what you want to specialise in when you grow up and you said, 'Oh...erm...the Mafia please?'" she tormented sarcastically.

"This goes no further, Ruby, do you understand me?" He suddenly sounded gravely serious and it made her shudder.

"I understand," she agreed, quickly dropping the attitude.

"Johnny Giavani here...he's...well...he's my father," he confessed. Her mouth dropped open and she slid away from him.

"No! No, that can't be. I held onto that file in Tom's office knowing my life was at stake, knowing that's what they wanted, knowing that I was willing to put my life on the line. I was even going to tell you about Carlito because I was worried that your client might kill you if you didn't find out who was leaking information!"

"And, Ruby, you have no idea how much I appreciate that. That is why I know I want to do all of this for you, treat this place like your home, get the qualifications you want and need and enjoy being young. It's the very least I can do for you. I want to give you a life because you sure as hell didn't have one before you came to my office. Make no mistake, Ruby, if Johnny here thought that I was leaking information or not doing what I could I would be taken care of." Johnny squinted like he didn't like the sound of that and then coughed and prepared to speak to Ruby. He spoke slowly.

"I was married to Alessi's mother. We have very strict values about respect for family, for your wife and loved ones and I loved my wife very much, Ruby. She knew what she was getting into. I never duped her but things got heavy and she was caught up in it. She wasn't as strong as you seem to be. She was pregnant and it scared her so much she went into melt down I suppose. She had a nervous breakdown and she wasn't the same woman. She lost her hair, she lost weight, she couldn't eat or sleep. I wanted to keep her but the mafia was my life, it always has been. It was all I knew but she wanted out. I couldn't just leave...so...because I loved her, and I knew it was what she wanted...I let her go. I saw to it that she disappeared. Names were changed, flights were booked and she gave birth in Italy. She died when Alessi here was in his early teens."

"Oh my god, Alessi, I'm so sorry," she told him looking sad. "You must have been devastated." Alessi nodded and managed a smile but it was clearly hiding pain.

"I had no brothers or sisters, Ruby. I was on my own. My mother never found anyone else after my father and she poured her heart and soul into raising me. She continued to suffer bouts of depression which knocked her off her feet for weeks at a time. She was a very troubled and lonely woman and I missed her very much. I still do," he confessed and Ruby wanted to cry for him.

"How did she die?" she whispered hoping that wasn't a question too far.

"She took her own life," Johnny explained. "And with nobody else, no *other* family, Alessi here eventually came looking for me. There are complex rules, ones that *you* don't seem to respect young lady," he told her firmly, "We had to wait to be introduced but when we were I welcomed him with open arms. I took him in, of course, he was my son and I'd always wanted him in my life. He was a clever boy and I wanted to use his services as a lawyer to help with the legitimate business deals, cases and paperwork." Ruby's eyes were wide and Alessi noticed that although she seemed saddened she had also slid into the corner of the sofa. She was afraid of him now.

"And this doesn't bother Danny?" she asked doubtfully. "You said you told him but he stayed with the firm? He stayed with you?"

"Ruby, brace yourself sweetheart," Alessi forewarned her. "Danny is *my* son. I told you I had children and I do...I have Danny."

"No!" she screamed again, holding her face in her hands. "Oh my god what have I got into! I've fallen in love with him, Alessi!" she whined in despair and he raised his eyebrows. "I threw myself at him and we made out on his desk. Oh god I nearly had sex with the mafia!" Now it was Alessi and Johnny's eyes that were wide. It seemed there was *something* that could disturb them and apparently it was *her* having sex! Alessi dropped his head into his hands.

"I'm going to kill him!" he mumbled.

"Like father like son it seems, Federico," Johnny commented with the insinuation that he'd failed to control his son.

"Federico?" Ruby echoed gleefully upon learning his first name. He looked up and frowned at her.

"It's still Alessi to you!" he snapped before looking back at Johnny. "And what's that supposed to mean? I've never done anything like that!" he protested. He sounded like Ruby trying to defend herself in front of his desk while he gave her lectures about virtue, shoes and Almond bloody Blossoms."

"Haven't you?" Johnny asked surprised. "You think I've never bugged you, Alessi?" Alessi looked horrified and whispered a number of obscenities in Italian, very unlike him! His eyes showed the desperate internal turmoil, his attempt to pin down exactly *which* incident Johnny was talking about. Johnny laughed a long low laugh. "At least your son has waited...*this time*. I think he's in love. Have *you* ever been in love, Federico?" he teased, giving Ruby a discreet wink. Alessi's face looked hard. He didn't like being questioned about his private life in front of Ruby. She was happy to listen, she was making mental notes to use against him in the future, but she was still very angry too. Would she have allowed herself to fall for Danny had she known the truth?

"So what do I do now, Alessi?" she suddenly demanded.

"Nothing has to change," he tried to reassure her. "You stay here with me. I will look after you and you will get the education you need and anything else you need too. You can have *whatever* you want, Ruby."

"Why? What do you want from me?"

"Nothing, all I want is for you to be happy."

"So I can have whatever I want?" she asked and he nodded.

"Whatever you want, Ruby."

"Why would you offer me the world like that? I don't understand, Alessi!" He took a deep breath and exhaled nervously. He had never looked so torn and she waited, eager to hear what was bothering him *so* much. What could be worse than having to tell someone you were the son of a scary mafia boss?

"Because I like you, because you deserve it, because I'm in a position to be able to give it to you and...because...*I* killed your father, Ruby."

34
The siege

Alessi reached out to place his hand on her arm but she shrunk away from him in horror.

"Don't touch me!" she screamed trying desperately to get her head around what he'd just told her. "You engineered *all* of this. You took away my dad and my home and then you offered me a place to stay. What do you want from me, Alessi?" she demanded. "*He* wanted me as a punch bag, John Billingham wanted me as his victim, Matthew wanted me just for the fun of it so what do *you* want?"

"It's not like that, Ruby, I swear. I heard what he did to you and I saw the marks he left behind. I just wanted to help. It broke my heart to see you suffering and it made me furious that you had to cope alone. I tried to offer you help but you turned me down and then he continued to beat you, you continued to come into the office with marks and you continued to try and hide them. I saw the injuries, Ruby, I was looking for them. I listened to him torture you. He physically and verbally abused you and then you started begging him not to look at you and that was the final straw."

She clasped her arms around her body tightly feeling uncomfortable. Johnny Giavani was watching her intently, his face serious and Alessi had turned to try and get closer while he appealed. "After what I heard in your bedroom the night Danny had to help you there was no way I was going to let you go back there again. He was like a time bomb and I wasn't going to stand back and let you be his victim. I *had* to take him out, Ruby, don't you understand? I want nothing from you, other than to help you succeed. I love you, Ruby." She cringed and scrunched her nose in disgust but he shook his head. "Not like that! I swear it's not like that at all. You are a beautiful girl who's had a really hard time and I love you like a daughter. You have a heart of gold and nerves of steel and I want to take care of you."

He reached out and she practically climbed over the arm of the sofa to get away from him. She was out through the double doors in the blink of an eye. The reception area was still being used as a lounge by Johnny's men and Mickey stepped into her path. She barged right into him refusing to be the first to move. He was slammed by her slight body as Johnny, Alessi and the other men watched on. She was clearly upset and Danny stepped towards the front door wanting to stop her from leaving. She detoured to avoid him, turning back towards the stairs. She whirled round and confronted him when he tried to follow her.

"Stay away from me, Danny Glover! You lied to me. You led me to believe you were normal but you're not! Don't try and follow me you may as well go, we're done here!"

She ran up the stairs in floods of tears and slammed the bedroom door behind her. She threw herself face down onto the bed, her endless tears soaking into the pillow. She sobbed not knowing what to do or where to go. She felt trapped, duped and stupid but she was suddenly snapped out of her depression when she heard three gun shots ring out. They echoed chillingly through the reception area at the bottom of the stairs and bad memories of Tom's office and Sergio's face flashed through her mind.

She pushed herself up and a hand roughly shoved her back down again. She struggled but was pinned by the weight of a man's body as she screamed into her damp pillow. Surely Danny hadn't followed and turned on her. Surely Danny wouldn't attack her because she'd said they were done, just because she told him to leave...*his own father's house?* An arm lay across her shoulder blades keeping her trapped and then her attacker buried his face into her hair, close to her ear.

"Gotcha!" he whispered. It was Mickey! She began a renewed wave of fighting but it was pointless. He lifted his arm to straighten and separate one coiled length of rope from another. She tried to twist and push herself up but he was heavy on her waist and the weight sunk her into the mattress. She couldn't even find a gap to wriggle. He grabbed her hands from the pillow and pulled them back roughly, tying them so tight she could feel the burn on her wrists. He then spun himself so he could face her feet. He bent her kicking legs at the knee and proceeded to tie her ankles together. "Right dilemma," he told her spinning back round. "Do we have a little chat now or do I gag you to keep you quiet and come back for you later?" She was sobbing and frightened.

"Please, Mickey, don't gag me," she begged and he laughed.

"I have to say as pretty as you are the mouth gets a bit annoying, Ruby, so I'm going to take a little break. You can have a think about things and I'll come back to pay you a visit in a short while." He rolled her over so he could straddle her and look into her eyes.

"Who's been shot?" she demanded. "What have you done, Mickey?"

"How many shots did you hear?" he asked her sounding only remotely interested as he pulled his gun and dusted it off with a handkerchief. She thought about it before answering.

"Three?" she whispered as her eyes began to fill with tears.

"Yeah you're right. I'd say it's official, you're all on your own in this big place now, where no one can hear you scream, where nobody cares if you do and where nobody misses you if you suddenly *stop* breathing. The only thing any of *us* might miss is our turn visiting *you*. I happen to know that Nico can't wait," he told her cruelly and her eyes widened as she realised just how vulnerable she was. She felt hopeless whereas he seemed immensely happy with how things had turned out. "Have some thinking time, Ruby," he ordered, tearing off a strip of tape and placing it over her mouth.

The thinking time started off all about Danny, Alessi and Johnny. Had he really killed them just like that? Why would he kill the two people who definitely knew where the file was? Surely he would torture them first. *That* didn't make her feel any better. She wondered what they would do with the bodies if they had been killed and then she wondered what they would do with the bodies if they hadn't. Would they still be downstairs in separate rooms or together? Would they have brought them upstairs to her floor and might she be able to communicate with them or hear them if she stayed calm and listened carefully? A shot rang out from somewhere in the building and it forced her to consider her own predicament. What were they going to do with *her?* Was this about the file or had they killed Danny, Alessi and Johnny because it was actually about something else? How far would they go to get what they wanted? She frantically tried to slip her wrists free of the rope but every time she moved them back and forth the burning was immense. When her hands felt wet and sticky she guessed she'd drawn blood.

Quite some time passed and it was getting dark outside. When Mickey left her he'd taken the key out of the lock and used it to lock her in from the other side. She heard it turning now and stiffened, dreading her fate. He came in with a tray of food and what looked like a cup of tea and placed it by her bed. Upon drawing the curtains he turned on the lamp and then stood and looked at her as she clenched her eyes tightly shut, petrified of what he might be about to do.

"I just want to ask you some questions that's all," he whispered kindly. He lowered himself so he was close to the head of her bed and peeled the tape from her mouth. "This is how it works, Ruby. I ask you some questions, being really nice. You give me the answers I want to hear and I continue to be nice to you. I won't hurt you and nor will I let anyone else hurt you either. You piss about with me, Ruby, you play games, and I *will* get nasty. Now do you understand me?" he asked and she nodded. "Good, well done, that was the first answer I wanted. You catch on quick," he grinned. "Do you know about Johnny Giavani's file?" She nodded. "I want *actual* answers so there's no confusion, Ruby, please."

"Yes," she whispered softly.

"Do you know how important it is?"

"Yes."

"Do you know *why* it's important?"

"It has information on it? I'm not exactly sure. Names or something?" she was scared of getting the answer wrong and rambled, showing her fear much more than she knew was sensible.

"No, don't worry, that's fine. That's a pretty good attempt at an honest answer. You see I know all the answers to these questions already. I know that Alessi bugged you the day Carlito and Sergio were shot. I was there when it was played to Johnny so he could have the proof he needed that Carlito was informing and working with his brother. I heard Danny telling you about the file and why it was so important. I heard your very sad story, boys can be so mean can't they?" he teased putting on a sad face. "I heard your waster of a dad beat you, over what I'm not quite sure. Just for the fun of it probably. Who needs enemies like me eh? Then I heard you tell Danny what you'd seen in the alley. You, Ruby, dropped yourself *right* in it. You had enough information to get a lot of men killed. You deserved to be shot that night. Anyway, enough of what I think. Your next question for a get out of jail free card is; where's the file now, *Ruby?*" She shook her head as silent tears rolled down the sides of her face and pooled in her ears. "OUT LOUD, RUBY!" he shouted, startling her.

"I don't know. I'm sorry but I don't know!" she protested. He jumped up on top of her and lowered himself to look into her eyes.

"Sure you don't want to tell me?" he asked and she did want to very much.

"I can't," she whispered. He gripped her chin tightly and pressed his mouth to hers. She tried to move her face but he grabbed her around the throat pinning her. His mouth was hard, his face bristly and painful, and he stunk of tobacco and coffee. He moved his mouth to her ear.

"Sure you don't want to tell me?" he repeated and she shook her head. He sat back, his weight over her middle as he looked at her, searching her eyes and contemplating what to do with her next. She was shaking he could feel it and she knew he could. "Hmmm," he murmured thoughtfully. "Maybe you just need more time. You're in luck because I'm feeling generous and I'm willing to give you some." He climbed off. "Are you eating?" he asked and she shook her head.

"I'm not hungry. Have you really killed Danny, Alessi and Johnny?" she asked sadly and he grinned.

"I'll come back in the morning. Sleep might help you remember where the file is," he suggested ignoring her question. He replaced the tape over her mouth and took the tray away, locking the door behind him.

She didn't sleep, hoping if she listened carefully enough she might hear something other than the boorish chants, laughs and shouts of Mickey's gang. By morning she had a plan.

Mickey followed the same routine as the night before. He came in carrying a tray and a drink and placed it beside her bed. He opened the curtains, turned off the lamp and crouched down beside her, removing the tape.

"Where's the file, Ruby?" he asked and she shook her head sadly.

"Mickey, I'm really sorry but I just don't know. They never told me, I swear." She begged him to believe her and he sighed.

"Are you eating?" he asked and she nodded. The last thing she wanted to do was eat but it would mean getting out of the restraints for a few minutes and an opportunity to get a little further than the bed. He rolled her onto her front and jumped on top of her, untying her in the same way as he'd tied her up just in reverse. He kept his weight on her until the last minute and before shifting he gave her a warning. "Try anything stupid and I'll take you out do you hear? Wait until I'm off you, count to five, and then get up slowly," he instructed and she did as she was told. He watched her intently while she ate, his eyes always somewhere they shouldn't be and then occasionally on *her* eyes. "It's a new day," he told her with a smile, "You want to get changed?" he asked hopefully and she looked up from her cold piece of toast and stopped chewing.

"No," she replied flatly.

"Shame," he grumbled his eyes lingering again.

"I *would* like to use the bathroom though," she requested. "I need the toilet." He frowned like he didn't trust her. "Time of the month," she told him uncomfortably and he rolled his eyes.

"Ugh bloody female hostages are a pain the arse, there's always *something!*" he moaned before nodding. "OK you get ten minutes and then I'm coming in. Oh and I'll need to give you the once over when you come out," he smiled. She didn't like the sound of that but agreed anyway.

Once in the bathroom she turned the taps on full and flushed the toilet before identifying that she had all the things she needed. She washed her face and sprayed herself with body mist before running the toothbrush over her teeth. She wanted to lock the door and stay in the large tiled room but she knew there was no point, he'd get her and she'd just make him angry. She came out and he was leaning against the wall looking at his watch.

"Eleven minutes, Ruby, don't push it. Turn and put your hands on the wall," he ordered and she did as she was told. He then ran his hands over her body and tied hers while she was standing. He led her back to the bed and lifted her feet, tying them too. The finishing touch was the tape on her mouth. She watched him as he left the room. That visit had been less stressful than she'd feared.

He missed out a lunchtime visit and came as it was getting dark. The same routine was followed by another request to use the bathroom and this time she made sure she was done in nine so as not to hack him off unnecessarily. She returned to the bedroom where he was waiting for her.

"Right let's make sure you're not carrying anything unaccounted for shall we?" he asked, placing her hands against the wall as he ran *his* all over her body. She clenched her eyes tightly trying not to react. He leaned in to her ear so close she could feel and smell his disgusting breath. "Nice body I can see why Danny likes you." Her eyes opened wide but she bit her tongue. That was enough *that* was all she needed to give her an inkling of hope that he was still alive. He had said 'likes' and not 'liked'. The present tense was enough to convince her that Danny *wasn't* past tense. She decided to stay calm and agreeable and then he would leave her alone, for now. Before replacing the tape he asked her again. "Ruby, where's the file?" She shook her head and looked into his eyes.

"I don't know, Mickey," she told him and he chuckled menacingly.

"Soon, Ruby, my dear things are going to get so heavy that you will be making stuff up just to try and stop me. After tomorrow nice Mickey's taking a break and nasty Mickey is clocking on. Prepare yourself, you're going to wish you *had* died in Tom Marshall's office."

Those last words stayed on her mind all night tormenting her relentlessly. The time passed slowly and her body started to suffer cramps and sore spots from lying in the same position for too long. Her legs got jumpy in the early hours and she just wanted to move, to walk off the growing frustration.

In the morning Mickey arrived with the tray and a slightly more frightening look about him. It was almost like his personality was changing ready for nasty Mickey. She could feel his energy as he leaned over her longer than necessary to remove the tape and he spent time touching her skin when he untied and retied her hands and ankles. He left her with a kiss and she wanted to spit so bad just to get rid of the pungent smell of him. Mickey felt like the weather and a storm was *definitely* brewing.

35
Don't forget to look under the bed

She now had only minutes. She knew that when she eventually picked her time there would be no going back. Mickey had warned her that if they found the file without her help they would get rid of her. She'd better hope they didn't find it before she talked. *Now* it was time.

She swung her legs round and placed them on the floor. She tried to wriggle free first but then berated herself for wasting the little time she had. She had a plan and she needed to stick to it, trying to escape by struggling was futile *and* dangerous. She shuffled off the bed and sunk to the floor, rolling onto her back so she could push herself along with her feet. When she reached the door to the en-suite she realised she was going to struggle. The handle was round and needed a good turn to open. Had it been a push down handle things would have been quicker and easier. She refused to let herself think that getting into the bathroom was impossible.

She kicked off her flip flops and then wriggled until she was lying on her back with her feet up and her bottom as close to the door as she could manage. She placed her bare feet either side of the round knob and inched it anticlockwise. She started to sweat and her head was spinning. The tape on her mouth kept her from getting the extra oxygen that she needed while exerting herself and she felt faint and nauseous. Eventually she heard a click and she cringed for her weight against the door caused it to swing away from her quickly. It would bang against the bathtub and then they would find her...*like this!* It would all be over before she'd even started. This *wasn't* in the plan! But as she waited, her heart almost unable to take the stress, the door came to a silent stop wedged on a towel that had fallen from a hook on the back. She forced herself to breath more slowly and calm down.

She wasted no more time as she swung herself back around and slid across the tiled floor. She moved to the sink and reached her bare feet behind it, using her toes to lift the glass she had placed there. She was relieved to find the candle she'd lit on her bathroom break still burning. Mickey's bathroom check didn't involve looking behind the sink for a naked flame. She'd sprayed body mist and he'd made some pervy comment about her wanting to smell nice for him. It had covered the smell of the lit match which she had dropped through the plughole in the sink. The matchbox had been replaced in the mountain of cosmetics.

The glass was already hot and she burnt her toes moving it to the middle of the floor. She then backed up to it and held her hands over the flame hoping she wouldn't set light to her hair or her clothes. It took some time and the heat singed at her skin but eventually the rope began to burn and the fibres frazzled. She felt one of the cords break and she rubbed her hands together loosening the length. She nearly burst into tears as it all fell away but there was no time for emotional outbursts she was far from being free.

She tried to undo the knot on her feet but it was impossible. Each time he tied her tightly with a fresh piece of rope and then used a knife to cut her free. She held the flame to the rope and waited patiently for it to give. She then picked at the tape on her mouth and peeled it away, less quickly than Alessi had when he found her in the alley. That had hurt! *Alessi,* she thought to herself. She was sure Danny was alive but what about Alessi and what about his father? She wondered if they were still in the house and then imagined them being taken to some disused factory where no one could hear *their* screams? *No time* she reminded herself and jumped up.

She had to get rid of the evidence just in case she was caught again. She didn't want her tricks uncovered. She used the candle to set light to the rope in the sink and then washed the residue away. She stuck the tape to her thigh, put out the candle with water and then placed it back in the candelabra hanging from the ceiling. She returned the glass to the sink, upside down, where it was usually kept for washing out her mouth after brushing her teeth. She sprayed some more mist and opened the window to let the smell of burning out before closing it and looking about her. Everything looked as it had when Mickey last checked. She picked the towel up from the floor and hung it on the back of the door, closing it quietly behind her.

Lifting the foot of her bed she exposed the storage space in the base. It had been a moving in present courtesy of Alessi. *'It's not possible to have too much storage space, Ruby!'* he'd told her and she'd huffed at him then knowing it was his way of saying *'Just keep your room clutter free and we'll say no more about it!'* It had stayed empty out of protest but now she could kiss him for insisting on something so functional.

She made her way to the window checking that nobody was stationed beneath. It was clear. There were plenty of places in the huge gardens for her to hide and she hoped *that* would keep them busy searching for ages. She took the swivel chair from under the desk and swung it with all her might against the glass pane. It shattered and she threw the chair out too. Hopefully by putting two of their limited brain cells together they'd figure out that she'd followed it. She used a shoe to break away the splinters of glass round the edges of the frame and then threw it to the floor. Running for the bed she climbed inside, pulling it down on top of her. She cowered in the cramped dark side space, waiting for a furious Mickey to come looking for her.

The time came that she'd been dreading. The first thing she heard was the door to her room fly open, the second was Mickey's snarling voice.

"Where the hell is she? How could she have got out of here? She was tied up the little...!" He trailed off to call the others up and they searched the room, tipping over her wardrobe and trashing the place. He was absolutely furious and she knew he would kill her if he found her now. How long till they thought to look in the bed? She wouldn't dwell on it else she'd be sick. "She's not here," he concluded sitting on her bed and running his hands over his head and around his neck stressfully. She pressed her face to the floor of the bed base and clenched her eyes tightly shut. He was so close yet so far away. If she moved or made a sound he would find her just like that. "There's no other option she must have gone out of the window," he concluded at last. "I want everyone searching the gardens and I don't want them back here until she's found. I want her do you hear me? I will torture her slowly in front of her little boyfriend and by the time I get round to shooting her she'll be *begging* me to do it! Find her...NOW!" he bellowed.

Oh god, what had she done? She heard his men file out of the room and the door slammed behind them making her jump. She at least knew it wouldn't be locked now, they didn't think she was in there. She had a hoard of angry men looking to be the one to return her to a very angry Mickey but, on the plus side, she now knew that Danny was definitely alive and somewhere in the house. She inched up the bed base slowly and peeked out, checking the coast was clear.

With the most infinitesimal of movements she turned the handle on her bedroom door. She could hear shouting from the garden and hoped that *everyone* was out looking for her. It would mean the house would be empty, though she doubted Mickey would be searching. He'd still be indoors, ready and waiting for her return. She inched the door open and checked the hallway. It was clear. The stairs were to her right and she could see through the banisters to the ground floor. Mickey came into view and she caught her breath and held it. He was pacing with a face like thunder. She desperately didn't want to find herself in front of him. He was ready to rip her apart with his bare hands.

When he disappeared from view she slipped along the hallway to her left and noticed in three of the doors the key was in the wrong side, like hers they had been locked from the outside. Three, her heart skipped a beat, were Alessi, Danny and Johnny behind those doors?

She opened the first door and slipped inside. She pushed herself forward and opened the door to the en-suite so that the light would illuminate the room. She didn't want to draw attention by messing with the curtains or the lamp. She could just about make out a figure on the bed now and she stood, dreading what she might be about to find. As much as she wanted to see Danny she wanted to see him alive, but the dark figure on the bed was still and lifeless.

She crept over cautiously and gasped upon seeing his face, Danny's face. His eyes were open, fixed blankly on the ceiling but her gasp soon registered and he turned to look at her. He squinted as if he couldn't believe what he was seeing and then his eyes filled with tears. She climbed onto him gingerly. His face was badly bruised and she ran her hands gently over the blue and green marks. She peeled away the tape and pressed her mouth to his, crying and horrified by his condition. He grunted painfully and she pulled away. She was leaning on him and moved back to lift his shirt. Huge bruises covered his torso like he'd been kicked over and over.

"Oh my god, Danny, what have they done to you?" she whispered wiping the tears on the back of her hand. He coughed uncomfortably before struggling to reply.

"I thought...I thought you were...gone. What have they done to you? Are you OK?" he tried to look her over but he was tied up and suffering.

"I'm fine, honestly, they haven't touched me. They certainly haven't treated me like they've treated you," she admitted feeling completely out of her depth. These guys were serious and they'd left Danny in a *very* bad way. She could see pure torment in his eyes as he leaned his head back and gritted his teeth against the cramps and shooting pains racking at his battered and bruised body. He gulped preparing to speak.

"Mickey told me he was going to make you suffer. He told me they all were. He said he would continue until you either told him where the file was or he grew bored, whichever came sooner, and then he would put you out of your misery. I wouldn't tell him where it was, I couldn't even if I wanted to because I don't know. He told me he was going to you next and then he left me here like this with the thought of...what he'd said he would do to you. Forty-two minutes and thirty-three seconds later I heard a shot and I didn't know whether to be sad that you were gone or happy that it was all over." She realised now that the shot he heard must have been the same shot *she'd* heard the night Mickey had first tied and gagged her. He had left her alone to *'think about it'*.

"He was messing with your head, Danny, he never hurt me," she tried to make him believe her seeing his desperation.

"I'm so sorry, Ruby, I couldn't do anything to protect you. This time I couldn't come," he wept silently and she wiped her face on her hands again and touched his lips with her fingers. He seemed slightly delirious. Even though she was there in front of him he didn't seem to believe it.

"He never did those things," she tried to comfort him. "He asked me for the file, tied me and left me in my room. He told me if they found it before I confessed he wouldn't need me anymore. He told me you guys were already dead. I heard three shots just before Mickey came to my room and I thought that you'd *all* been killed right where I left you. I thought I was the only one left and that's why they were keeping me alive."

"But do you know where it is, the file?" he asked her and she nodded.

"Yes, Alessi showed me."

"Will they find it?"

"Never," she told him certainly.

"But how hard can it be to find a great big pink file, Ruby? They will find it eventually. Maybe you should just tell them and pray they let you go. If they find it, which they will, they will kill you because you didn't co-operate. They will kill *us* anyway. We know too much and we threaten everything they stand for. They want all the power and they can't have it as long as we're here. It's just you now, baby, please for once think of yourself and get out of here. You should never have been dragged into all of this. I hate Alessi for keeping you. He should have fired you on the spot when you saw his clients. Hell you never should have got through reception, you didn't even have a bloody appointment! What's with you, Ruby? It's like you were determined to get yourself killed right from the start!" he complained.

"I'm telling you, Danny, they will never find it because they are looking for the wrong thing. *They* are looking for a big pink file with the wrong name on, the file *I* watched Alessi burn the other day, every last bit of it. I helped him to wash the ashes down the drain," she smiled cheekily and he frowned.

"He did what? Is he mad?"

"I helped him scan everything so we could save it all to disk. It took all night and then we deleted and burnt *everything*. It's all safely stored on a CD marked Pavarotti's Greatest Hits. I don't think they'll be stumbling over it any time soon."

"What now, Ruby?" Danny asked quietly, mulling over the latest information. "What's the plan?" She shrugged feeling unsure.

"Are the others alive?" she asked giving herself some thinking time.

"I don't know. They shot Johnny right in front of us," Danny explained. "They took Alessi away and then they gagged and tied me. They beat me in here right before going off to deal with you. I don't know if they're alive. Mickey is probably using all of us as a way of getting one of us to talk. Alessi and Johnny will never talk, no matter what they do to them. I don't know if I'd have told them after what he said they'd do to you. Maybe I would have if I'd known as much as you do but you, Ruby, *you* know. What are you going to do if they get you? Will you tell?" She thought about it and then looked into his eyes.

"I will never let them get their hands on anything that would give them more power. I *hate* Mickey. I knew he couldn't be trusted. I thought Bardo was different, he seemed OK, but he's with them too. I don't want to end up in Mickey's hands but, if I do...I won't give," she promised determinedly and Danny looked at her in desperation.

"Please, Ruby, I think you should. You will never get out of here otherwise."

"Just keep quiet OK? Trust me I know what to do." She pulled the tape from her thigh and he protested but she placed it tightly over his mouth. Leaning over him carefully she pressed her lips to his head, lingering to enjoy him for what might be her last time. She then slipped off the bed and pulled the en-suite door closed. The room was black again and just before leaving she whispered into the darkness.

"I love you, Danny."

She crept out into the hallway and over to the second door. This time the curtains were open and propped up in a chair with a drip running from his arm was Johnny. His eyes were closed as if dozing and he had a plastic mask covering his nose and mouth. An oxygen tank rested beside the chair and a lamp lit the room dimly. There was a bandage taped to his bare chest and he looked pale. She crept over and placed her hand over his. He was semi-warm and as he opened his watery green eyes she was too scared to look into them. He reached up painfully and pulled the mask down.

"Ruby, what are you doing here? Do you know what they said they would do to you? Do you know what I've sanctioned just to keep secret a file that could have every single one of my family members incarcerated or killed? One young life, a few hours of suffering in return for tens of my most valued and loyal brothers. That's how I looked at it, Ruby, that's how I reasoned. You should be dead by now and I could have stopped it. The guilt has been killing me faster than the bullet in my chest but you're here, how?"

"They haven't hurt me, I escaped," she reassured him. "They think I'm in the grounds somewhere and Mickey is waiting for someone to bring me back so he can do just what he's threatened to do. I understand why you wouldn't tell them. I wouldn't tell them either. I just needed to know you were OK." She plucked up the courage to look into his eyes and was surprised for what she hadn't expected to see was any sadness at her loss.

For the first time she felt like she had a place, somewhere where they might not be able to protect her from *everything* but where they would mourn for her or suffer *with* her if it came to it. He had said it was a matter of numbers and that made sense. Why would they keep *her* over the majority? Did that mean that if it came down to better odds she stood a better chance? His eyes told her that she did and she placed the mask back over his face and rested her hand over his. "Just stay strong a little while longer, Mr Giavani. I don't know if I can do anything but what I do know is that I can try." He nodded and pulled the mask away again to speak. It seemed to make him tired.

"*You* can call me Johnny, Ruby...when others aren't present of course."

"Of course," she nodded with a cute smile. His stern face gave a little and he smiled back turning his hand to squeeze hers.

"My son looks upon you as a daughter. I wasn't so sure. I mean *broody*, at his age!" he laughed and then gasped in pain. "But I can see it now. I have gained a granddaughter, my first. Ruby, please take care they *will* kill you."

Ruby stood and left the room without another word. There was no time to look upon anyone as family. She had lost enough of that already. She put her hand to the key of the third door and was just about to turn it when a hand grasped her mouth and an arm wrapped itself around her chest, pulling her backwards into the bathroom. The door shut and as he swung her round to lock it she saw his reflection in the mirror. It was Bardo and she was petrified. He let go of her and she backed up to the sink, gripping the edge and looking for anything to defend herself with. She wasn't being dragged back to Mickey without a fight.

"You're one cocky little ragazza, do you know that?" he laughed.

"I don't speak Italian, Bardo!" she told him defiantly.

"Well how about I translate for you. Mickey is ready to pull you limb from limb. He has all his men searching every foot out there and you're in here *right* under his nose. I'm surprised he hasn't smelt you out himself, he's like a dog, Ruby, he *smells* fear!"

36
The Ruby prize

"I've got her!" Bardo announced as a greedy smirk spread across his face, the triumph was *all* his. She screamed and struggled as he threw her to the floor at Mickey's feet.

"Call everyone in, let's have a party," Mickey ordered dropping to the ground and grabbing her quickly. He pinned her up against the base of the sofa with his hand around her throat. "Do you want to tell me where the file is before...or after?" he asked leering over her and she shook her head.

"I don't know," she whispered helplessly.

"You don't know whether you want to tell me before or after or you don't know where it is?" he tried to clarify his eyes dancing with glee at having her back in his clutches.

"I don't know where it is," she spoke softly but then feeling trapped and wishing she could just obliterate him she looked up into his eyes, seething pure determination and hatred. "And if I did I wouldn't tell you!" she snapped. He raised his hand and struck her, the impact so powerful it threw her to the floor.

"Nice work, Bardo. I think maybe we'll have everyone upstairs in Danny's room. I'm pretty sure he'd like to watch this," he laughed and she screamed rising to her knees to beg.

"Please, no, not in front of Danny. He hasn't done anything wrong. It's me you want to punish not him. Can't you just settle for torturing *me?*" she pleaded.

"He did wrong when he got himself born to Alessi. That's good enough for me. Now get her upstairs!" he ordered pushing her away with his foot.

Bardo grabbed her roughly and dragged her up the stairs with a fistful of her hair. She found his hands and clung on to them to keep her hair from being pulled out at the roots. He unlocked the door to Danny's room dragging her inside. Mickey was right behind and gripped her by the arm to keep her from running to his bedside. It was a grand presentation that she was now *officially* Mickey's. Danny struggled and tried to shout out before crumpling in to the pain again.

"I'm so sorry, Danny," she apologised. "I didn't want for this to happen in front of you. I know you can't do anything. Please just close your eyes and go somewhere else, anywhere but here. It will be over soon."

"I doubt that," Mickey told her with a laugh. "It's a reunion, Danny, and look what the cat's dragged in or should I say, *Bardo*. Shocker eh one of your best men turning on you like that, stabbing you in the back. Maybe you should take the tape off and give him one final chance to tell us where the file is, Bardo?" he suggested and while Danny nodded desperately Ruby clutched at Bardo's arm and pleaded.

"Please Bardo, no! You have what you want now. You found me and brought me back, please just leave Danny alone. Please just give me this one thing, you have *everything* else."

"Err not quite *everything*, honey, we're still a file down," Mickey reminded. "Perhaps Danny might like to tell us where it is?" Danny nodded eagerly then groaned out in agony. "Ahhh now we're getting somewhere. I knew the girl would work on him."

"No, he's lying!" she protested. "He doesn't even know where it is! He's delaying that's all. He will tell you where to look but it won't be there. He's playing games with you, Mickey, can't you see that? It just means I will have to wait longer and you won't get what you want. Just get it over and done with already!" she screamed at him, close to hysterics.

"How do *you* know he doesn't know where it is?" Mickey growled gripping her jaw tightly.

"Because...because I'm the only one who does. Alessi told me. He never told Danny because he knew you would expect him to know and try everything to get it out of him. He hasn't been able to tell you even if he wanted to. Whereas *I* helped Alessi find a place to hide it. He thought you would think I was the last person he would confide in, just some girl, just some office junior with no links other than landing a crappy little copying job. He thought you would press me then give up and his secret would be safe." Bardo looked from Danny to her and then to Mickey.

"It's your call man. I know what *I'd* do."

"*What* would you do?" Mickey asked cautiously, buying himself some thinking time.

"Well...I don't fancy listening to Danny's objections, might be a bit...distracting...don't you think?" he suggested and Mickey pondered his words as he searched Bardo's face for a long moment. Finally he nodded in agreement.

"Leave the tape on," he ordered over his shoulder now concentrating on Ruby. Danny tried to object but Mickey paid no attention, his was now on Ruby. "So you know where it is?" he asked her slowly. She took a deep breath to steady herself *this* was about to get nasty.

"Yes I know where it is...but don't get too excited because *I'm* not telling!" she told him stubbornly. He laughed a guttural sinister laugh and tilted his head from side to side, taking in this determined little girl with way too much to say for herself.

"Oh you will, believe me," he promised. "Looks like you're all mine now, sweetheart." He looked around at the five other men in the room. "Or should I say, *ours?*" he sniggered.

She shuddered. Her body was shaking from deep inside and she ached with dread as she tried in vain to look brave. Mickey grabbed her arm and put one hand on her shoulder forcing her to the ground. "You can stop me any time you want. Just tell me where the file is and you're free to go," he told her as she pushed herself backwards towards the bed. Danny was still struggling in protest and writhing in pain but she couldn't look at him, she felt too sorry.

She glanced at the faces around her and though Bardo looked indifferent and Nico, Pete and Dave more than eager the other, Bobby, who had searched her bag for ID on the bus, looked uneasy. His eyes made contact with hers and he quickly looked away guiltily. He fidgeted and she could see the sweat forming on his brow.

"Look man," he spoke out. "I'm not happy with this. Can't we just...I don't know, lock her up, chuck her out, get rid of her...something...but not this?" Mickey grabbed her wrists so she couldn't escape while his attention was diverted and turned to deal with him.

"What?" he asked sounding agitated and impatient.

"This isn't what I signed up for, man?"

"Oh yes it is," Mickey nodded vigorously. "What do you think you signed up for, nine to five, bank holidays off and nothing outside of the job description? If that's what you want, get yourself a job at Subway. *Whatever it takes*, that's what *you* signed up for and right now it takes this so, *yes*, you are up for it," he corrected him. The man nodded uncomfortably and Mickey turned back to her. "I think Bardo was right objections *are* distracting and what with you being so eager to get started and all..."

"No! I can't. I can't do this. I can't stand and watch this..." Mickey let go of her with one hand and reached inside his jacket. He pulled something out, something small, black and shiny. A gun! Ruby screamed out. She struggled against his grip using her free hand to try and grab the weapon but the crack came and she knew it was already too late. The one who dared to speak out, the only one who couldn't do it to her collapsed to the floor and the others didn't give him a second glance. Ruby began to sob.

"Oh my god you killed him! You killed him!" She fought against Mickey and he quickly replaced his gun to get a firmer hold of her.

"Yes. Yes I did and the next bullet has your pretty little name all over it...that's assuming nobody else has any objections?" he called out over his shoulder and got a unanimous.

"*No!*"

Danny was still making noises and fighting the restraints but Mickey laughed as he mumbled under his breath.

"I wasn't asking you."

Mickey moved his hands to Ruby's waist preparing to get her torture started

"Wait!" someone else called out and he gritted his teeth furiously.

"IS THIS ANOTHER BLOODY OBJECTION?" he shouted, proceeding anyway. He planned to ignore the man who only a few minutes ago seemed more than happy to be part of it. Mickey quickly yanked Ruby out of the corner she'd squeezed herself into and wrestled with her until she was flat and straddled securely. She was going nowhere but to Mickey's annoyance the voice from the sidelines came again.

"Mickey, just hear me out yeah. This isn't an objection but we need to be certain about where this is going."

"Do you need me to spell it out for you, Dave?" Mickey asked snapping the locket Danny had bought her away from Ruby's neck. He looked over the picture of Almond Blossoms inside and then flung it across the room.

"No I don't mean that...I mean what happens *after?*" Mickey had tried to ignore him but now he was finding it hard to concentrate. He let go of Ruby's hands, knowing she would never escape from under him, and turned to face his accomplice.

"After?" he asked him slowly like it better be good.

"Yeah...I mean...You're expecting her to cave and tell you where the file is, right?" Mickey glanced at her, smiled and then nodded.

"Yep that's the plan."

"Well what if she doesn't?"

"Well she will, *obviously!* She certainly will before it gets round to your turn because you're thick and she'll definitely be giving in before then. Who knows what *you* might do to her! *And,* and I'm humouring you here Dave, if she doesn't then I shoot her, simple as!"

"But if you shoot her that only leaves Alessi and he's definitely not going to tell. Then you shoot him and *nobody* gets the file."

"YOUR POINT!" Mickey shouted getting impatient now. He hadn't intended for it to be so damn complicated. They were going to storm the place, beat each of their hostages until one of them broke, grab the file then torch the place. It was going to be *that* easy, except it hadn't been.

Nothing had gone according to plan and he was now getting seriously agitated.

"My point is," Dave explained. "She's more valuable alive than she is dead. If you're planning on keeping her alive after...*this*...then there's a chance, given that she's proved that she's more than capable of escaping, that she will get away...and talk. I'm not going down for this. If it's staying here between us then fine but you have to promise to kill her after. I'm not doing it if she stays alive. I'd rather go the same way as Bobby than be accused of..." BANG! Ruby covered her ears and squealed as another shot rang out but her eyes were on Mickey and he hadn't pulled his gun. She looked over and the second guy was on the floor. She looked about the room and Bardo's arm was at his side, holding the weapon that had delivered the fatal shot.

"What did you do that for? He was one of our best men?" Mickey protested, completely stunned.

"He was putting me off and I'm *trying* to concentrate," Bardo grumbled. "I can guarantee nobody else will be objecting now." They looked at the last two men, Nico and Pete, who shook their heads slowly, eyes wide.

37
Candy from a baby

Mickey took a deep breath and sighed in frustration, turning back to Ruby.

"Do you see how many men you've cost me? Do you see how much time and effort you waste? Yet still you lay there with your mouth shut, determined to do this the hard way. Are you sick? Are you *stupid?*" he seethed at her but being as stubborn as always she shook her head.

"No, I'm not stupid and I never have been. I know *exactly* what I'm doing...do you, *Mickey?*" she goaded fearlessly, questioning his capabilities as a leader in front of his men. Danny's eyes widened just as much as Mickey's, though Mickey was laughing in astonishment and Danny was thinking she *must* be sick...in the head. *Why would she do that?*

Suddenly a voice called out from outside of the room, a voice that Mickey *wasn't* expecting to hear.

"Mickey, if you want the file then why don't you just come out here and get it?" It was Alessi and Mickey frowned, turning to look at Bardo.

"How did he...?" he began but Bardo shook his head staying silent. "Is he armed? You did take everything off him right, before you tied him?"

"Yeah, of course I did. What kind of idiot do you take me for?" Bardo argued seeming defensive and Mickey nodded.

"Right," he raised himself off of Ruby and she immediately scrambled to her feet. He suddenly realised she was free and he looked indecisive, unsure whether he should take her too.

"No worries, man, I've got her," Bardo told him helpfully, grabbing Ruby roughly and pulling his gun on her. Mickey nodded then pulled his gun on her too and pointed it at her head. She felt like she might collapse but Bardo held onto her tightly, forcing her to stand and face his leader. Mickey cocked his weapon as he stared into her young blue eyes. Using his weapon he pushed her shirt open enough to expose the wound on her shoulder and she closed her eyes and bit down on her lip hard. He looked thoughtful as he tried desperately to formulate a plan. He contemplated just shooting her on the spot. She was a pain in the arse, a distraction, and a mouthy one at that. However, he also knew that she was a valuable bargaining tool when it came to Alessi and Danny. He un-cocked his gun to her immense relief.

"I'm going to let you live...for now," he concluded. "Right you two," he pointed out Nico and Pete with his gun. "One goes out into the hallway and the other stays here with us," he ordered. Nico automatically stepped forward and opened the door slowly. Pulling his gun he pointed it towards the ceiling just in front of his face as he looked round the door into the hallway. He checked in the direction of the staircase first and a gunshot echoed out. He crumpled to the ground, dead. Mickey looked anxious as he turned to face Bardo.

"You said he didn't have a weapon!" he sounded accusing as he glanced at Ruby still held firmly in his arms."

"No, *I said* I took what he had on him. This *is* his house, Mickey. He's bound to have other stuff here. You expect me to try and find all of that as well as the file *and* her?" He gestured towards Ruby with the gun and she cowered and yelped in his arms, fearing he might shoot her just like that."

Mickey took a deep breath. "So...he's armed...but there's three of us and one of him. How hard can it be, right?" he asked looking for reassurance.

"Exactly," Bardo agreed. "Send *him* out. At least we know he's on the left hand side now," he suggested helpfully and the other man frowned, understandably unhappy with the latest plan.

"Why me? Why don't *you* go?" he asked Mickey who looked furious. This was *his* siege! The man realised his mistake and quickly looked at Bardo. "I mean...why not him?" he corrected and Bardo narrowed his eyes like he'd be sorry for that.

"Mickey, you want me to go and risk losing Ruby, that's fine. I found her once and brought her back to you but if you want to risk losing her again then that's your call. If she can get out of a locked room while gagged and tied I'm sure she can manage mastermind here," he snarled glaring at Pete like he could kill him with his bare hands. Bardo had a good point and Mickey agreed instantly.

"Either you go, Pete, or I get rid of you myself for being *completely* useless. It's about time you showed us what you're made of because you certainly haven't done much so far." Pete looked worried. He was going to die for sure going up against someone like Alessi.

"Look, use the shaving mirror in the bathroom to see where he is before stepping out, you'll definitely get him," Bardo suggested, letting go of the grudge.

"Yeah, cool," Pete agreed. "Thanks and...you know...sorry," he apologised.

"No worries," Bardo nodded. "Forget it."

The shaving mirror was located and Pete stood in the doorway as he edged it out gingerly. He used it to look left and then right. He then looked left and right again.

"He's gone. He's not here," he exclaimed stepping into the hallway and turning back to look into the room. A crack rang out and in seconds Pete was on the floor too. Mickey turned to look at Bardo. It didn't make sense.

"He said Alessi wasn't out there," he despaired holding his hands out wide, his gun loose and pointing towards the floor. Bardo turned his gun away from Ruby's head and pointed it at Mickey. He placed his free hand over Ruby's eyes and then fired. Ruby screamed and went weak in Bardo's arms but he caught and turned her so she could hide her face against his chest.

Alessi dropped down from the loft hatch just outside Danny's door and landed steady on his feet. He stepped over the bodies of Pete and Nico and moved around Bobby and Mickey, who were slumped in the middle of the room. Pushing his gun into his waistband he scooped Ruby out of Bardo's arms and into his own. He placed a firm kiss on her forehead and both of her cheeks before begrudgingly allowing Bardo to have her back. He needed to see to Danny.

He hovered gingerly not wanting to hurt him and took a flick knife to cut through the ties on his wrists and feet. He then peeled back an edge of the tape on his mouth and Ruby stepped forward eagerly.

"Wait, Alessi, let me!" She knelt up on the side of the bed and inched the tape away carefully. "Just for the record, should you ever need to de-tape us in the future, ripping it off *really* hurts," she told him and Alessi smiled and apologised.

"I'm sorry, Ruby," he cringed.

"I'm sorry too, Alessi, for the way I was with you in the dining room, just before all this kicked off. I don't hate you I was just shocked and scared. As soon as I heard the three shots and thought you were gone I knew where I really wanted to be. I want to be with you, Alessi, if you'll still have me?" she asked cautiously and he shook his head at her.

"Ruby, if you want out, honey, I can arrange it. I was selfish and I should never have..."

"No, Alessi," she stopped him. "Please, I don't want out. I want in. I know this is how you guys live and I want to be part of your lives. I'm willing to take the good with the bad. I feel like I have a family, for once in my life I have a place. Please don't push me away now," she begged and he held the back of her head.

"I'm very happy to have you, Ruby," he smiled warmly. "I'm honoured to have you in our lives." She grinned and slid off the bed so that he could look after his son but Danny wouldn't take his eyes from hers. Alessi and Bardo sat him up and assessed his injuries, a few broken ribs and some very bad bruising. Alessi immediately called for a doctor and some people who could help with the clear up. He flipped his phone closed looking from Danny to Ruby. "I'll give you guys a few minutes. Come on Bardo let's go check on Johnny."

Danny and Ruby watched them leave and then sat, neither quite knowing what to say.

"I have some serious gaps that needed filling here, Ruby," Danny declared, breaking first. He looked pale and tired. She perched beside him trying to hide her shaking hands in her lap but he found them with his and held them tightly. "What happened? You left me here and then they brought you back..." He couldn't go on, the memory was too distressing.

"After I left here I found Johnny. He's been shot like you said but they've kept him relatively comfortable. I then went to find Alessi and that's when Bardo caught me. I was ready to fight for my life but he wanted to talk to me. He said that he didn't want any of this. He'd been here initially to bring Johnny to see Alessi for a meeting and that's all he was here for. But the building was taken over by Mickey and his men and Bardo was dragged into it. He was the only one that didn't know it was going to happen and his family were threatened in return for his co-operation. He reasoned that we would all be held captive while the property was searched and then it would be over, that's what Mickey told him, but it got out of hand."

"Yeah just a little!" Danny snorted raising his eyebrows and Ruby felt sorry for him.

"He told me that Johnny was shot, Alessi was bound and gagged and you'd been beaten while I was held prisoner. He said Mickey had every intention of torturing me until I eventually broke. He wanted to help us but he couldn't do it alone and they'd all been stripped of their mobile phones. They were warned that if anybody was seen trying to escape the grounds they were to be shot instantly. We came up with a plan together, not one I was overly happy with I have to say. I mean I couldn't be completely sure which side Bardo was really on but I didn't have too many choices. He said he would deliver me to Mickey like he'd found me and Mickey would be over the moon. It would cement Bardo's commitment and show he had no allegiance to you guys or to me. He would have to be rough with me, be as normal as he could. He needed to show it was for real else he would be shot and I would be all Mickey's. He promised that whatever happened he wouldn't let Mickey do any of the things that he'd threatened to do to me."

"I wish I'd known that bit!" Danny breathed still trying to come to terms with what he'd seen.

"I'm so sorry, Danny. We both knew that Mickey would want an audience. He'd said as much when he ordered the search party. We took the plan to Alessi and he agreed to it. He got a gun and took his hiding place before Mickey's men came back in. Bardo was to take down as many men as he could so the odds were better. Fortunately, well kind of fortunately given that he wasn't prepared to hurt me, Bobby got himself killed for going back on the deal and Bardo used some stupid excuse to get rid of Dave. Bardo said that when the time came he would keep hold of me. He said he would be prepared to take a bullet for me. Alessi hid above the loft hatch just outside this door, the idea being that they would look left and right but were unlikely to look up. That's how he took down the last two men."

"And that just left Mickey," Danny pointed out and she nodded.

"Exactly, and that was as easy as taking candy from a baby. All that bravado, the big talk and bullying and he points his gun at the floor and practically gives Bardo a clear shot at him! I knew he was an idiot," she smiled and he smiled painfully back at her.

"So you had to be up here for the plan to work?" he asked and she looked up into his eyes, cringing at how bad he must have felt for her.

"Oh, Danny, we knew he would bring me up here to you. Bardo said that if Mickey didn't suggest it *he* would. I didn't want to put you through it but that's where the loft hatch is, it was the only way. I nearly backed out when Bardo first threw me at Mickey's feet. When I saw the hungry savage look in his eyes the last place I wanted to be was up here in front of you but it was the plan and, by that point, I really had no choice anyway. I was Mickey's hostage again." Danny frowned and cupped her sorry face in his hands.

"Ruby," he whispered. "I can't imagine going through anything worse." He didn't go on, he couldn't go on. He just ran his fingers over her mouth, gripping her hair and pulling her into his chest so he could bury his face into the top of her head. "You're something else do you know that?" he told her.

"Yes she is," a voice agreed from the doorway and they both looked up to see Alessi leaning casually against the frame with a hot drink in his hand. "She's one of the family now so keep your hands off her until you've received my blessing, young man," he warned. Danny grinned at her wide eyed expression and looked back to Alessi nervously.

"In that case if she's...erm...up for it," he shrugged unsure of the official wording, "May I date Ruby please, *Mr* Alessi?" he teased and Alessi cringed.

"Up for it? Danny, you're practically a lawyer! You go to court at least twice a week, you draft very good legal arguments and all you can think of is *'up for it'*? Well I'm not sure I'm happy..."

"Yes, I'm up for it!" Ruby declared, much too eager for Alessi's liking and completely ignoring his little outdated ways, or the fact that he was still standing in the doorway! She lunged at Danny, throwing her arms around his neck and kissing him passionately. Danny groaned in pain but tried to accommodate her as best he could while Alessi shook his head with disapproval.

"I take it that's your answer then is it? I wouldn't dream of trying to contain Ruby and, *apparently*, it's impossible anyway. I'd have loved to see Mickey's face when he realised she was gone just like that. One minute tied and gagged and the next seeming to have flown from the window like a little bird.

"Uh huh," Danny agreed still glued to Ruby's lips.

"Right, I'll just go then shall I?" Alessi asked realising he was now a spare part.

"Uh huh," Ruby responded, still kissing Danny wildly.

"And in my own house too!" he grumbled as he made his way back to the living room to dig out some *very loud* Mozart and to check on Pavarotti's Greatest Hits.